The Midas Consequence

The Midas Consequence

A novel by Michael Ayrton

Doubleday & Company, Inc.
Garden City, New York
1976

Library of Congress Cataloging in Publication Data

Ayrton, Michael, 1921–
    The Midas consequence.

    I. Title.
PZ4.A986Mi4 [PR6051.Y7]   823′.9′14
ISBN 0-385-08470-6
Library of Congress Catalog Card Number 75–14804

To Basil Wright

I

Rushes

Pushing a toy perambulator with one wheel distorted, the old man moves down the wayward path, one of many which have come into being on the building-site. This patch, intricately scribed with tracks cut through scrub and dried grass by men with wheelbarrows, cyclists taking short cuts, juvenile bandits brandishing plastic fire-arms and campers seeking to be near the beach, is strewn with clumps of hardware, invested with brambles and aloes. It is not a rubbish dump but, even so, it has attracted all manner of discarded utilities, each rustily protesting its loss of function and gesticulating its defeat in the field. In and out among boulders and dilapidated machinery, the old man paces like a marabou stork, bowing slowly over each junk clutch and occasionally shooting out a lean brown arm with a pecking movement to retrieve, what? Difficult to see at this distance from the jetty but maybe part of a gas-stove, a crankshaft or a piece of marine flotsam flung beyond the beach by some spring storm.

On the dusty road separating the seashore from the old man's curious hunting-ground, a jeep, packed tight with a concentrated camera crew, is moving slowly and halting often, because his explo-ration of the building-site is being filmed. Thus, cries of instruction, punctuated by the sharp clap of the board indicating the title of the production, the date (3 April 1973) and the number of shot and take, are faintly audible to those gathered on the jetty, who are closely observing the sequence. None of this appears to affect the old man, who may well have forgotten that he is on camera, for he, too, is concentrated.

He is leisurely as he fills his baby-carriage, but the group watch-ing him intently from the jetty is conscious of observing a ritual and three of the four seemingly indolent spectators become tense with speculation each time the figure on camera stops, slaps at the flies which buzz in the shadow of his straw solar-topee and stabs down to come up with something. When this happens, the spectators exhibit a slight but positive concern. They are, with one exception, inappropriately well dressed for the seaside. Two are nervously well dressed. The exception is a good-looking young man, ostentatiously casual in jeans and singlet, in order to prove by this uniform that, unlike his companions, he is part of the place. The visitors naturally recognise in him a person of talent, if not without vanity.

The fertile field of rubbish is not going to last. Men will shortly come with more wheelbarrows and with a bulldozer and a concrete-mixer to lay foundations for the long-awaited annexe. All that are required are the building permits and then from the labyrinth of sea holly, mercury, mallow, myrtle, thyme, rock roses, boulders and jetsam, there will rise a blockhouse box of a building as undistinguished as the *Hôtel de l'Univers et Libéria* itself.

As to the *Hôtel de l'Univers,* ugly it may be but it is recorded in *Michelin* as a restaurant worthy of a détour and therefore contains a gold-mine in its kitchen, shining as brightly as two stars in a concrete shell. A blot on the landscape, it squats close to the beach, only separated from its jetty which shambles into the shallows, by the coast road, across which, on this and every evening from spring to autumn, except on Mondays, waiters dart, clattering as they reach the timbers, and trot among the tables shaded by an insecure pergola of palm fronds laid across poles. As a place for eating an expensive meal, or for finding the skeleton of an old bicycle, it is beyond compare in the neighbourhood.

At present only four people are seated on the jetty, but they are the scouts and outriders. The full court for this evening will arrive later. Meanwhile, Nella Schlegel, *née* Roccafalco, the Contessa, whose huge sun-glasses are designed to mask all but her expressive nostrils, her mouth petulant and chin determined, each in its way showing small signs of strain, sharply snaps open the dialogue.

"My God, Hansi, what is he doing out there?"

Her husband does not reply. Instead, from the untidy, chic young man with the talent, all indolence, grace and easy-earned suntan, comes, not for the first time that year, the cryptic rejoinder, known to those in the know.

"He finds."

"For what does he seek, to get so dirty?"

"He does not seek, he finds."

4

"Ma . . ." says the Contessa who has heard, impatiently, that quotation from Picasso before and considers it hermetic. The shrug and the long, slim hand flashing dismissive, earns from her husband, Herr Hans Schlegel of Zürich, notable publisher of books, a reproving glance, only to have it blocked dead by the implacable shield of Nella's sun-specs. Hansi, who is all buttoned tight in his correct business suit, takes no offence but smiles slightly from the apex of the coffee-table stacked with books upon which, metaphorically, his solid buttocks are securely set, he having published them.

"Nella," he says, too exactly without accent, "they are metaphors that he finds."

"What he finds," adds the young man, not without a note of envy and too explanatory, "he transforms."

Nella is shy, of course, but not to be patronised.

"What is to be transformed from a toy-cart filled with garbage?"

She receives a courteous reply from the elderly art dealer who, for so many years, has patiently enlightened the unsophisticated.

"Such an *objet trouvé, ja?* . . . Some little girl's lost plaything could, in metamorphosis, a little girl itself become."

"Or perhaps a sculpture of a little girl pushing a toy perambulator in which case the pram at least will not be much trouble except to the bronze-founder."

Such remarks, even from young men of talent, are not acceptable in the opinion of Doktor Adolph Ritterbaum, dealer, savant and one of several keepers of the sacred flame. The beak of his ancient and often genial turtle's face clicks shut.

"Is possible, *ja*, is possible," he says, abruptly.

There is no question but that this quartet shares the pleasure of being highly informed, even if one of them plays the philistine. They are an élite with nicknames. "Hansi," the publisher, "Addle," the long-time dealer now a sage, and "Jeannot," the young painter with the talent. All are now smiling slightly except Nella, newly come to court and impatient of this artistical priesthood. She has been dragged all the way from Rome, too far for a lion-hunt in hot weather. Besides, when it comes to the arts her sophistication requires of her no more than the acknowledgment of supreme success. She has no need to penetrate the bizarre mechanisms whereby an old man, sweaty with a pushcart, has gained pre-eminence.

5

"*E poi?*" pops from her with a note of irritation and Addle, ever the peacemaker, applies, with a sure touch, his smooth, didactic emollient. "It is quite strange, my dear, is it not, that such an assemblage as he has gathered in his little *carrozza* can become something for which any museum in the world would compete?"

"A *carrozza d'oro,*" says the Contessa languidly and, rising, the sun catching all her shining trophies, charm bracelet and rings flickering, she walks along the jetty to look out to sea. Addle's sad old eyes follow her, catching the flashing of her larger ornaments. Jeannot's eyes follow her, catching the flexing of her little bottom under Pucci's, the most final cry of an afternoon dress. The button eyes of Hansi are fixed on Addle from beneath frowning eyebrows as stubble-pale as his cropped short back and sides.

From the entrance to the restaurant, the old man, no prospector but gold-miner extraordinary, patron of the Universe and famous even in Liberia, comes with his tiny chariot, trailing waiters like lampreys. On his way through the building, he has added to his hoard a musical instrument, erstwhile part of the restaurant's décor, and bright with Brasso. This bombard, product of the antic mating of a cornet with a trombone, each coil and piston gleaming, shines out from the pram, that collapsing cockleshell borne up by wire wheels, one of them bent.

Catching up the veteran trumpet, the Master flourishes it, puts it to his lips and blows. Nothing.

"Capo," says Addle gently, "try, with the lips pursed and the tongue in the hole, to spit."

The old man grins, teeth long, strong and separate. His face is oiled leather, each wrinkle a muscle in its own right. The stygian eyes blaze and are then shut tight. He inhales hugely and tries again, tongue familiar with holes, and vastly gratified when the instrument sounds a stertorous if short note. The group relaxes and applauds this brazen bull's fart. Capisco, the Man with the Golden Horn, has made his entrance.

The above is written in the historic present, since those present are in the presence of history and is by way of being the *avant-propos* or pre-title sequence, nowadays called "the teaser."

Let me, since I scripted it, first define my own rôle in the production, for I, temporarily at least, am the juvenile in this one-night stand in the continuing story of Capisco's place. I am, of course, the good-looking young man who has been here for some time, living in a ramshackle, desirable property up behind the Universe and Liberia and owned by its proprietor, Monsieur Isidore Poitevin, *capo mafioso* and *grippe-sou*, who is here a featured player and has the eye of a buzzard. I, on the other hand, am a painter of talent and even genius and have the eye of a detached observer of the human comedy. I am not the lead here. I am an understudy and scene-shifter, neither director of this spectacular nor puppet-master. I am the aspirant, not the star.

As for the staging of the production, the restaurant and its annexe-to-be are established, but now we get a long, panning shot, carefully set up to avoid the gas station and the two cafés, the caravan-site and the little bungalow boxes not on wheels which litter the length of the coast road, so that all we have on camera is the sweep of the bay, the beach, the cliffs and the great matt silver, almost still sheet of the Mediterranean, *mare nostrum* and cradle of all arts.

What will develop, once the credits have come up on the roller caption, is in some sort such a *commedia dell'arte* as Diaghilev staged as *Pulcinella*, with ragtime ingeniously injected into Pergolesi but no longer shocking now, save where Stravinsky is supplanted by the bull-roarer blasts of the Master, still blowing but now with his straw hat held over the mouth of his instrument in the manner of the men of the massed brass of the big-band days.

But what we have here is no musical, but rather a glamorous happening, a *fête galante* or more precisely a court masque graced by ingénues twittering like starlings and jewel-bright as humming-birds, pointing their uplifted breasts, nipples cocked, not at the shepherd boy who is a prince in disguise, but at the king enthroned as a god. For this is not a spectacular, but an epiphany.

All will be seen initially to be done with insouciance, and now the scenery described darkens into evening as the act drop dims, bringing mystery to cement and cementing mystery, for soon we shall see some of the rest of the cast advancing into shot under strings of golden bulbs at forty watts each, hung from the pergola.

A long table has been set on the jetty and generously spread for

7

the nine featured players, whilst around this high altar, but at a decent distance from it, are smaller but not less elegantly served tables for the walk-ons—a whispering chorus of those who have come to see and be seen, all pretty and pretty casual as to costume and all moderately glamorous themselves.

And now, sliding out of long low cars, or sloping over the sandy beach, come those who feature in the opening sequence, four of whom we have seen welcome the star, of whom I was one and am the prologue, partial narrator and minor protagonist, being employed to move the chairs and play the dupe—having, I suspect, been duped out of shot. Where I am heard in the first person singular, I may strike a note of irony and even bitterness, since my best lines will be cut, but such are the wonders of cinema that those who, in another age, would have had to come downstage and confide their lines in soliloquy across the footlights may now be heard "voice over" whilst smiling and conversing in defiance of one another, so that what they are thinking comes to you direct from the sound-track all unknown to the rest of those present.

Therefore the antics of Harlequin, the duplicities of Columbine and Scapino's tricks, are joined in with other rôles perhaps including Polonius, Candida, Brett upon whom the sun also rose, Juno with paycocks and little Kane with his rosebud sledge, each according to the player's self-engendered image but where all may be seen in seeming amity, and each one, being somewhat singular, will speak in the first person as they wait for Godot who is on set at all times. Only he, however, is first and truly singular and for the time being will keep his thoughts to himself.

This then has been the ante-masque and now, as the principals in the first reels take their places, an exposition of who they are and the parts they play will follow as each is carefully lit. As to the plot which will eventually be carefully edited to contain, in acceptable measure, laughter, tears, pity and terror, it opens with a device, formulated by whom but Capo, based upon the traditional game for young and old called Consequences.

So Capo is seated at the head of the table and there he is waiting, benevolent and impatient, in a very close shot so tight in on him that you can see, or at least surmise, the very nature of his power, distilled as it is from a talent sufficiently superabundant for it to have relieved him of the necessity to concentrate his genius for some years past. Critical amnesty, long won in the golden aura reflected from the figures realised at auction, has confirmed him in his place. Vanity, co-existent with warmth, conceit bubbling in a colander pierced with irony, rivalry teasing where no rivalry exists—except that Picasso and history still live—prestige glittering in the beholder's eye, caprice caracoling pre-eminent, all these may be read by the discerning in this very close shot of the head, the bony, black-eyed, monkey mask of Capisco, lit from below by the fire in his belly.

And now they are come. First Héloïse, who is my girl and, despite my footwork and long-sustained protest, now my wife.

Beautiful, solemn and determined to foster me is Héloïse and unaware of my tactical avoidance so far of the fate of Abelard. Even as she approaches I recognise the risk yet again, but there she is. Kisses exchanged with Capo and Addle, vague smiles for the interloper Schlegels and not much smile for me. Héloïse who is nick-named "Kir" because of her taste for a mixture of white wine and cassis and her tendency to blush to exactly the colour of those liquids combined, is exceptional, viewed from behind. A lovely arse she has, which Capo pats goat-grandfatherly. Walking along behind Kir, as I often do for pure pleasure, I have the feeling she leads me about like that live lobster Gérard de Nerval used to take for walks attached to a silk ribbon, because it did not bark and knew the secrets of the sea. The analogy may not hold up since I often bark and do not know for certain any secrets, but the view is superb.

Now, following Kir, comes "Lens," so called because she is a camera, and now, following her fourth divorce, she has decided to remain Mrs. Leonora Lodge, a working girl of a certain age and very highly paid for pix and captions. To Lens, life is spelt Time-Life and in her time she has been one of Cap's inamorata, which perhaps she remains for life, but she is far from past her prime, therefore much to be fancied, and a talent-spotter, where the talent has already been well and truly spotted. Lens, from her occupational hazards, is a lush. *Life,* after all, has folded.

And from the big car, parked by Pancho, Estelle arrives. Estelle who, by dignity, has earned no nickname and who is Cap's perhaps last fish shot in the barrel and lovely. Estelle is Demeter in full autumn, a corn goddess imperturbable at perpetual harvest and she I love without reservation and have no smart remarks to make about, brittle-wit as I may be. So when Estelle is present, there is much scraping of chairs and darling such ages and you look wonderful and kindness at least from Estelle and even Cap is, at one level, momentarily overshadowed.

That is all for the title sequences, except for one player who sidles in off the beach and in under the credits so unobtrusively as to be almost imperceptible and she is called "Moustique" because she is long-legged and shy and industrious and priggish and not because she stings or at least, if she does, no one has felt it. She is Mary Ellen Whitaker, a scholar whose light needs no bushel to hide under, but who hides none the less in fear of violation by the truth as opposed to the facts, feeling as she does that there is no room in her life for both. Moustique, here employed by the good Hansi to contribute the learned apparatus to yet another book on Capo's drawings, now seats herself next to Estelle, like a mouse hesitating on the threshold of a granary.

These then are the Consequence Players although by no means all the consequences of play. They are the Heads, who think, the Bodies, who promote lascivious thoughts and imply actions, and the Legs, who run about for Capo, and it is he who has divided us casually into those particular extensions from the general human condition, on a sudden caprice to get him through the evening. So there are, with Capo, nine of us, of whom I am the other one who can really draw like Raphael, if I care to. And all of us are seated and joke merrily through dinner, except Moustique who is silent and Estelle who says very little and Nella who is very cool and precise but seems to grope, somewhat in the dark. This may be because she is still wearing those vast sun-glasses.

Capo, determined to demonstrate that he has more drive and panache and needs fewer clothes than anyone, displays his compact musculature only now on the verge of fragility. Convincingly, he shows how the spars and cordage of his frame can still carry crowded canvas and yet release, like a catapult, an energy which blinds the spectator even to think about it. Capo is cheerful. This atom-crusher in the striped T-shirt and shorts exists for real. Basking in his magnetism, he is, as always, on his mettle to prove it molten. Relentlessly unbored and apparently tireless, he prods his way disinterestedly through a meal, modest in all but price, not so much eating as recomposing the design of the food on the plate, incising the tablecloth with fork prongs, building spilt salt into low reliefs and organising the twin red rings left on the cloth by his wine-glass into a bicycle upon which half a radish, apple pips and matchsticks are presently mounted to present the winner of the Tour de France, strenuously riding uphill.

Capo talks, falls silent, looking sharply at where his words fall among the rank and file. Often he looks down at his hands which move and move.

"What do you think, Cap?"

"Yes."

"Yes, what?"

"Yes, I think we shall now play a game which I shall begin and which needs strips of paper to draw on."

Paper is instantly conjured up by waiters scenting viable souvenirs to come. Plates now destitute of the *tarte aux fraises* which followed the *terrine de foie-gras* and the *homard Libéria* and cheese and salad, are swept away.

So now, on film, are to be seen fluttering and denials of ability and different degrees of excitement and in the air is to be sensed the scent of gain, for all here are waiters of one sort and another, except Estelle and the Master himself. So nine people have slips of paper but of course no pencils and then pencils and Capo begins to draw.

The director of this production, who is called Sandy, is a great one for jump cuts and low-angle shots and rather overgiven to frozen frame; but with Capo drawing, frozen frame is right so we get it on all cut-aways from Capo and meanwhile you will at once see Capo at his magic and hear him speak but you will not hear what passes through his mind at this stage of the game for that is reserved for Part II and comes after the commercial break.

Everyone else at the table will be given the dubious benefit of a "voice over" on the track and thus, as they draw, each in his or her capsule of self-conscious quiet, you will hear what they are thinking to themselves, but not Capo whose silence is golden. So, for the time being, I shall continue to compère the proceedings, doing my best to narrate without undue prejudice.

Capo has begun to draw with his left hand, perhaps by way of a self-imposed handicap, but also, I fear, because his right hand is already under the table, on the knee of his dear friend, my wife. Both Cap's hands are always on the move and nowadays he tends to look at them in action as if he were a little surprised at the independence of their behaviour. I think he does not like to see them in repose and I have heard him say that they look like bleak little landscapes to him. He is right, they are relief maps of his age. In repose, Cap's hands are stubby, wrinkled, blotched with liver marks, striated with blue veins running across their backs among the wiry hairs, the knuckles pushing urgently up through the skin like barren hills. Cut that . . . edit it out . . . a silly comparison. These landscapes, somehow primaeval, are very far from infertile. Block the simile and try another. Cap's hands are like tigers; an animal act. They are performers; Capo's Prestidigitators now displaying their well-known exposition of aerial hopscotch but tireless and terrible in their grip on knife, chisel, brush, etching needle or whatsoever else they clench on, including Kir. Squeaks proclaim this.

So far as I can tell, the right-hand set of Capo's acrobatic troupe of fingers is working up under Kir's skirt as is customary and Kir is whispering fiercely to him, while a taut little not-in-public-Capo, stop-it-Capo, battle is engaged, with Capo grinning and drawing, left-handed, above the struggle and Kir, Kir-coloured, is blushing. I smile pleasantly at her and find to my irritation that I have a stand moving up on me. Such is my form of jealous response to a not infrequent dinner-table occurrence, when Kir is accidentally placed on Cap's right hand.

Since no one else, so far, is drawing on his or her little slip of paper, all eyes are on the Master, where else? And all are craning to see, upside down, the head that he will draw in consequence. It is of course, a portrait of Kir, what else?

"This done, children," says Cap, "and it is not yet done, I shall fold back my head leaving the lines of the neck visible over the fold, much as you will see if you look at Addle's stringy old gullet over there. I shall then pass it to my charming neighbour on my left who will attach her elegant little body to it and so on, round the table and to and fro until, time passing, all here will have contributed heads, bodies and legs to the nine sheets, except, I suppose, Estelle."

"Yes, darling, except for me."

"It will be social intercourse at the highest level," says Addle, who is no doormat even for Cap, who retorts in character.

"You will not get these treasures to sell, let me tell you, but you may contribute to them, which is a privilege for a tradesman. But, to continue; all done, the papers will be unfolded to the consternation, delight and amusement of us all. Any questions?"

"Why are we doing this, Capo darling?"

"To produce results gay and comical and as meaningful and surrealist as Breton and Tzara, once upon a time, tediously found them to be, when playing with Dada."

"Surely surrealism was not insignificant as a movement, *Maestro*. You were part of it; Picasso also." Hansi is shocked at such iconoclastic anti-iconoclasm. He looks very serious for one who is supposed to be being gay and comical.

"My friend, when I think that I played that game in the thirties, I am like to vomit. Maybe even Pablo, who no more than shook surrealism out of his *muleta*, whilst making passes elsewhere, tired quickly of that charade. It was not his *corrida*."

"But surrealism is now revived. People are most interested in it. The prices a Picabia fetches . . ."

"It is the function of dealers to deal, my friend. Addle will tell you that when a man was about the place at the right time doing an in-thing badly, they have only to wait to revive him, at a more modest figure, in the shadow of those who were doing it well. Picabia was one such. He was 'amusing.' He was allowed to be about because he had money and was generous with it, therefore 'stimulating.'"

Capo is a trifle irritable and inside his act as usual; in this mood, he shoves his needle into his own history. I suspect his exploratory fingers have discovered that Kir is wearing stretch tights. This would certainly madden him, belonging as he does to the era of the stocking-top and the journey home across the thigh unimpeded by anonymities of close-woven fog. Be that as it may, Capo is now lecturing. The diners are all awed ears. "Pablo," says Cap, "is another thing altogether. He is the *torero*, awarded the tail and both ears

13

even when the sword flies into the air and the bull, not dead, is spewing blood. The kill is made by the critics and the dealers who dash in with their little *puntillas,* one lot to explain and the other to merchandise the *cojones,* back under the seat tiers, *al sombra.* That, children, is the extent of my Spanish and that much I got personally from an American literary man, an *aficionado* who used to know Gertrude.

"In those days there were three of us on the posters, Pablo, Georges and me. We were rivals, or at least Pablo was everybody's rival and he forced the pace. Georges had none of it or, if he had any sense of rivalry, he was so quietly conducted that you couldn't tell. He moved about inside a still-life, did Georges, slow, cool, French, noble, and now dead, for making everything so patiently beautiful. Oh, what a Normandy Georges made out of frying pans and fruit bowls, giant pigeons, violins, easels, palettes, tablecloths, woodwork textures, bread rolls and suchlike. He had the seasons turning for him and he swam in his fish tank like a flattened fruit moving slowly but determinedly through a jug. No risk of cracking the china. Nothing ever got broken in that immaculate studio."

"But a great painter, for all that." Braque is not someone I will hear slighted even by Capo, even by a Capo full of impish fun, with his hand up my wife.

"Great he was, child, great indeed. There should be a law against great, quiet Normans who paint great, quiet, peaceable pictures and make such small, tiresome, incompetent sculptures. Even Georges' signature lay like a fish on a marble slab."

The table remains silent. There is no one here prepared to provide witty or informed comment. Moustique is too shy, Lens is already too drunk, Hansi too reverent, his Contessa too ignorant and Addle has heard it all before. That leaves Kir who is fully engaged elsewhere, Estelle who is Estelle not interrupting, and me, and I am watching Cap drawing left-handed. So Cap talks on.

"Georges' signature was a still-life element. Where he put it, it stayed put. Pablo bounces his about, but Georges' signature always looked like a statement of intent from a sheep valued for its wool rather than its mutton, 'Bra-a-a-que' was a fricassée of the lamb of God. And he signed everything so carefully, before seeing it slid into a baize-lined slot in the secure interior of the armoured car his wife made him buy to move those precious *objets d'art* from the Braques' to the vaults, to the dealers and so by train and plane to the museums and the collectors."

"What," I ask, "has that to do with Braque's signature? Everything you do, Cap, is signed, sealed and delivered in much the same way."

"Jeannot," says Cap, his pencil gliding silky round Kir's profile as, carelessly, the left-handed likeness comes up on the paper, riveting the eyes of everyone, "signatures are very potent things. They are gilded signs like those that used to hang outside shops before people who wanted bread or latchkeys or whatever, could read the word 'baker' or 'locksmith.' They are now for people who cannot read works of art. They are the signs Addle goes by."

"Dubious proposition," is Addle's retort to that, but his old neck retreats into his collar.

"Let me tell you a story." There is no stopping Capo in flood. "Sitting here, in this very restaurant, which points out to sea as if the cooks had only to reach down and pull in the *oursins* and the *langoustines*—which they do not do, since the fish comes from the market—I recalled, the other night, my last trip to Paris, where I visit the dentist and seldom anyone else, now. The idiot Pancho let the car run out of gas on the rue du Bac and went off with a can, so I went for once into Maeght-Gravure and there was a show of Miró etchings; each a coloured blob or two and a large etched signature and that was all. Each etching was thereafter numbered and signed in pencil so, MIRÓ, Miró. So game, set and match. Round the corner at Jolas was a show of Max Ernst with all the pictures signed under a pseudonym, as it might be Rose Selavy if it had been Duchamp. But no! Pablo, they tell me, showed three hundred and sixty-seven etchings at Leiris, a bit later, with no signatures; due maybe to pressure of events, not having the time to sign fifty prints from each of three hundred and sixty-seven plates, at his age. And he was right. He can afford to be. Signatures are ugly, magic blobs. They usually disturb the composition but such are the phosphorescent enigmas of fame and age and so on, when it's a matter of signatures. As for rivalry, there's no question that old Georges was fond of Pablo and Pablo was sometimes well disposed to Matisse, and Chagall is not fond of any of us, but for myself, I don't know. I don't envy anyone. I certainly don't envy Chagall, nor the Mighty Matador, nor anyone of our sort of age still alive. Pablo still has the speed and the wrists, but would he go up against a big bull any more; one without the horns shaved? His is too old. As for me I have no rivalry. Also I am not so old or too worried about perform-ance."

A snort from Addle, which Capo ostentatiously ignores. None the less he stops lecturing. The drawing has so gained his attention that his right hand has joined in. He passes it the pencil. So far as I can see, from upside down and along the table, he is now suddenly im-patient. His right hand is fast held on the pencil and all the smooth ease of the sliding, tentative, left hand, back-hand, is gone. He is about to ruin the sweet, near likeness of my sweet Kir. He doesn't look at her.

"I'm not looking at you, Kir. I'm inventing you and it's time someone did."

"Oh hell, Cap."

"No, you'll see, it'll be you."

"Couldn't you make it pretty, Cap, just for once?"

"Naturally, it will be pretty. It will be more, it will be sweetly beautiful. It will be a Boucher. It will be a Fragonard, all thistle-down. What about that, huh?"

"Oh hell, Cap."

But Capo is now fully committed to his drawing and I can see from his hunched shoulders that the electricity coming off him is nothing to do with the courtiers who sit still and no longer even feel the need to look flattering. The marks come on to the paper in con-tinual cross-reference. No longer the smooth, knowing contour, the sliding line of the adagio dancer which is Cap displaying, as Picasso now does, his careless mastery. It is drawing and it is unexpected. He puts in the eyes, moving his pencil from one to the other, relat-ing them across the bridge of the nose. The visible ear goes in like punctuation, the nostrils are commas. The cheekbones counter-balance one another, yet avoid symmetry. The lips, precise in plane, are delivered under the tip of the nose, sharply but delicately. It is all going rapidly, from where I sit and it is speeding up, but Capo is cross-hatching which is a sign that he is really drawing and not just using the lovely line. Cap's fingers start romping in the hair.

His hand comes back off the paper and circles, then sinks down on to the eyelids, off again, pausing, measuring the forms with his eye and his memory, knowing how it shapes. Then again down and tight in on the iris. Eyebrows he snaps in like swallows flying and the contour moves surely through the hatched modelling, down the cheek and into the neck. Out of all this comes Kir to the life and for a moment her image stays that way.

"Oh, Cap, that's lovely."

Fatal, the fool girl should never have said that. Capo's face when he looks up at her and then down into the neck of her shirt, wears his clown look. The circus is due to start. I almost reach for the drawing, to save it.

"Kir," says the clown, as if his invisible buttonhole was about to squirt her with water, "it is a lollipop, a marsh-mallow and a sugar plum."

"But, Cap, I am a sugar plum."

"From here you look like two expectant apricots. Your nipples are like little hammers." Kir's hand flies up to her shirt. "And if you are a sugar lump, you need absinthe poured over you, don't you, or you will have no kick."

"Oh, Cap, do leave it as it is."

"So here is the absinthe."

"Cap, please."

"You are not supposed to be looking. Stop looking at my drawing. It is secret. I am not looking at it."

"Oh, Cap. Well, do look at it."

"Why? It's very bad."

The tease now on, Cap begins the work of destruction. His fingers might be Keystone Cops, everyone a comic. They seem to rush into the ring with bags of flour and buckets, custard pies and strings of sausages and in a flash Kir's face has vanished under the slapstick.

"Oh, Capo." It's pitiful to watch, but the sugar plum is gone. "Oh, Capo."

"Capo be damned," says Capo, "watch the birdy."

The mess of thumbprints and blurs he's made begins to reshape itself. It looks entirely incoherent. Suddenly, to the wild amazement of the spectators, now openly gawping against the rules, joeys and all manner of mysterious beast-handlers and bareback-riders seem to have got into the ring and are clearing up. Gone is the old jalopy. The brickbats, the bucket of paste, the bladders on sticks are gone. At climax, the pencil point snaps and Capo produces a felt-tip from a pocket. With it, he moves Kir's features about like pieces of a jigsaw, cheek into nose, left ear into left eye. The ear is now an eye and so he puts in a new ear. He turns the whole head, masking the confusion of earlier features with a wild burst of hair and sets out on the profile reversed. Out of all of it Kir re-emerges, to the life, but no Boucher.

Kir looks as if she might burst into tears, but Capo does not notice. He is groping in her bag, where he finds a lipstick and with it he adds two little touches to the lips in the drawing.

"See, there you are," he says, gratified. "I have invented you. Now this is what you look like. But you shouldn't look. It should not be seen before we are all unfolded."

"Oh, Capo."

"Well, it's your lipstick."

"Cap, I could spit."

"So you should, child, it is your spitting image and besides you are too young to know what you look like. It is for me to show and for our friends here to say and for your husband to judge what you look like. And for time to tell."

"Capo, darling, don't be so pompous."

"Estelle, my love, I am never pompous."

Nevertheless he is folding up his drawing and passing it to the little Contessa who takes it as if it were a precious relic she does not know quite what to do with. She looks anxiously across the table at her husband, who smiles and nods.

Nella's little gold-tipped claws hold the paper while, with her free hand, she carefully clears a space on the table in front of her, where she has eaten enough to keep two roadmenders satisfied for a week. And there she reverently lays the folded Capo.

"What's-his-name will help," says Capo courteously. He means me and he damn well knows my name. "Young man next to you," explains Cap. So Nella, smiling, turns to me for help, turns her whole chic little body and lays her hand on my arm. She is what is called all mute appeal and very fetching with her silky little paw attached to her sleek, small arm joined at the shoulder where the ball in the socket is smooth as a pebble and so on down to two very small, worthy of speculation, breasts. She smiles as if she were practising. "You will please help me with my body?" she asks. "At any time," I say, and she switches off the smile.

I put on my idiot face and gaze blankly into space.

"Capo, darling. Moustique is telling Hansi that you have hidden all your last year's gouaches and won't let him put them into the new book. And they are so good."

"Certainly they are good. They are superb. What do you mean 'last year's'? Do you think they are bottled plums?"

"Aren't they, darling?"

"*Maître,* we didn't mean . . ." This from Hansi Schlegel, of the art books.

"I am not ready to show them to anyone."

"But, *Maître,* the book . . . ?"

"Why not, darling?"

"Because they're no good."

"Addle, darling, you tell him, you've seen them."

"Most interestink."

It is the smooth voice of the Doktor-Professor, Adolph Ritterbaum, Capo's old friend and contemporary, his once and future dealer. If he says "Most interestink," he thinks they're no good except as merchandise. If he says *"Wunderbar,"* Capo should burn them in Addle's opinion. If he just says *"Ach, ja,"* he thinks they are good, and Capo will see him dead before he lets him have his new gouaches, or at least he will keep him waiting.

"Capo, do stop it."

I see he is at it again, climbing the long road along the stretch tights, like a thirsty man in a desert sliding on the dunes towards the oasis, despairing of finding the pool and palm fronds under the shifting sands. "In days not so long gone," I can hear him tell it, as he so confides in me when not otherwise occupied, "the explorer would reach the silk line, find the base-camp of the snap coupling and then move gratefully over the bare slopes with a new confidence. Where now, under the south col, lies the sanctuary? All is now blank, anonymous, intangible as mist in this nylon Sahara." To hell with that metaphor and to hell with you, my master and mentor.

There is much hanging back among the makers of consequences, sitting with their little slips of paper, but some are now drawing. They are just a few of Capo's friends, his loves, his sycophants, his parasites and panders; those who, loving Cap, dwell in his vast shadow and seek to prop themselves up there with their heads, bodies and legs.

On my left, the Contessa is making her presence felt. I would expect her to be radiantly social and of *le gratin*, Parmigiano or Roman perhaps. Not perhaps content with the earnest, respectable and perspiring Hansi Schlegel, notable publisher of books at great expense, in the grand tradition of Vollard, Skira and others. Good Schweitzer Schlegel has hand-made clients for rare editions, each numbered, signed and printed on hand-made paper by the likes of Lacourière, of Léon Pichon and of whosoever else is best at proofing and printing the gravures. Removing such a volume from the bank, each one of Hansi's fortunate clients must take a bath before slipping off the slipcase and handling, if not reading, the text of the *édition de tête*, with the extra proofs of the etchings on *papier d'Arches*, with the *remarques* in the margin and the value of the *objet de valeur* in mind. No desecration of these virgin pages, which must not be cut, is to be made by little, beringed paws even if they are those of the publisher's wife who is socially at a quite different altitude.

Next to Nella is What's-his-name or me, less well known as Jean Choiseul, so called "Jeannot" by everyone. A painter, an esteemed colleague of the Master's, whose pictures, no less than his sculptures, are very much his own except, occasionally, when they closely resemble his, blast them, to my intense and ridiculous chagrin.

Beside me sits Mary Ellen Whitaker, whom Capo also likes, which seems to frighten her. She is a learned girl who knows more about art history than she dares to admit, having written several books, including one about Capo, although I suspect she prefers Picasso. She can hardly be induced to speak and when she does, her voice rises beyond the capability of the human ear to receive. This high, thin note has earned her the nickname "Moustique" from Capo who says, in his kindly way, that she resembles a bifurcated parsnip, which is quite untrue. Moustique is here because she is under contract to Hansi, whom I hope she stings, to do a new book on Cap's drawings, and she means no harm. I like her, Estelle likes her, so far as I know even Lens likes her and Hansi will surely like her if she proves useful. He has primed her to get unpublished drawings out of Cap and she will succeed, without straining her voice. Her book will be excellent and will embrace most of contemporary art, since it is about Cap. That covers the subject, except maybe for Picasso. Who else is still alive? Me, unless you count Chagall.

Then there is Addle whom Capo has known through most of the twentieth century, trusts implicitly and mocks endlessly. He is vastly old and resembles an active, carnivorous tortoise. Cap often tells him this. He, more than anyone alive, has made a fortune out of Capo, which he richly deserves for all that legwork in the early days. It has bent him over, but then he is a dealer and maybe bent from bowing customers out when he has skinned them. I wish he would take me on. Sometimes he shows signs of it, but he is careful and perhaps too old to want to be bothered. He is seated as usual next to Estelle, at whose bosom he glances up warily and often, as if he fears it might explode. It is a bosom to do more than glance at and Capo boasts that it gives her the presence of a majestic ostrich. She is magnificent. She has a body like a body and she does not know what Capo would do without her. Nor does he.

We now come to Mrs. Leonora Lodge, who is drunk. She is not seated but, as always, is skipping about with her little Leica, clicking at history for some magazine. It is clear enough how she came to be called Lens, but if she has a shutter I have yet to hear or see it. That then is the family gathering.

"Contessa, you are our guest of honour. I deliver my head into your hands," says Capo, behaving suddenly like a head-waiter.

Watching him pass his head to the Contessa, with this courteous flourish, I see him suddenly eroded as if almost old, which is impermissible, even momentarily. It strains him to play the cynic and I sense he has been thinking cynically, snap, crackle, pop. This mood is one that he often adopts when he begins to feel himself creak. His mind is nowadays perhaps less active than his fingers which, still galvanic, seldom cease their dance. They are at rest now and he is a little slumped, looking at Estelle who is looking into the distance.

Meanwhile Nella has managed to remove her sun-glasses and is revealed with her patrician nose naked. She is as precisely and sharply drawn as a Watteau *en trois crayons*. The etheric tape is, I imagine, recording her confusion, for it is at this point that the director has introduced his well-worn "voice-over" convention which is the direct product of years spent in making TV documentaries. This production, let me say in passing, he hopes will loft him into the Ken Russell class or, let us hope, quite a different one. You never know. So Nella . . .

Most embarrassing. He really is. Marvellous of course for his age and really a little absurd but so forceful. What would it be like? Too late? I don't think I could.

How can I? How can I draw a body, when I can't draw at all? And on to his head. Everyone knows I can't draw a straight line. And Hansel is looking at me hard and *willing* me not to spoil Capo's drawing. It is really ridiculous to make me play this foolish game. The young man is waiting for me to make myself foolish at this drawing and I am perfectly frozen just to think of putting my body between the *Maestro's* head and this young man's legs. Everyone is looking at me except the little thin blue-stocking with the little thin voice, who is herself drawing, and of course Hans, who no longer looks at me. I wish Hans had not made me come, but I suppose I did want to come, I must admit if I am truthful. The photographing woman is taking snapshots of us, me next to Capisco. Well I shall show prints to Massimo and of course to Luciana and Clara and all of them and I suppose to Gian-Lorenzo, who will look disinterested.

I am no longer very sure of Gian-Lorenzo who no longer telephones so ardently or so often and is becoming so busy in the afternoons because of the economy and the troubles with the shareholders.

I suppose I must sketch something. The sheet looks so blank, so new, so virginal. And there are those two little lines on the fold, by Capo. *O dio mio,* how awful. How does one make shoulders? I will make little marks so and then; no that is not right. Again, yes, better. I must think of a suitcoat by Amies and as they make drawings for Vogue, very slim. What shall I do? I shall put this for the waist and then arms, well sort of arms. It is a child's drawing. I really cannot.

That young man is looking at me undressed. Gian-Lorenzo would be furious whereas Hansel is glazed just to be looking at Capo who is . . . I can see exactly what Capo is doing. It is really fantastic at his age. The young man is waiting. I must compose myself. It is better now that others are playing.

"Please forgive me, I am so slow."

"There is no hurry and anyway it is just a game."

That was nice of him. He has kind eyes and nice hands. His hands are remarkable. I am sure that Capo thinks very highly of him too, or he would not be here at dinner. I am sure he will be very good, will perhaps become famous.

"Oh, I cannot draw a straight line, you know."

"You have no need to draw a straight line."

"Oh."

"Let your wrist go loose."

"Yes? But it is too absurd."

I feel this young man would rather like me. And it would serve Gian-Lorenzo right, but how impossible. Jeannot she calls him— Gianni, Gian-Giacomo. I suppose artists do stare at people, else how would they come to draw their portraits? It is as Clara told me when Marino was doing the head she is so proud of. "He stared and stared and stared," she said. "It was quite delicious to receive such attention." She would say anything. She is really rather vulgar, but he does stare . . . perhaps it is to be revenged on his little wife, who is so occupied with Capo, and blushing, so pretty.

I have to put the tops of legs, which will make the skirt mini. Well, it must be mini, like English girls wear, really too short. Hans would be censorious if I were to wear such a skirt and I cannot get it right. It looks like a small table-top below the coat and this young man is waiting so patiently. The Lens woman is looking at me and Estelle is smiling, so superior, but of course at her age, even if she is a beautiful woman, I should not like to be so heavy although in a way it does suit her, but to dress must be a great problem. She is right to establish her own style but for myself I should find it a little too different, not that it could matter to anyone so self-possessed.

Gian-Lorenzo likes me to be very chic and of course his wife is not, poor woman. Gian-Lorenzo . . .

Capo is outrageous, handling the girl with the odd name and now, since he is not drawing, trying a little with me, although not impossibly. I doubt if I could. He'd be so *rough,* so imperious, so— well, wiry. Of course, it is flattering. Kir, what a peculiar name, from the drink I suppose, cool in a way but pink from the cassis. It does suit her and she did drink quite a lot of it. Charming, I think, although she hasn't spoken to me; rather lovely with those pretty breasts, like Carla.

Gian-Lorenzo is always trying to have us both together, Carla and me. He says she wouldn't mind and he's probably right. Then, of course, it might help. I'm sure he'd make more time. I don't know. It would be rather exciting to watch, and then Carla and I are, at times, together in the country, so that he could, too. But I think it must be ended.

It is curious, I have drawn my own body: too thin and yet not sagging at all, of course. Well, I cannot see how to add to it.

And so it goes, you see; a pattern emerging from this caprice of Capo's. It will probably work out that those he thinks of as Bodies will be drawing bodies and those he thinks of as Legs—the leg-men who run about for his fame and promote what no longer needs promoting—will be the promoters, the commercials on legs. One of those is now me naturally and the others will be Addle and Hansi and Lens, who is I suppose no longer a body to Cap, and even Moustique with her long, beautifully straight shanks, by her unrecognised as legs. But now that I think of it, Addle and Moustique and perhaps even I may qualify as Heads. Hansi will try to be that too, but Capo . . . Capo will be all the heads and all the bodies, in a sense, except for Estelle's which like the earth he still assays to traverse as a pilgrim on his own legs no longer quite so lithe as once. But is his staff still valiantly held in his hand on this journey? Estelle will not draw or be drawn in. She remains above and beyond, thinking of what? It is difficult to conceive.

The Contessa has slipped me her body, very carefully with her left hand, as if it were a note of assignation. Meanwhile she is giving me the eye, maybe from force of habit. Capo having passed her his head, which may be all she will get from him, is unusually still for the moment and she is clearly nervous of adding to those two long lines coming over the fold. Sensitive of her. I do believe she is a little awed to be tagging her elegant little frame on to the old goat's head, which is his own even if a portrait of Kir. Anyway, she has made some careful very straight marks and has folded them over. A pin man? Or is it her own refined and Voguish shape that she has presented me with? Her movements are most deliberate and most studied; the cigarette is held in the long fingers so, the glass so; the elegant little legs are crossed just so and the profile is not angled without care; the whole fine-boned structure is very firm. She is making quite sure that I notice her all the time, although doubtless I am, to her, far too unimportant to be noticed myself. At dinner she shook, from a great distance, droplets of cool conversation on to the table between us, pearls like aniseed balls. "You too are a painter? Such a marvellous talent to have . . . How I wish . . . My husband is most interested in all the arts. He is so creative . . ." And the empty glance and attention to the lobster, but abstracted and without appetite, yet eating away.

"I know so little . . . my husband . . . yes, in Milano, but of course I spend so much time in the country. Milano, so noisy, so . . . crowded, you know, and so . . . well . . . provincial. You too are making a book for Hans?"

The lady knows well enough he wouldn't ask me, not yet anyway.

"So difficult unless the name, you know," and then the chat about how marvellous Cap is. What a surprise. "You must show me your drawings. Perhaps some time . . . You come ever to Milano?" And then she apologises for her drawing although of course I cannot quite see it. Perhaps she is genuinely shy. I try another tack, steering back into the cool conversation.

"Schlegel Verlag produces very remarkable books."

"Don't you think so? Hans takes such pains, you know, over every detail. He would be so pleased to hear you say you admire his work."

"I truly do. Particularly the Grünewald drawings and of course the new edition of Valentiner's *Tino da Camatino*. I have both."

Nella looks quite amazed. She stares at my stretched smile. I remove it and look serious.

"But these are art historians' books. Surely contemporary painters don't study such ancient things."

"Some do."

"I mean don't you prefer the moderns?"

"Don't tell anyone, but no."

Now we have a secret and share conspiratorial smiles.

"Amazing."

"Not really, I am a modern."

"Myself I am not. Not truly. I like of course Picasso and of course Matisse and that generation, but the *avant-garde* I do not really understand, even when Hans explains what they are doing."

"I fear that I do understand them."

"Explain them to me."

"What, all of them? It would take weeks."

"Then you must certainly visit Milano."

Nella is not adept at looking demure. She is not shy, either. Kir, I sense, is looking daggers, but perhaps I flatter myself. I don't glance up.

"Well, at least explain to me Duchamp, whom my husband is now doing and of whom I make nothing. Is he important? He must be, or Hans would not do him."

No indeed, Schlegel would not underwrite the unimportant.

"He is the joker in the twentieth-century pack," I tell her. "And yes, he is important; historically important because his influence has been enormous as an image-maker, or at least as an idea."

"He is really a great painter?"

"Certainly not. He painted several sensational *avant-garde* pictures before 1914 and then gave up painting for good, except that he didn't quite although he took up chess instead at which, report has it, he was no great shakes."

"Is that all?"

"No, he is more than that. He is—or was—an inventive manipulator of metaphysical games with a gift for exploiting his own irony, a secret man assured of his inevitable celebrity, which he regarded sardonically. He made puns."

"You are not explaining. You are teasing me. Also you are rather pompous."

"No, it is Duchamp who teases but I admit I am being rather pompous."

Nella frowns. She thinks I am joking.

"But what did he *do* that my husband can make a book from?"

"He produced startling objects, under various pseudonyms, some of which he very laboriously and intricately made, but some of which, like a garden spade or a bicycle wheel, he simply bought in shops and exhibited on the grounds that the act of choice on the part of an artist was all that was needed to make a work of art. That opened the sluice gates."

"How?"

"He turned the Emperor's New Clothes inside out, without taking them off. He then packed them in a small valise."

"You have lost me." Nella is glazing with incomprehension and I can't say I blame her.

"He was a man of genius," I say, lamely, wondering why I have been plugging the old monster Marcel like this and using his own sorts of ambiguities to do it. "He was a wit, a dandy and filled with disdain."

"Was he a great artist? How could he be?"

"A great *flâneur,* certainly. He was crazy like a fox, anyway."

Nella looks coolly at me, well aware of where I have placed myself in the pomposity stakes, as an expositor.

"Thank you," she says sweetly, "you have made it all perfectly clear to me."

"I have?"

"I too am crazy like a fox," Nella says, and smiles like one.

Difficult evening. Even without Duchamp's ghost to send me up, evenings at Cap's shrine are always difficult, a fight with myself not to seem to want anything but the pleasure of the company. Must not be drawn into showing off, as I just have. Must not be so bloody cultural. Must be *cool.* Capo is looking at me to see if I'm drawing Kir's legs on to the Contessa's tentative and contrived body, brittle as a breadstick and narrowed smoothly down to wear clothes beautifully, as designed by St. Laurent. But I'm not going to draw Kir's legs on to it; I'm going to terminate the whole thing in a neat bow. I shall draw a neat, careful evening-dress tie, over and under and a gentle tug at the ends to knot it, as worn, and so much for sex, here at this delightful restaurant overlooking the slick and silver sea, among these charming and important people, any one of whom could untie me with a little enthusiasm for anyone but Capo. It seems I must wait a while for the Contessa's body, which is clearly giving her trouble. She has taken it back.

The head I've drawn now, on my own sheet, while I'm waiting for the Contessa, is very trad. No expressionismus. None of your fine frenzy being demonstrated—look at me everyone—at the top of the table. I draw Cap drawing, Cap's head all bone and wrinkles and that fucking, bloody marvellous old faun's look and so I put horns on it. Then I take off the horns—who cuckolds Cap?—and turn them into long ears. Not that Capo's any kind of donkey, but I had to turn the horns into something, once I'd started. And I have passed it on to Lens, folded under, and she is making vague passes at the paper with a stub of pencil taken from her suitcase of a handbag.

I wish now I hadn't put those ass's ears on Cap. Too late. It will look malicious and he will know I drew them. And God knows I don't want Cap to savage me. I wish I'd drawn Kir's head. A chance for a gesture lost, but she was looking down, with all her concentration, at Cap in action, mashing up the body he's been building on to Hansi's doubtless empty little head. He's reached the chopping-block stage again, so I expect his part of the drawing was great, half a minute ago; just like the first one, Kir's portrait. I can't see what he's doing now but doubtless it is the brave meat axe of the felt-tip pen, the pulling apart of all the blurs and scribbles which have bled out of his fingers on to the paper, and the recatching of them in his infernal net. Whatever he did, he's passed it on.

The way Cap's bending forward now, I can assume he's got his hand up her skirt again. She knows it gives me a kick and she knows I'm ashamed of that, too. Estelle's watching.

"Jeannot, darling, where is my bag?"

"I'll look."

"I think Capo has it, darling. I gave it to him just before we began this absurd game, for his pills."

"I'll get it."

"He has to have his pills absolutely regularly, don't you, Capo darling?"

"Huh?"

"Pills, darling."

"Ah."

A slight readjustment: Capo disengages from Kir and heaves up the beach bag, rummaging. Estelle smiles at Kir. Kir is blushing, head lowered over the space below the head I have passed her, tongue moving carefully over her lips as she applies the pencil to her body with the skill of a delinquent errand boy. She looks beautiful with the lights gleaming on her hair (Christ, what a phrase!), touching more gold glints into it than seems usual. (Well, if I am going to be mawkish, I'll be mawkish.) I think I am wearing a silly grin. She has a small wine stain on her shirt.

The Contessa is giving me the full frontal view of her and her fine feral face with it. And where did you get those great big eyes, Nella, so dark and luminous for a little stick insect, a mantis of old Milan? The praying claws, held up together breast-high, have folded over her second paper and run along the fold with a particular finality. Once folded, stay folded. Kir sent her the paper for legs and legs she has drawn and Lens is taking a candid camera shot of that exchange. I wish I didn't want anything from anyone except Kir. What do I want? From Cap, some sort of evident regard, some recognition that I am not just an amiable kid insecurely attached to Kir. From the promotion monsters, Addle and fat Hansi? Some promotion. From Moustique? Oh, I suppose a well-placed, serious article in a fat, influential magazine—"Jean-Jacques Choiseul—A New Talent"—something like that. From Estelle? A little more unchaperoned time with Cap. And so on and so on. From Kir, I want just Kir. I wish to God I didn't want anything from any of them, except Kir. I wish I wasn't so damned impatient.

"Jeannot dear, get my bag from Cap, will you?"

"Of course."

"Tell me, darling, how do you like Cap's present?"

"Christ, it's splendid. You know how we feel about it."

What I don't want is presents and especially not that bloody great present from Cap, the puppet-master. He knew, he fucking knew, what that would do.

"He was up all night doing it, while you children were away. He insisted, although you know how tired he gets."

"Tired? Tired? When have I ever been tired, my blessed melon head?"

"Oh really, Capo darling, what a thing to say."

"Estelle, my celestial heifer, my milch-cow, my golden apple, my June-bug Juno, I love you, don't I? And who could ask more?"

"Oh, Cap darling! Oh, thank you, Jeannot, he always gets my bag under his feet."

"Princess, anything of you under me is all I seek."

"Oh, Cap."

Round the table, drop the bag, back to your seat, you utilitarian bastard, and start in on a body for Addle's wise old snake's head. Most interestink. I shall give him Estelle's great Demeter torso. ("When you have finished, dear, climb up and embrace me," as some large cow once said to Voltaire, or maybe to Addle.)

I wouldn't mind the climb. It would take Cap's mind off Kir too. Happy Hansi shall be the recipient and leg-man for this cornucopia.

"What is this present of which we speak?"

"It is a *grisaille,* Contessa, which Capo did for Kir and me, on our studio wall."

"Hansel, *mio caro,* did you know of this?"

"No, *cara.* It is a recent work, *Maître?*"

"Last week, and please do not call me *Maître,* I am not French." Hansi is unnerved but struggles on.

"In what style?"

"Mine."

"Of course, of course. But I mean . . ."

"It is a major work, Herr Schlegel, I hope to reproduce it. I am writing on it, now." Moustique to the rescue.

"In the new book?"

"That must depend on Monsieur Capisco, Signora Contessa. The book will be of drawings from 1950 to the present."

"Why not a frontispiece for our book, Signorina Moustique?"

Moustique looks prim. The truth is that she has not seen our present, our very own wall-sized Capisco, which is as big a drawing as Cap can ever have done. She tries a gnomic smile on the Contessa and does not answer.

"I think it very fine, this mural. It is complex. The master is not often allegorical and at so many levels." Addle has not seen it either, but feels he must seem to have.

"Allegorical? My Gahd. Can I get pictures? What allegory is it, Cap? What the hell is it?" Lens is filled with drive.

Bloody Capo is grinning like an ape. He has the back of Kir's neck in one hook and the narrow nape of the mantis in the other, so that he's spread out, arms stretched, like a withered Silenus. You can practically see those long, swinging brush-strokes, Rubens fashion. Warm light on his old skull from the fairy-lights and light behind him from the restaurant. Chiaroscuro, clear-obscure as if there was anything either clear or obscure about the old satyr except his damn talent. Two heads, one in each hand, a double consequence.

"My children," he says, "it is a large drawing; charcoal, chalk, wash and anything I could lay hands on by way of medium. It is of Alcmene whose misfortune, or you might say good fortune, it was to receive the embraces of the god Zeus, who had disguised himself as her husband; her husband being away at the wars. Very confusing. Husband comes back. Girl exhausted. Husband ardent, girl not so ardent, the divine event having taken three nights and maybe more, since old Zeus made the moon stand still while he was at it. No wonder the good general Amphitryon, fine young fellow as he was and well hung as they say, found himself bemused. Nothink allegorikal about it, Addle old friend."

The mantis delicately disengages, unhooks her neck from the clutch of the master, whose left hand, coming free, begins to model a small piece of bread. The twitch on him as usual, he unclenches my dear wife so as to get both hands working at the crumb. A small dove in dough begins to emerge between his fingers. Pinching out the wings without looking, he is still grinning. He is inserting his pills into the bird's head for eyes. They are small and bright pink.

"My Gahd," says Lens.

"Capo, darling, how absurd you are. And take your pills."

Capo swallows the bread-bird, pills and all.

Well, think about it. Kir and I have this monstrous great masterpiece all over our studio wall, drawn direct on the plaster. A onenight stand for Cap and there it is heaving itself over us whenever we're in bed and whenever I'm trying to work. End vat does it represent? Think that over too. A Greek dummy, all helmet, armour, cockstand *et al*, and *inter alia* a duplicate divine *Doppelgänger* having it off from behind and well up, in a tent with the luscious Alcmene, daughter, let me tell you, of Electryon, king and ground landlord of the realm of Mycenae. Eventual result—the birth of Heracles! And portraits, of course, of whom do you think? Spitting images of who dares spit?

Then there is the very present matter of the present landlord, the proprietor of this very restaurant, honest Poitevin, who has conveyed to us that since he owns the cottage, so he owns the Capo, so we are merely renting our present with its portrait of Kir and double portrait of me, and it is worth maybe ten or twenty times the price of our studio cottage and love-nest, on which we owe rent. I bang Demeter's nipples into place and pass the body over to the publisher, the art-loving Hansi who is not publishing anything of mine.

"Nothing will yet be unfolded," commands Capo, and Moustique, the least unfolded among those present, knees clenched as mother taught and as habit at the desk has maintained in the Fogg, the Met, the Bibliothèque Nationale and elsewhere, has the tape spinning, all unknown to her, within inches of her *terra incognita*. She is unawakened, as they say, hidden in learning, but respectable having earned respect, a butt for Cap inevitably but not one he will damage, since she is no sycophant despite her alarm. If, as might perhaps happen, she got fucked suddenly, it would be the unmaking of her. She would be what was once called "ruined," which is perhaps something she desires but no one with any heart would risk. I feel quite sure that I know what she is thinking. She is all propriety and reverence, impressed, overwhelmed to be here, an Artemis fearfully unarmed, a St. Ursula . . .

Mary Ellen Whitaker, just what are you doing here? Why didn't you stay home in the hotel and go over your notes and wash the salt out of your hair and oh, do your other chores like writing those letters home? But you can't resist it, can you; you just can't resist being part of a little moment of history? Mary Ellen, you are a real snob, that's all, and so you despise yourself. So what? So, you're here and it's just awful. As usual, it's just awful. Doesn't Herr Schlegel feel how awful it is, sitting so fat there gleaming with pride to be at dinner with *him?* He does not, no indeed.

Why does Monsieur Capisco have to be like that? Oh, I know he has to . . . with that vast energy, that power, but well . . . why does he have to be like that in front of all these shallow, decadent people? Why, they're parasites, all after some advantage. It's disgusting. And so are you, Mary Ellen . . . so are you. You're honoured, aren't you? No use to say to yourself that all you need is the work of cataloguing, to analyse, to relate one drawing to another, or you'd be washing your smalls this very moment, back in your hotel room. Oh Lord, it's so undignified.

"Say to the court it glows, And shines like rotten wood." Who said that? Glows is right. Look at it glow. Dignity, who needs it here in this great little restaurant with its marvellous cuisine and these talented and lovely people. Get the setting; the moon-rise over the sea: Claude. The lights of the café: Van Gogh, or maybe early Bonnard. The table: pure Matisse. Just about everything glowing and shining. Who on earth said that line about the court? Why do I have to have it so dignified? It's not rotten, just rich. Why don't I adjust to it and be calm, poised, sophisticated, urbane, like Signora Schlegel sitting so at home up there, between Monsieur Capisco and Jeannot, with her elegant, really elegant, address? Mary Ellen, stop kidding yourself. You just aren't *mondaine.*

Harold always said I just couldn't adjust to people in other walks of life and I guess he was right. "You stay on campus, Mary Ellen," he said. "In the University Museum you fit. In the great big world, you don't. Social aplomb you don't have, but Mary Ellen, you're cute . . . no, I mean it . . . you're really a very cute girl. You could be a real doll if you just fixed your hair and everything."

Well, I sure couldn't adjust to Harold, although Harold could write. I mean really write; but he wasn't gentle, and well, I just couldn't, not at first. He was so urgent. We sat there in his room and he had those great prints on the walls and we talked and talked about Spinoza and Kant and Sartre and heaven knows what and he really *knew* about things and it was exciting, and then he jumped me. I felt such a fool, and oh my lord! I upset the coffee on my skirt. Oh Lord, and that was so long ago; my senior year. What can

I do about my hair? I have my notes to go over in the hotel room, I could maybe just kind of slip away . . . and wash and set my hair.

"You must your head make now. You have already made a body for Jeannot."

"Why, I just don't know, Doctor Ritterbaum, I haven't tried to draw a head since my junior year in College."

"Come now, my dear young lady, surely it is not for you troublesome? Drawing is your speciality."

"Why, not drawing, Doctor, writing on drawings."

"I know, I know. It was my little joke. I know well your work on Capisco. You have insight. Also on Giacometti and the little Schiele book . . . very good. I say to write on drawing is to understand drawing. So, young lady, draw . . ."

This dear old guy is being kind to me. He's nice, I guess, even if he does look like a Daumier pen and wash or maybe a Breughel. "Breughel!"

"You are speaking with yourself? You say Breughel and you are right. It is such a scene from Breughel, if more French, but rather even more from the early Titian . . . Bacchus and Ariadne . . . not so?"

"No, yes, I mean no more wine, thank you, I just don't have a head for wine. I'll be drunk."

My voice goes up like a bat, dammit. I can't help it. I squeak. Oh God, I must not squeak. But the scene here is like a Breughel and not the Peasant Wedding . . . more like Dulle Griet, the mad St. Margaret looting in the Mouth of Hell and me as her, looting culture like the zany in the veiled tin hat loots metalwork, but in my case, no sword. I really believe I look as cute as that, with my hair under the drier. Mad St. Meg, I remember, confronted the Devil who had got himself up as a dragon and for that he ate her, but her crucifix stuck in his craw so he threw up. That, I feel like. But to Breughel, Griet was *Fortuna* with the unstable proceeds in her cook pot; such junk as Cap collects in his and I from him, in my analysis. Or I could say that Griet was Mother Courage with her pramful of bits and pieces, like Cap. I could do a very scholarly treatise on these implications, to prove that everything means itself and other things as well. After all, it does.

I wish it were quiet: like Velasquez is quiet. Ineloquent. But that's not Cap. He burns with a hard, gem-like . . . The hell he does. He just burns and glows and shines and fans his own bonfire and all those beautiful people are so much kindling to him . . . matchsticks glowing, maybe rotten. I remember the line now; Sir Walter Raleigh: "Say to the court it glows, And shines like rotten wood" something . . . something "If church and court reply, Then give them both the lie." I guess it's a lie and I guess the reigning monarch knows that, but why does he have to have it this way?

Madame Capisco is smiling at me and saying nothing. She doesn't mind what he says to her, but I mind what he says to me and I can see from his grin that he's going to tease.

"My little insect," he says, "give us the benefit of your sting. See if you can bring up a lump on the paper and make it itch."

Everyone laughs, of course. They are all waiting to see me look foolish, all watching me. I don't speak. What can I say when I know my voice will go up and up until it strangles? Oh damn . . . damn. "Insect," he calls me, "Mosquito." Always nicknames. Does he know how often his drawings are graphic nicknames for drawings, nowadays? And it is he who stings, not me, with his clown's grin and his needles. I suppose he quite likes me, by the way he looks, even if he thinks I'm an insect. I'm privileged to put my little, thin proboscis into his lordly dish and pen thin comments on his lovely and his lousy drawings. Maybe I can glow and shine a little with a rotten drawing of my own.

Well, so okay, so I'll draw. What? Something to make him laugh, but not at me. What'll I draw? Something fantastic . . . a zoo-morph . . . a little grinning monster out of Breughel maybe? It seems to go with the scene. Mary Ellen, come on now . . . So come on, girl, draw.

We are halfway round the table, seeing that Estelle shows no sign of joining in our antics and so far the game has gone without overt ill-feeling, even from me. Cap opened with Kir down to the neck, a feat the more remarkable since I am sure that he was feeling her up towards it for much of the time. He passed his head to Nella who maybe did herself skeletal justice and so the consequence passed to me and I ended it in a neat bow. Meanwhile, as reported, I began a portrait of Cap and gave him horns, scrubbed them and made them into ass's ears and regretted it, so passed this item to Lens who gave it a body and pushed it across to Kir and there is Kir with the tip of her tongue stuck out and following the action of her pencil slowly, slowly. For manners, now and again, she is holding off Capo.

The mosquito who is a shy girl of furiously quiet endeavour is crouched, wings folded, antennae aquiver, starting a consequence on her own with who-knows-what to guide her diligent hand, but leaning for sure on the remembrance of the Flemish and German masters c. A.D. 1510 in which she majored, and relying on her raw Kansas courage, which she pronounces "kerge." That painstaking image neatly folded over will go to Addle or maybe to Lens, because nothing is simply going round the table but also across as well as up and down.

Hansi has compressed his features into the centre of his face and wears his wide brow wrinkled as if he were reading the contractual small print. Addle is saurian serene and both are thinking how to start, while Capo is waiting for Lens to finish and pass him her body, which is something he doesn't want any more, with my head on top, which is of him and something he won't like. He doesn't get it because Kir does and is slowly finishing it off. As for me, I am like Cap, ahead of the game, but now Hansi has done some scrawl and naturally passed it to Capo to do a body for him, as a token of his deep desire for a body of Cap's work, whilst Nella is fretting with her make-up and hoping not to draw anywhere else henceforth but on to the subtle curves of her exotic Roman lips.

Now that I look around, I see that all save Capo, who is grinning, have their mouths pursed up in the way that football players do at half-time when they suck quarters of lemon. Even Estelle has pursed lips, because she has taken a pomegranate from the fruit dish and is severely cutting into it with a blunt fruit knife. I cannot tell why she should attack this intractable fruit, which is hell to manage, save that it is an object sacred to the goddess Hera and that Estelle can manage pretty well anything. And she is through the rind and the seed bursts out blood red. Lens, who is a pro, gets a snap of that for her album with its God-knows-what circulation.

Estelle doesn't play children's games, not even Cap's, but I imagine she has the tape recorder now notwithstanding, and her gravid thoughts may well be seeding as if they were microfilm of the sacred books which ravishing Tarquin once sought to buy, to his cost, from the Cumaean Sibyl. Every time this Etruscan monarch made a bid, the Sibyl upped the price by burning one volume and asking the same going rate for the remainder. It would make Hansi weep to think of it.

For Estelle, the lighting is adjusted so that she can see everything a little out of focus, making it endurable. Only Cap, down at the other end of the table, is sharp and clear to her, in his own lime-light, and she is not looking at him but at the pomegranate. I think Estelle has her hand on the dimmer, changing the intensity of light and pulling focus at the same time because she is without the hysterical charge which the consequences are setting up in everyone else. Thus she alone is not keeping the circuits on the blink and is not contributing to the overload which may yet blow the main fuses.

What Estelle holds, and she has held Capo with it for quite some time, she holds in common with archaic Greek sculpture. It is a gift of indestructible energy contained in a monumental calm. To her, perhaps, it is not only Moustique who is an insect here, although Estelle would not hurt a fly. Whatever that noble bulk of a Piero della Francesca madonna contains by way of thought, it will now at least silence my frantic chatter for a while. And it will also alter the pace.

He is not quite well, my Capo, and not good about taking his pills. With men who are never ill that is to be expected, but at his age . . . and he has eaten practically nothing. I shall have to make him fried eggs, when we are alone. Well, he will not listen to me, although he will accept from me what he has not heard me say, since he knows perfectly what it will be. To be a nuisance to Capo is to be upset by his performance, knowing, as I should after this much time, approximately where his truths hold, under his funny hats. I wonder a little if he has quite clear thoughts any more, up there where he has got to, but perhaps on the plateau, with all the climb behind him, he could try to rest. He admits nothing, but I think, in the work, he rests a little.

It is astonishing how far Cap will go in reacting to circumstances he has not himself created. I remember when I was very young, at Cannes, in the year when Serge had just died, that Capo strained and strained to be rough and casual about Serge's death. Capo always seems gay when he is upset, or moved, or not working well, but I did not know him well in those days. I did not respond properly, not being secure then any more than now, if now more convincing, perhaps. I had no idea that I had any answers or could be one answer for Cap. So he got up and went away and stayed away for five hours. I thought he had left me and I cried, not knowing that he was in the hotel bedroom next to ours, which was someone else's room. There he was, drawing and drawing on the hotel notepaper and screwing up the drawings and throwing them out of the window and trying to telephone anyone who would come and not assume that he was upset and let him make jokes. It was only when I looked out of the window that I knew where he was. All the paper was on the lawn outside, screwed up like snowballs.

So I went in to him and took his head and held it to me and he tried to put down the telephone receiver, being unable to get it to his ear, with my arms round him, so that we got twisted up in the wire. Capo began to laugh, out of his sense of duty to himself, and went over and locked the door, so that presently Stravinsky, or Kochno, or whoever's room it was, began to bang on the door and Capo shouted at him and whoever it was went away.

"Let him go, Cap," I said.

"He's gone," said Capo.

"No, I mean Serge."

"Oh, him," said Cap, disinterested. But when I looked at the drawings on the floor, the ones that hadn't gone through the window, they were all caricatures of Serge, playing with boys. "I'm sending them on," said Capo, "in case he gets short of ideas for ballets." At which I put the telephone back on the hook.

In the morning a little pageboy came to our room with all the screwed-up drawings from the garden, piled up in a pyramid on a silver salver. That wouldn't happen now; Capo throws nothing away nowadays. The pageboy backed out of the room, in case Capo should jump on him, and Capo, who was in bed, leaped up, stark naked, and tore after the poor child, to give him an enormous tip. They ran right through the hotel.

Sex is a great duty to Capo. If I hadn't been there, perhaps he might even have jumped on the pageboy, if only to preserve his own *amour-propre,* his image as they would say now. But I doubt it. Cap doesn't like boys, although he likes girls who will pretend they are. Truthfully, he never really liked Serge, who did like boys.

I expect I must seem very stolid to those people here. I have so little to say and all they want me to talk about is Capo. Knowing how angry he would be for fear I might give some little bit of him away and let them get at him, I don't do that much. So I seem very dull and I sit still. It doesn't matter.

The difficulty has always been to make him feel more or less safe. Cap doesn't believe in his own fame, that it is truly earned, except now and again. He's like this fruit I'm holding, tough in the skin but filled with seed like blood.

When they were very young, before I was even born, Capo and Pablo and, in his prim way, Georges and after that a lot of painters, began to smash up Cézanne, althought I think Capo was the only one who felt that that was what they were doing. It was natural to Pablo and easier, and easier for Georges too, both being primarily painters. But Cap is really a sculptor, despite his having to paint and do everything else as Pablo does. Pablo and Georges went into Cézanne through the landscapes and still-lifes. Capo went in through the portraits, the faces of Madame Cézanne, still and sculptural. "There was this bloody building," Capo said to me once, "blocks all fitted together and held there with the colour cementing the tones even in the portraits and something had to give or we'd all have been walled up." Pablo thought it was Cézanne's anxiety that made him interesting and Pablo could never resist needling someone's anxiety. Capo however was anxious and felt he was trespassing. I'm not sure he ever forgave himself the Cézanne-bashing. Cap's not Pablo. But both of them and Georges too got into Cézanne; "getting into the cracks and pushing sideways for landslides," Capo said. And he rearranged all the splinters and fragments that fell, much as Pablo did, and built them back altered, but Capo kept the anxiety which Pablo ignored while Georges was not much anxious. Capo is still anxious about building everything back when it's altered. He's been like that with me too, as long as we've been together. I've been pulled apart and reassembled over and over again, being in some measure the building he lives in. "You never change," he tells me.

So he chops at me, but he can't leave me splintered, as Pablo would have. He has to put me back together each time.

The time Capo started to "harden up" Rodin was not so different, because Rodin was always breaking up his plasters and putting them together differently, so it was quite natural for Capo, but Capo made more of Negro sculpture than the others, after Derain showed it to him. Being a sculptor, he couldn't leave it where Pablo left it. He did other things with it and called the results "carapaces," although he doesn't like to be reminded. He never gave me a carapace and I should have found it so useful.

Being a sculptor, when Cap started, was difficult. There were painters, but very few sculptors. No one much knew what Degas had done with sculpture then, because he kept his little wax models private, and otherwise there was just Rodin and official art and what Capo called "my revered and corpsed compatriots" by whom he meant the long-dead Donatello and Giovanni Pisano and those. In a way too, Capo made sculpture out of the recollection of Masaccio who had made painting, in his time, by looking at sculpture by his own revered and sometimes corpsed compatriots. Then there was Brancusi, whom Cap admires although he used to call him the "Romany Machine-Tool" and maintained that everything Brancusi did was done on a power-lathe, in secret. But then Capo isn't really a carver. He's a bronze-man, a builder-up and cutter-down of wax and plaster, a maker of soft into hard. He invents and builds and destroys. "With stone," he says, "how do I get rid of the evidence or put it together differently?" Rodin was like that. He didn't carve but hired Italians to aggrandise his marbles from plasters and bronze maquettes.

Of course Capo has that chisel of his, with a pomegranate hung from the handle, but he's a penetrator, not a carver. I don't think he forgives himself the destruction, not of his own work but of his "thefts" as he calls them, when he is boasting. I don't think he forgives the Cézanne-bashing, when he thinks about it. Often he doesn't think, doesn't care to think, now. He hangs on to being protean. When he begins to lose his nerve, he gets especially protean. No one else knows that Cap sometimes loses his nerve. No one who hasn't really been with him; not even Addle who's been there longest. Cap works beyond the risk, "wrecks it to save it."

When he's frightened he lashes out against the fear that he may be drawing in his horns. Those horns of Cap's, all gilded now and twined with vine leaves, are ram's horns, not bull's horns like Pablo's. But I think Capo would rather have been a builder, like Cézanne, before it got to be too late. Yet it was hacking at Cézanne and hardening up Rodin that gave him his points of departure.

I've spilled pomegranate on my skirt. He's put down Kir and picked up that little Contessa, just when Jeannot was going to get upset. That's not like him.

"Addle, do you think Capo looks well?"

"Never better, my dear."

"I just wondered . . ."

At one time Capo used to bring his girls to bed with me, which surprised them. I had only a limited response to these girls at the outset and some curled up like frozen snails, but sometimes, well, often enough, they uncurled and I liked it so long as Capo was there to watch, of course, but I wouldn't have, without him. He stopped when he thought he couldn't have us both, one after the other. I said, "Capo, you don't have to every time. We can make each other, or you can do her or me, without both," but he didn't. "Vanity," he said, "is vanity and I need mine," and he would say he couldn't feel anything any more below the waist which was demonstrably untrue as he would afterwards admit could be proved. Now he says he has to play singles. Or he says he does but I don't feel so sure he does. I'm not sure he plays any more. He doesn't look quite well.

Some time ago Pablo got married and his friend Dominguin the bullfighter said, "But why marry one?" And Pablo said, "Why not? When I'm older I'll get another one, younger." Capo is not like that. He doesn't trade them in, he adds them in, like Kir who got married to Jeannot. Like the story of Amphitryon and Alcmene which made Capo laugh so much that he broke into Jeannot's little house when they were away on honeymoon and painted a picture of that myth all over the wall of their studio in one night. And now the poor children don't know what to do with it because it's so valuable. They can't afford to be angry, but I think they are; or anyway Jeannot is.

I don't think Capo had Kir. I think he just wanted Jeannot to get worried by the myth and maybe he wanted to believe he could be young enough to be Jeannot and better than Jeannot to Kir, at least in the dark, which is what the myth is about.

The ways in which Capo and Pablo are different is something I think about. Pablo is all Spaniard, bulls, minotaurs, pride, flowering wounds, irony, Goya and rivalry. Of course he has no rivals now except Capo and the dead, so he goes at the dead with pics, *banderillas* and his sharp, bent sword, to kill. Pablo has mocked his own love of Velasquez and Delacroix. He mocks being the great artist. He mocks the recollection of his own potency. Capo is too Italian for that, although his Corsican blood is a thing he shares with Napoleon. Capo is a man of the Aegean by nature, a bull-jumper rather than a matador. Also he is not so old as Pablo.

The Cézanne-bashing had Pablo as pacemaker and the only rivalry that has ever truly existed between Capo and Pablo is the male one. And what, I wonder, do they think? There's only a mouthful of the essence of any man to be squeezed out and sprayed in, even if it tastes like oysters. Apart from bulls and rams, the rivalry only extends to the length and thickness of the catalogues of their retrospective exhibitions. Pablo is worse about this. He was furious when Matisse got a bigger catalogue than he did when they each had retrospectives in that museum in New York.

The museums are something peculiar. Even I can remember the times before these big one-man museum shows really got going, but once they began they became very important. Before that the painters and sculptors went to museums to learn, as Cézanne said they should incidentally, because that was where it was to find and to steal. Pablo and Guillaume Apollinaire actually did once steal sculpture from the Louvre, or so it's said, but the stealing with Capo, and with all of them really, went on through the eyes. Capo carries his museum on his back fairly comfortably, with all the weight of his revered and corpsed ancestors in it. Pablo invades his, with an axe, but Pablo is a fierce one and Capo is not so fierce as he makes out. He has, under all his carry-on, all that appearance of improvisation, a concentration on ordering the look and relationship of things that lie outside himself. He does not have Pablo's rhetoric, nor his dazzle. Capo is less the acrobat, more the high-wire artist, clowning a bit nowadays on the tightrope, but balanced, I think. I don't believe he'll lose that.

Watching Capo work when he's not putting on an act, as he is now, is like watching a fisherman mend his nets. They are nets torn by great marine monsters and he mends them with a needle. And he himself is the monster who has broken the nets but he mends them, whereas Pablo, who is also a monster, glories in the gaping tears and leaves them be, or tears them wider. Capo has destroyed much of what he has done. Pablo, I have the feeling, never destroyed enough. But then Pablo is a painter, and maybe even more a graphic and when he makes sculpture he rolls it out like a baker or a pastrycook and puts it straight into the window to be taken and eaten, not worrying about it or who eats it. Capo, being a sculptor, who also turns out paintings, worries, because the speed of the cooking and the precise heat of the oven is different and perhaps more important for him. He worries about his digestion yet he takes his cakes back out of the window, not finding them good and eats them himself and they give him wind. I don't know why I am thinking like this about Capo and cooking. Perhaps it's because he's eaten so little dinner.

Jeannot, who is always on about Greek gods, which is why Capo teased him with that picture on his wall, says that Capo is an Apollo behaving like Dionysus. I am not sure I know what he means.

"Addle, what did Dionysus do?"

"Eh?"

"Dionysus, you know."

"Do? He was a drinker . . . god of wine, also very destructive and dangerous but much loved, *ja?* He came from the east with panthers and maenads and satyrs and goats, very disorderly. Very powerful."

"Like Capo."

"Not so. Not like Capo. Capo is from nearer home. In Capo there is no blood lust demonstrated. So far as Capo has a god in him, it could be Hephaestos except that Capo is not lame and is certainly not thrown down from Olympus, as in the legend. Perhaps he is Zeus who was a great collector and an unreliable husband."

"Addle, don't be sly!"

"I assure you Capo is not Dionysus, whose Apotheosis, or epiphany, Euripides insists, was as a bull."

"Apollo, Jeannot says."

"In a way, *ja*, in a way." Addle speaks absently since, rather unwillingly, he is drawing now.

Did I say that? I could have done. I suspect the body that he is tentatively attaching to Moustique's head, passed quickly to him as if in secret, and now folded over even more decisively than his own, is something of a limp Klimt, a stray, sad shade decoratively bred in the Jugendstil. I suspect that he is conjuring up a female wraith, stroking away at her contours with his soft pencil. At any rate he is folded over it, nose to table, his neck moving gradually in and out of his collar. He is peering at his piece of paper as if it were a dubious lettuce leaf. If, when he has finished his diaphanous doodle, he passes it to Hansi we should get a conspectus of the north alpine tradition from Bosch to Beckmann. Meanwhile Addle is withdrawn into his shell and on to the track there should come a Wiener-Waltz as backing for Doktor Ritterbaum's silent soliloquy.

A god, he is not. Capricious he can be and a genius, but not a god. It is too late for him now to be a god, when gods are all museum exhibits worshipped for aesthetic investments. Perhaps it is altogether too late to be a god now, unless one is a young Jesus with a guitar and even then, a short run. The children do not want Capo nowadays, nor the others. Duchamp did that and perhaps that is how it had to be—a joke. A joke god. To Estelle, of course, Capo remains a god. With feet of clay? No, feet of gold is better, but she would not accept that either. A god . . . Dionysus? Zeus? Apollo—he was orderly and cruel—I think not. More of the earth, this man whom I have so long known and who has made for me such a fortune and so much else, although I have done something to make him such a god as they used to think he was, before even Capo became something of a joke, or maybe beyond a joke.

When I was young, in Austria, where there was serious and strict education, in those days serious, we learned properly of the Greeks. Not only of gods and heroes but of victims of gods, and we were made to know clowns as well as heroes. It was not of gods only, but of their victims, their playthings, that one learned. I think that Capo is more the victim, unknowing, than the god, unless perhaps by now he knows. And of both gods and demigods a victim, because of Pablo coming in. Pablo is also not a god, but he has been the one with horns and panther skins who owes little to Apollo and much to Dionysus, although Pablo was never a drinker. It could be said that Capo and Pablo and Juan Gris, poor boy, and Georges received their gifts from Dionysus. No, not Gris. He was truly an Apollonian and not Georges who owed to country gods his seeming tranquillity, but Pablo certainly. He received the gift from Dionysus, and for Capo, for both of them, it was the absurd gift given to Midas. It was the golden touch. The Midas consequence.

Perhaps it is not so. Midas left nothing but his greedy story and his dead treasure, washed off in the river Pactolus. They, Capo and Pablo, will both leave more than that, but who am I to think in this way? Am I a river? Well, perhaps I have been such a stream in which the gold dust was washed off. Much washed off on me, certainly. And it was I, so far as taking Capo's work and passing it on has been concerned. Such idle thoughts and fancies. Yet seeing Capo wandering about in that rubbish out there, this afternoon, I thought to myself, Addle, here is Midas in his rose garden and Midas has you to wash out his gold and watch over it. You are his gardener and it is you who cares for the gold, not Capo. He has the touch: I have the trade.

I am a happy man, except that I am as old as Capo. Only when I was starting, and then when the wars made it hard on a Jew, did I have difficulties. Only temperament in others have I had to worry about and lack of money at times, when Capo had the temperament and the others also, since they, not I, had the real worry about how good was it, matched against their gods and, I suppose, each other.

I had energy and I believed in them and I believed in Capo even when he did not quite believe in himself ever. No one else knows about that.

Once Pablo said to Braque, "We make shit," which upset Braque very much and Madame Braque even more. When Capo heard about this he said, "Georges makes the most serene shit in Europe, what more does he want?"

"Shit?" I could be shocked then.

"What else do we squeeze out of our guts," said Capo, "roses?"

"*Ach,* Cap," I said.

"It is your business to make it smell like roses, not ours."

"That perhaps, yes. But for me that is not so hard."

"You are a natural hairdresser, old friend," said Capo, "with your sweet-scented toilet water to pour over the body politic and your brilliantine to rub into their prestige and your lacquers to set their confidence and your little clippers to trim them with."

"Who benefits?" I was displeased.

"Who? You mean me? What do I need?"

"Hah."

"A little food, a few materials, a place to work, what else. And besides, you keep me short."

So that was perhaps thirty years ago when he had only one studio in Paris and one at St. Jean and the villa outside Arezzo. He still owns all of them, as well now as the other places and the castello up the road from here, with the zoo in the garden.

"Tradesman," he said, "go peddle to your public."

"I peddle to your public."

Capo is ambivalent about that public, which is perhaps natural since nowadays he only sees it in the distance when it comes to look at him. This he likes, which is why he has iron railings round his house and Pancho on guard and why he goes all summer to the public beach also. For fifty years, nearly, the public, as opposed to Cap's followers and the critics and those of the *avant-garde,* regarded Capo as a rogue, a charlatan, or a joke, or mad. Now the public loves him for being so old and so vigorous and the *avant-garde* does not. The museum directors love him and the dealers love him and the critics seek to make him into history so that they can love him in a scholarly way, but his followers are gone.

"The public loves you," I told Cap, last summer, when he was complaining.

"They are alone in that," he said to me, "and in any case it is Pablo they love, for being old and so vigorous." Capo can be melancholy. I think he is melancholy now, and Estelle sees it. I shall pass my little drawing to Lens who can put legs on it. She is braying

and she is drunk. I do not like drunk women. They can be most embarrassing.

Lens does not seem to know what to do with Addle's folded-over
body. "Where are the leg places?" she asks.

"Here and here," Addle tells her, prodding at the strip of paper
across the table with a spoon. "There," says Hansi, pointing. "For
God's sake," says Lens, searching in her handbag for the pencil in
front of her. *"Garçon, un whisky-soda."*

Looking round now I see that the whole table is drawing and
there is a batch of folded strips of paper piling up in front of Capo
and the conversation is very general except that Cap is silent and
Estelle too. The rest of us are being animated and who knows what
voice over is going on to the soundtrack with so many of them at it.
It will be quite an editing job.

Lens cannot think how to start and I can't think how to stop and
I have drawn four fragments of no consequence, whilst Capo has
naturally made all manner of gay and brilliant improvisations and
can hardly wait to get to work on other people's drawings, in his
manic way. The waiters are waiting and even honest Poitevin, the
proprietor, is among them waiting, and the chefs have come out to
get in on the event, and something is beginning to go wrong with
the evening. Hansi is clearly wondering how to lay hands on the
scraps of paper, once Capo has worked them over, and Addle is, I
suspect, thinking of some way to prevent the Capisco overflow from
gushing, since he sees himself as the guardian of what art gets out
and the proper judge of its quality. These mixed-up memorabilia
might prove a problem. Kir is very pink from something Cap has
said and Lens is very white. She is groping for her spectacles which,
Estelle has pointed out, are lying on the table next to the whisky-
soda. For the moment Lens has the ball in her court.

A production. I could be a feature, yet another one. And I get so
tired of thinking that way; tired of thinking in sub-titles about
Capo who has been tired of me and sub-titles for God knows how
long. Why doesn't the boy bring my Scotch? I shouldn't need it, but
I get so goddamn tired. I stay on, I keep coming back and sitting in,
don't I, and for what? Because I'm a pro? I say that. Capo is news,

47

always news, always hot. And between Cap and me is the griddle, the grid, the goddamn great iron-barred thing over the coals with me on it, like a lamb chop, burned hard on the outside and bloody rare inside and perfectly cooked, or stewed, I could say.

When Cap and I were together, when it was my portrait he drew and twisted up and took apart and then made in plaster with bits of sheepskull bedded in it and the cardboard one bent and cut, which that bastard Lodge got away with, I didn't get so fried, did I? Not in those days which were the good days. Now I do. Maybe it was the life I led. My career. "Your career, your little click-click-Kodak career is a collage," Cap said. "Stick it together and you have a photo-montage and you are too much a photo-montage already." But I had to be independent of Cap, seeing that Estelle was already there anyway. I couldn't just be an item stuck in his album, but I could and I was, whether or not I took the assignments they gave which, never mind Korea and Suez, always came back to "Why not a new line on Capo, after all you have the entrée and so on," and I'd say okay and back to the click-click of Capo. Capo making wax models or Capo at the bronze foundry or Capo with his children and, and . . . Oh God, to play second fiddle, okay, but to be just in the string section and at the desk in the back under the brass is not. So okay. If you can't lick 'em, join 'em and I joined Estelle, who is sitting here next to me like a damn statue off the Parthenon, wearing her worn look as if it gave her antiquity and not just age. It's the material. Next to Estelle, I feel like plastic. She's got no fire, Estelle, no go, no zing. She just *is*, without working at it. Is that what Cap wants maybe, a matrix, a fireproof oven to incubate his motherfucking genius in? He looks shrivelled up. He looks like an old clown, fiddling at that girl, while Lens burns, and now showing her his bright, brass horn, wherever he got that from.

I hear myself in N.Y., when they say "What's he *really* like?" And how should I know? I was there and he had me and Estelle was there, and could I fight at that weight? She looks at me now as if I'd been entered for the fights, but strictly the prelims. But I tell them, "Well, it was great . . . he's just great," and they look at me as if I'd made it, made the champ himself and still got my looks so now I'm news myself. So the champ keeps it up, even now. He can't part with anything from his collection. No discards for Capo; just the gold-plated trophies on the mantle and do they tarnish? No, they stay bright as buttons, don't we? Gold doesn't tarnish.

Estelle makes out she never bore any grudge. The hell she didn't. Buster, on my left, is making signals and I don't feel so good. And what have I drawn on this damn consequence? Chaplin's funny boots, turned out sideways, what else? Chaplin is what I always draw: Charlie, the Capo of the silver screen.

"Mrs. Lodge," says the Swiss cheese, "I wonder if, together, we might make a volume of photographs of the master? Could we discuss this?"

"Sure, sure, great idea, just wonderful." As if no one ever thought of it before.

"This evening is most memorable, and you have made a most complete record of it."

"If they come out."

"You are joking. I know your work. I would like to tell you how much I admire your talent."

"Thanks. Yeah, they'll come out, why sure, they'll come out." Out they will surely come, the little prints, and a volume they will surely go into and into the glossies too and ten per cent to Joe. And they'll be good. So they'll be good, so thanks. Only the Lens is not so good.

"Lens darling, are you sure you feel quite well?"

I have been waiting for that question. She asks it every single time I see her and she means it. I don't even ask myself any more why she won't drop dead and I don't expect to feel quite well.

"Sweetie, I'm in great shape. Just a little bit tired."

"You should take care. You live so hard."

"It's the rat-race, sweetie, I guess I'm sort of used to it."

She pats my hand and I smile, click-click smile, before my face breaks up and falls off, but it won't. Now she'll say, "Come and see us tomorrow, when we can be peaceful," and she does. And of course I'll go. I always do. I'm truly, deeply fond of Estelle and I'll go and see "us" tomorrow and there will be Cap's new things and Cap's jokes mainlined into me, hooked as I am, and Estelle will take trouble. So what else will I do? Who do I love in the world, for God's sake, apart from Cap and Estelle? Who else is anyone who seems real?

I have this metallic sort of taste in my mouth again and Jeannot, Jeanikins, is hollering up the table to me and I don't seem to be able to fold up these little pieces of paper very well. Addle is looking at me too, so at once I am in there hiding behind the Leica and click. With film as fast as this, I can damn near shoot in the dark. Addle looks concerned. A nice old guy. I could do a story on Addle, maybe for *Life* if *Life* hadn't folded. My analyst tells me I use my camera to avoid confrontation. Maybe I do. There are people here who use their faces to avoid confrontation. Estelle does, but to do that you have to look like Estelle, or be like her. So far as I can see all the people gathered round the table have their faces smoothed out, avoiding confrontation by letting it glance off the surface: except Capo and a lot he cares.

Jeannot is a lot like Ben, not just to look at. Ben, when I was first married to him and things looked bright and nobody had ever heard of him, nor me for that matter, but things were going for us. When was that?

Jeannot has that same fierce-eyed look and the same smooth arrogance, which is to hide his insecurity, natch. And he's stuck on Cap, just as Ben was stuck on the All-American Poet, Frost, which kind of dates us. Always hanging around the old man and not really liking him. Can you have calf-love when you're adult? Because that's what it's like and what it was like for Ben. Jeannot can't believe that Capo won't show him a mystery which, being solved, will solve everything. He knows he can't, but he can't believe he won't. And it's as if Cap has Jeannot gold-plated, stationary, and as static as a motor mascot. Kir ought to get him out from under and Cap ought to let him out. But Jeannot is hypnotised by Cap. He thinks the sun shines out of Cap's ass. It's like Ben and that old bastard, Frost, and I understand it. Oh Jesus, don't I understand it?

There was a guy I did a feature on in Germany: big noise on animal behaviour. This guy had jackdaws, geese and for all I know wombats and wolves following him round, falling over him and sitting on his head. He said they were imprinted; that they were fixated on him and sure enough they couldn't let him alone. Some went in swimming with him. It would have driven me nuts, but he thought it was great. Capo has Jeannot imprinted and I suppose he thinks that's great, but I think it's been for long enough. Jeannot's a big boy now and I have the feeling he is showing strain. It's rough on him but, like the old man said . . .

I guess I'm screwed up, mean maybe, maybe tired. In Estelle's shadow I can lean back a bit, out of this gay throng and just sit here awhile. Maybe nobody will get at me. Ben was no good, the poor sweet dope. He quit and walked out one night in the Crillon bar, when we were there with Sam, and went home to the barbiturates and that was Ben. I guess it's nice here with Cap and Estelle and anyway I'm out of film.

And now Hansi is, I observe, thinking to himself as you shall hear, while for the rest of us it's all very gay in this reflected glory and gilded company. It's what Lens would call wild. But somehow it's ominous too. Hansi is helping Lens to fold up her paper and has spilled a little of her whisky and is apologising and being helpful because Lens is stewed and he is mopping at the whisky and Lens screams at him, "For fuck's sake, let it alone. Jesus fucking Christ, get your mits outa my Scotch."

Hansi recoils in alarm. Estelle says, "Lens, darling," and Capo, moving as with the speed of light, picks up his trumpet thing and blows into it like a triton. This device works, since everyone's attention is attracted, more or less. Some seem to be in states of shock.

Lens is safe behind her camera, now that recovery becomes general, whilst Hansi has retired into his consequence. He looks severely shaken, as well he might, being on the receiving end of one of Lens's shrieks and Capo's blast, and he gives the impression of having more buttons holding him in than previously. He stares at Capo, who is carefully putting his instrument back in the toy pram, and then, stiff as a puppet, he begins to draw with his fingers clenched on the pencil, white to the tips.

Why did she do that? Is she insane? I meant no more than to assist her and she screamed like that. It is horrible to do such a thing at the dinner-table. I do not know what would have happened if Capisco had not blown that remarkable note on his oliphant. I think Mrs. Lodge would have become hysterical. She might have caused a terrible disturbance, whereas now she is quite calm again and has at once photographed him, winding his oliphant. Astonishing that she should have caught up her camera so quickly, but that I am sure is most professional of her and I am sure she will have taken a most unusual picture. She is what they call "fast on the draw" in American.

It is most extraordinary that Capisco should have discovered an oliphant in this restaurant. Astonishing that there should have been an oliphant in the dining-room here. It is a very rare instrument although this one can hardly be an original example. I myself cannot remember seeing one except in an engraving of the seventeenth century, shown to me by Madersteig one evening in Verona. The oliphant was of course used by huntsmen in the service of the Byzantine Court but I should hardly think that a specimen would survive until today, especially here, in a restaurant. But then everything this evening is strange and magical. It is magical that I should be sitting here drawing an image on a paper, which I shall presently give to the greatest of living draughtsmen to complete. I should not have believed it possible. Even more unlikely, Nella, who cannot in any way draw, has added to a Capisco drawing. Amazing. It is not a thing that a bookseller would expect to happen to him or to his wife, even if she is Nella.

I am afraid that I am not making a good impression upon my fellow-guests. I am not a person who shines in such circumstances. They think me stiff because I cannot share their jokes and I am of course not quite at ease. I am seldom at ease except with bookish people and at the office. But I am so happy to be the guest of Capisco and he himself is so natural, so unpretentious and life-enhancing in his manner, making, as he has, such an event of this children's game we are playing at his behest. It will be an evening to remember with Nella and to tell our friends about. She is so beautiful, my Nella, and so elegant. I am so proud of her, seeing her so much at ease in this exceptional company. She is so relaxed that she casts me many sympathetic glances. Apart from Nella, Herr Ritterbaum is really the only person here with whom I can easily converse, or could if he were my neighbour at table. I am most grateful to him for effecting this invitation and even more grateful that he has spoken so highly of our books to Capisco that we shall be allowed to publish the new drawings. The book will be as well produced and the reproductions as perfect as I can have them made and then perhaps I shall be sufficiently familiar with the Master that he will agree to make etchings for a classic so that I can publish something which will be historic; something to rival Vollard. I shall wait to ask Herr Ritterbaum, or perhaps Miss Whitaker, if this might be possible. Miss Whitaker is very precise, very correct, and I am again grateful to Herr Ritterbaum for commending her to me. It will be a good association, valuable to us both.

To be able to draw is something I have always envied, really to draw like a Klee or, even more, a Schiele. It is Schiele whom I find myself following here and that perhaps is why this drawing which I am now making portrays so thin, so anxious a face. I do not know whom I imagine I portray. It is a slender man to whom I have given a wreath of vine leaves: somehow appropriate to this occasion, I think. He is a man but somehow a little resembling Nella and yet someone else. It is not bad, truly not so bad. And Mrs. Lodge is now quiet. I shall not address her further for fear of another outburst. Madame Capisco is soothing her and so I need not speak, but may concentrate on my drawing. Almost everyone is now drawing. It is amusingly like the life-classes I attended at the Kunst Schule which I had all but forgotten. It is like the lessons my father had me take when he believed I was to be an artist, before I decided I was not so gifted and went into publishing. That was a long time ago and besides publishing is also a talent.

Nella is very much at home with our friends here, this evening. It is natural of course that she should be. She does not seem overawed, even by Capisco himself—and the young painter to whom she is talking is clearly taken with her. I wonder if he has ability; I have not seen anything written about him. Clearly Capisco thinks warmly of him and he may be a coming man. I should ask to visit his studio, if he would not be offended. I shall ask Nella what she has discovered about him. She is exceptionally observant and if not perhaps knowledgeable in the arts, most sensitive to them. And so I have finished my drawing, nearly but not quite of this unknown person, and shall pass it up the table to Capisco. It is a wonderful moment.

You have now met everyone of consequence here tonight, except for Kir who is the last link in the circle going clockwise round the table to begin and end on Capo.

You have doubtless recognised the director's device, which is to isolate the individual players on sound so that you will hear them soliloquise, voice over, from cunningly edited tapes while he pans and tracks about the table on camera, with all manner of long shots and close-ups and two-shots and what have you, to show them all drawing at once, as in fact they have been doing. Also he will zoom in and out over them and over me while I do the links. That is what a zoom lens is for.

Myself, I should have favoured more dialogue and longer takes with far less bloody zooming in and out, but it is early to judge. These are, after all, only the rushes. And I must point out that there are two different kinds of consequence, even in terms of the game and quite apart from any other meaning to be attached to the word.

I guess that the heads, bodies and legs we've all been doodling at are simply the first round. There will be spoken consequences to follow; verbal consequences in the next reels where someone says something, and his neighbour picks it up, and then the anecdote goes on round the table or somewhere else, with whatever consequences result. I would have said, if there had been a script conference, that this could be dangerous, but, as usual, I should have been ignored. In any case it was Cap who improvised the game, not caring that maybe others would join the party for the second round, invited or uninvited, and the director is going along with it. When I caught his eye, he just grinned and winked at me. So I don't know for sure how it will go tomorrow, but I have an uneasy feeling that it's all been too pretty damn smooth this evening. Just the one predictable howl from Lens. Otherwise all sweetness and light and mild embarrassment, encouraged by the old Proteus at the table-top.

As things are now, only Kir is left drawing and Cap is becoming impatient that Kir is so slow although he should know it was the infighting under the tablecloth that slowed her up. Kir is still drawing legs on to Len's body, I think, with my head of Capo on top and I suppose Cap will grab it and touch it up the moment he can. Meanwhile there is a little heap of folded consequences lying between all of us on the table and the waiters and the chefs and honest Poitevin are hovering and even Pancho, Cap's Figaro and charioteer, is hovering; if anyone so heavy in the shoulders and so dignified can be said to hover. It has become very quiet. I suppose it is quite late. I wonder what Kir will do with those legs. I suppose they'll be her own. It's odd how people, if they don't make the same image every time, make self-portraits when they don't know what to do next, when they have to draw and don't want to. And Kir's legs have had a lot of attention this evening. Or maybe just because of that, she might have drawn something quite different: she has a gift for fantasy. God though, she's taking her time. Everyone else has finished and all the other little folds of paper are in front of Capo and he is waiting quite still, like a sacred crocodile, to dash into them with irony and measureless superiority to go over all of them with his felt-tip and make a meal of them. Kir doesn't seem to be thinking what's she's doing, her pencil is going round and round and the tip of her tongue in unison with it. She looks childish, pensive and earnest, as if working very hard at lessons.

I have to get Jeannot out of all this, somehow. Not just this evening, but altogether. He doesn't want to be out, I know, but he wears that kind of anxious calf look more and more and he wants someone he can blame to push him, which is me. It's not Cap altogether who's holding him, although Cap doesn't loosen his grip on anything or anyone once his tentacles have taken hold. It's the magic circle and the grandeur of being Cap's sort of heir-apparent that Jeannot can't resist and Cap can't resist Jeannot not resisting so it's a magic vicious circle. I think Cap is truly fond of Jeannot and fond of me too and used to both of us which counts for a lot. Cap is a fond man, despite his act and despite the intolerable burden of his fame, which he carries so easily since there is nothing intolerable about it.

Of course Cap tried to have me long before Jeannot turned up and when it was more important to him to have every possible girl than it is now. He only tried once, when I was practically still at school and living so near and was absolutely dazzled that he just spoke to me, but even at the time I thought that "I must draw you" line was pretty trite. Still I went up to the castello when I was asked —who wouldn't—dressed up very carefully and with my hair done and everything. But when it came to it, I didn't let him because he took me for granted or, well, I just didn't, and he was awfully surprised and put out so that I felt I ought to have let him and by then I hadn't. I was scared and he is terribly old but it wasn't really physical, I mean he isn't repulsive or anything. I even wanted it in a way for rather dreadful reasons like hinting to Suzanne, to make her wild because she is so stuck up. But then I thought that Madame Capisco might suddenly come in and be furious and that I wouldn't be asked to the castello any more, which Suzanne would tell everyone of course and embroider. Silly, really since she ran off with that mechanic from St. Rémy, just after and wouldn't have had time to crow. Still . . .

Cap had me half undressed and had made my hair a mess and I was rather fighting him when he suddenly got up and went to the window and shouted down to Estelle to come up and "bring the anti-freeze" and Estelle came up and looked and said, "Cap, darling, put her down: she's frightened," but Cap wouldn't. Estelle spoke very sharply then and there was a sort of indeterminate tension set up between them which left me right outside it, but nothing happened except that Estelle put down her gardening gloves and the trowel and sailed out into the kitchen and began to bang pots about and break the crockery and Cap began to laugh. I dressed terribly fast and while I was doing that, Estelle came back with a Kir and made me drink it which is how my nickname started. Then Estelle said, "Capo darling, put it away," but Capo wouldn't because it was still standing up hard and I couldn't look.

"It's much too big for this little girl," said Estelle soothingly and went and put it back into Cap's shorts, adding, "It takes getting used to, darling. Put it away for now." And Cap at first looked very pleased and then rather glum and he winked at me but he seemed rather nervous too, which is the only time I've ever seen that. He was also very ostentatious about settling his shorts and I couldn't think what Estelle must be thinking. I felt sure she must really be furious in a very controlled way, but she wasn't. Capo was. He began to make a fearful, uncontrolled scene, working it up with shouts and grandeur and getting very upset in a deliberate sort of way until Estelle sighed and picked up her gardening things and went out. I ran down the stairs after her and out into the garden, where she had already gone back to weeding. I thought that neither of them would ever speak to me again and I was crying and horribly embarrassed until Estelle looked up from the zinnias and smiled and said, "Come again on Sunday," and went back to her weeding.

I didn't know what to make of it and never even mentioned it to Suzanne or to Anne-Marie, fortunately, but of course I went back on the Sunday. Cap was in the big studio, working in plaster, but the moment I arrived he stopped and washed his hands and said "Undress at once." Estelle was sewing by the window and all she said was, "Why don't you, dear? Cap wants to draw you." So I did, but I thought: what next? What next was that I stripped and Estelle went on sewing and Cap started to draw on a very large sheet of paper pinned to a board. I just stood there naked, waiting for Cap to do something else, but he didn't and I stayed still for hours and Cap seemed to get more and more irritated and began muttering and starting again on new sheets of paper, while Estelle just sewed. It was weird.

After hours and hours, Cap got up and went back to mix more plaster in a bowl, saying absolutely nothing. He slapped the plaster on to the figure he'd been making and then began to hack at it with a knife and then to file at it with a cheese grater, which calmed him down. He began to sing. It was very warm and I wasn't much worried any more and I went and peered at all the drawings on the floor, where Capo had flung them and none of them was of me. They were all drawings, from different angles, of the head of the half-finished figure he was working on at the far end of the long room. I wasn't very pleased.

"I think you inspired him," said Estelle, putting down her sewing, at which Cap gave her a fearful look and went out. "You see, dear," said Estelle, "he gets worried about getting old and not being a ram so readily and we can't let him feel like that, can we? It disturbs him so."

I didn't know what to say, so she went on to explain that Cap believed all his power lay in his sex and all his strength and talent, however absurd that might seem to us to be, except that it wasn't quite. I said of course I knew it couldn't be, but Estelle explained that it was the only flattery he could still really enjoy. "He's had the rest of it for so long, the fame, the money, the admiration and they don't do anything for him any more. So he keeps saying he's finished and he works and works harder than ever and all that gets him is more fame and more money and no criticism, but also no proof. Anyway he hates criticism and won't tolerate it, but he doesn't really believe in all the praise either and that drives him mad. You don't have to sleep with him, you know," she added, without looking up from her sewing, "but please pretend you'd like to, because you see he likes you and he doesn't like most people unless they're very clever, or funny, or he's known them a long time."

It all seemed very peculiar to me, but for Estelle's sake I've played up ever since. No, that's not true. Cap is a bit irresistible in himself and also he makes me sort of want to honour him and I have only the one way.

Then Jeannot turned up and rented the cottage from Poitevin, to make it more complicated. Because at one and the same time Jeannot took me away from Capo, who had taken to showing me off as his, although I wasn't, and this made Cap very sardonic and competitive and Jeannot very ambivalent. Still, after a while we got married because of my mother. Jeannot was very good about it, if ironical. He really wants to share me with Cap although he insists he doesn't and makes jealous scenes, while Cap, who doesn't really care, teases Jeannot without mercy, but also shows him great favour and gives him drawings, especially the huge one on our wall, which is very confusing because of our not having any money much. Anyway, part of Jeannot wants Cap to have me and enjoys thinking about it and believing that Cap has, and asking me about it when I'm in bed with him and not believing me so I have stopped saying and now pretend, even though I've only ever had one other person and that was quite horrible and I only really want Jeannot. Jeannot feels that Capo is entitled, simply by being Cap, although it also excites him—Jeannot I mean. It gives him a sense of being more than equal to Cap, at least in that way, and making a tribute to him as well. Which is all very difficult but there it is.

I can honestly say that I only want Jeannot, but that wouldn't be honest. I do get intrigued and excited by Cap almost in an experimental way, since he is Capo, apart from wanting to please Jeannot, of course.

So when Cap puts my hand on him under the table, like this evening, I do and of course when he feels me up I respond, because of

Jeannot, I expect. Jeannot thinks I have tights on this evening, which I haven't, and Cap's fingers are Cap's fingers and a bit magical and especially drawing me like that just with his left hand because of touching me with his other one. He never drew me before. There wasn't very much of Cap to hold, at least not for long, but in a way, while it was there, I felt it almost springing right up him and along him and down his arm into the drawing and I was thrilled.

But I don't think it's right for Jeannot. He looks so furious and baffled and excited as well and that makes me excited and Capo thinks he's doing it and round and round. I suppose Estelle understands. She has a trick of saying something to divert Cap when she thinks it's the right time, but I think Jeannot and I ought to get away from here, except that there's this huge painting that Cap has made on our wall, which is a problem because of Poitevin and our not being able to take a huge wall with us, if we move. And of course to leave it behind would look so ungrateful and in any case it's beautiful.

What with Jeannot glowering over there and Cap showing off and looking at my breasts and making remarks about them, I haven't drawn these legs properly. I couldn't think about this silly game and I can't draw anyway, so knowing everyone would want something funny, I've made the ends of the legs into a knot. I've made a huge complicated doodle of a knot and it's supposed to look like that Gordian one; the one Jeannot told me Alexander the Great cut; so I suppose it's a symbol of being knotted up or something. Jeannot had better cut it.

Now all the consequences are drawn and piled up, folded, in front of Capo and the table is cleared and there are two cameras, one shooting mute, and everyone is waiting for Cap to unfold the consequences of this evening except for Lens, who seems to have gone to sleep. And suddenly I am angry. I am angry with the whole charade and furious with Cap who is too big to play such games.

Poitevin and the waiters are perched over us like jackdaws. All the people at the other tables have come crowding round and Cap is looking fiercely at them. Suddenly he gets up with all the drawings and stuffs them into his pocket. Hansi looks desperate. Addle's neck has shot out of his collar and he looks jurassic, a pterodactyl, not a tortoise. Kir clearly thinks it must all be her fault, for taking so long, but Kir usually thinks everything is her fault. As for Nella she is motionless and looks as stiff as an armature. "Not a very good game perhaps, darling," Estelle says calmly, and Pancho collects her bag and I try to collect my wits.

"Out," says Capo sharply, *"vai!"* He doesn't shout, but he is glaring at the spectators who are clustered around like blow-flies. Then, silence.

Poitevin, who is shrewd, backs up, signalling the waiters who dissolve as smoothly as a good optical. The gilded walk-ons are slower but, with Capo looking at them, they break up into busy groups and begin to slope away, although not so suddenly as Moustique who just vanishes onto the beach and into the dark. Cut.

With the rest of us it's all dignity and calm, and a long zoom out. Pancho and Estelle process towards Cap's elderly Hispano-Suiza. Cut. Addle takes Hansi by the arm fraternally and out of shot they go, with an air of high seriousness and distinction, deep in discussion. Cut. Nella looks at me, offers her hand with formality and remarks that they must drive back to the hotel and a kind goodnight to all, who may be heard by now talking easily, but very quietly, about meeting tomorrow, when we shall, they are sure, see the consequences apart from Cap's new drawings if he allows it. Dissolve to Pancho who comes back for Lens while the Schlegels make their exit with polite whispers. Other cars are heard starting up out of shot and the lights on the pergola go off so I assume it's a wrap and the crew is listening to the director saying something consequential and busy about tomorrow's call but, whatever it is, it sounds remote and incoherent. They've killed the lights and now the full moon is contending with the restaurant for control of what lighting remains except for a bright frame which is the interior of Cap's car, with Pancho sitting stiffly at the wheel and Estelle with Lens in the back. They, too, are quite still. One is dead to the world and has her head resting on the other, who is a world in herself. For a moment, the group shines like a museum exhibit in a well-lit glass case and then Pancho switches on the headlights and switches off the inside one.

Capo, for once, is not on display and not in the museum. He is standing alone on the road, between the jetty and the restaurant, and looking out at the vacant lot where the metaphors were found. The moon has bleached it and it has become an aquatint, pitted with deep blacks where, with sharp gestures, standing out like urgent but equivocal protests, the junk holds its own court in metamorphosis. I have an idea that it could have been the best shot of the evening, but that's documentary for you.

The old man has put on his hat as he trundles his little pram towards his car, the brazen horn he carries on his shoulder picks up the light from the restaurant and it shines out like gold.

A Cable:

UNIT SOBER RUSHES AIRFREIGHTED AI ARRIVE 820 AM STOP TAPES
GREAT STOP NARRATION LOCAL BOYGENIUS OK ONCE EDIT
PISSANDWIND STOP GENNY BLEW ENDEVENING SUGGEST RETHINK
BUDGET AS MUST RESHOOT SAME LOCATION DESPITE UPSCREWED
RENTAL RESTAURANT STOP CASTELLO SETUPS PENDING STOP CAPO
GREAT TO CAMERA TEMPERAMENT ALLOVER NO VOICEOVER STOP
WAIT AND PRAY

SANDY

II

Master Positive Reel I

Is Capo dead? Am I finally gone to glory? Has my time come? I think I am dead. I am finally and absolutely still, therefore dead, so it must be morning and I have been having that dream in which I have died, so that I am lying here laid out and dozens of postmen keep coming with telegrams and letters from all over, which Estelle is very reverently placing in a neat pile on my belly. The pile grows and grows until I am covered with paper and the messages come through to me. DEEP AND HEARTFELT REGRETS STOP WE HAD GREAT TIMES GARY COOPER. (No, that can't be right; he's dead.) LE PRESI-DENT ET MME DE GAULLE PRESENTENT LEURS REGRETS LE PLUS . . . (That can't be right, either; he's dead; did she send it?) One from Malraux; nothing from the Picassos, of course. FELICITATIONS STOP ENTRE DONC STOP HENRI MATISSE. The cables flow over my legs and then letters and then the newspapers with the long obit-uaries and then special magazine issues, until I am entombed. Then I wake up.

I have woken up, but I am keeping my eyes shut so that no one will know I am still alive, but perhaps I am not dead because I can feel the sun on my legs and stomach and chest. Why have I woken up? Because I can hear the intense sounds of everyone in the place concentrating on being absolutely quiet and not waking me up. Es-telle is whispering to, perhaps, Lens; Addle has arrived and, I sup-pose, the Swiss couple and the rest of that lot. And there will be Pancho keeping everyone away from this part of the house, which is sacrosanct, of course, because I am asleep. Together with Pancho will be old Gasparo and the boy who is the great-nephew, whom I fired and who is still here, and the crone Teresa who is Jacopo's great-aunt and the maid with the little birthmark and Gabriella who is married to Ernesto and Ernesto who is wholly dishonest and Giovanni's cousin and What's-his-name who is . . . Why am I rehearsing the list of this troop as I wake up? It is the noise, like heavy breathing, of their being so reverently considerate that drives the whole gang through my head, because there are so many of them, for one reason and another. Also there are Estelle's lame dogs who are probably poets and mothers with babies, but they are kept in the far wing in case they make noises and disturb me. There are a hundred and forty-nine rooms in this place, some of them empty, I suppose. I don't know. I do not understand why there are not a hundred and fifty—and all empty.

It is an encampment, a tribe of blood-sucking gipsy-, art-, or artist-loving parasites. It is a three-ring circus.

I open my eyes carefully and the sun, streaming in, suggests that it must be the early afternoon. Everything shines golden in it, the bronzes, the gantry, the dustbins full of plaster, the bones and shells, the bits and pieces, the moulds, the finished plasters shellacked golden, or bronze sprayed with gold and black so that I can see what they will look like when they are in metal. I must be on the camp-bed in the big studio, which was built in 1360 as the hall of audience for the Duke and is now the haul of junk for me. There is my new perambulator with the wheel bent and my large bugle, which I learned to play last night. They are at the foot of the bed like childhood Christmas presents. I can see them between my feet.

I am quite flat, except my belly which is like a heap of wheat. Awake now, I can see my gold-bronze belly and the very tip of my poor old pale, gold prick sunk into its grey underbrush, then two lumps of red golden, knobbled knees and then sallow, wrinkled feet with the toes bent about and all being further gilded by the sun. I am a landscape looked down upon from a high face. I look metallic or maybe I am sawdust, or maybe tan-bark. My belly is a circus ring. Belly circus, a rumbling metaphor and down there, coyly hiding, the ringmaster, poor old cock, who used so readily to strut in his red coat, with his purple top hat at an angle, commanding the equestriennes and ordering the animal acts. He is asleep, as all good ringmasters must, I suppose, sleep after many performances. He has his bald old head down. As for the clowns, they are all elsewhere, and the animals are in the garden under the window, except for the marmoset, Ariadne of the golden fur, who was on a window-sill, crouched among the little bronze maquettes of my baboon, but has now leaped on to my chest. It must therefore be half past two, or thereabouts.

Somewhere about must be that film crew, setting—what they call —up. Another dozen people, milling round, shooting what they call "cut-aways" or whatever, bits of local colour in artful compositions including my Matisses and the Rodins, the Bonnards, that vast bloody Balthus, the Greek pots and the rest. They will be shooting the Pisan marbles and putting their bits of apparatus down on Marino's wooden horse, which he *would* give me, or on that Englishman's reclining figure in elmwood, which is very good in its way.

I have shut my eyes again and Ariadne has climbed up my face and is sitting on my head, wishing that I had any hair there for her to explore for fleas. No fleas: they are all outside the room, setting up or sitting down and waiting. No hair: Capo is bald as an egg, a golden egg on a plate as indulgently offered by Herodias to Salome: a head as an offering to a belly-dancer from a client.

I do not think that the head over there on the turntable will do. It is very large and slack and not integrated. The nose is not urgent enough. It is too symmetrical. If I reach down, there should be a chopper by the bed and I shall presently get up and hit the bloody head along the side of the nose with it. That will teach it. But not yet. I need coffee. First I need coffee. Why does no one bring me coffee? God knows, there are enough people in this bloody *certosa* to bring an old man a cup of coffee.

"Coffee, Cap darling."

"Huh."

"Coffee. It is three o'clock in the afternoon."

"Nonsense."

"The place is full of people."

"Send them to hell. Tell them I am dying."

"Capo, darling."

"Estelle, tell me. Isn't the nose too easy on that head?"

"Which head?"

"That one down beyond my feet, on the turntable, the big plaster."

"Yes it is. It is too symmetrical."

"Ah."

"The nostrils have no vigour."

"Huh?"

"And it does not seem to me that the skull is fully realised."

"Now for God's sake, melon-tits, must you play the critic at crack of dawn?"

"Well it's not finished, after all."

"Give me the coffee."

I must get up or the coffee will spill onto my neck. She overfills the cup every day. She is insensitive to a creaking old man's bones. So I heave up and scratch my balls and my head and prepare to take the coffee, when Estelle tells me.

"Capo, I didn't tell you. The film men were in here yesterday fixing little box things."

"Where?"

"Over there in the corner, somewhere. I don't know where else."

"Why? I don't want people messing about in here, I told you."

"Well, they asked and I wasn't thinking. You were on the beach."

"What are the things?"

"They said they were videotape things, whatever videotape is."

"A videotape is an instrument, my sweet-arsed concubine, for recording on tape with."

"What?"

"What whoever is being taped is doing and saying."

"You mean us—now?"

"For fuck's sake, yes . . ." I get up, stark naked, bollocks swinging, to look for the contraptions and blunder about to find them and there is Estelle laughing and spilling the coffee. There are dozens of places they could be hidden in this junk-pile. I have a good deal to endure. I bark my shins. I knock the riffles off a bench and all over the floor. I tread on one very painfully.

"The tape-machines, you cow. Where are they?"

"Somewhere about, darling," she tells me and I see that she is sitting blandly on the bed laughing like a hyena at the greatest living sculptor hopping about like a trapped wallaby. I stop. "Estelle," I say awesomely, "do you realise that the things must have been running all night and all morning as well? Do you realise that when we got home from that fearful dinner at Poitevin's, I worked six hours stark naked on the big, standing, double nude and I did it naked because I was hot? Do you understand that I built up the thighs on top and the tops of the calves, because you have to build on top of

68

the forms, with standing figures, to give them thrust? And have you not known me long enough to realise that when I am building up, I sing?"

"A very revealing talking picture, this will be," says Estelle solemnly, "and in living colour."

"I sing the same couplet, or snatch, over and over again, don't I? You've said so."

"You do, darling. You do and it's quite obscene."

"It is not obscene. It is because to give the forms thrust, you thrust them up, like pushing up into a woman."

"I know, darling. That is what you sing about. It is quite disgusting."

"Oh, bloody hell."

Estelle gets up and comes over to me and to get into shot for sure. She winks carefully at all four corners of the studio, which are cluttered up with God knows what that workshops get cluttered up with; a confusion that could hide anything including movie-cameras. Then she gives me a tender kiss and tweaks my prick. "If they can't use it," she says, "they'll doubtless cut it." And she pulls on the poor ringmaster and then lets him go and makes her exit slowly swinging her noble buttocks with the monstrous dignity of a hippopotamus.

I drink the rest of the coffee and I splash my face in the wax-cooling tank because it, the weather, is still very hot and I go to work again, having found the chopper. I chip the side off the nose and mix plaster and build up and use a chisel on the underside of the forehead, over the eyes, to make the bridge of the nose more convex, cutting in under the brow to keep the bridge in shadow, so that the nose juts like an axe. And then riffle with the sureforms, because the plaster is still damp from the build and would clog a rasp, which would mean wirebrushing every two minutes. And I have not been at this for more than a few minutes when the door opens and there is Jeannot not with Kir but with Nella. What is this? "You should have come earlier," I say to her, "because as you can see I have nothing for you just at the moment as I am working."

Nella giggles and says *Maestro* and Jeannot says "Sorry, Cap, but you're wanted," and he looks very indeterminate.

Wanted. "I'm wanted." For Christ's sake do they think I come when I'm wanted? What am I, a clown in a circus? Well?

"Tell them I'm in the lavatory and tell them that I shall be there for some time and tell them, if they have a tape-machine thing in there, exactly where they can plug it in." And that is where I go, because that is where I can think undisturbed, more or less, and when I come out I shall put on a pair of shorts. Ariadne sits on my shoulder, as I move through the far end of the Duke's hall of audience, leaving the present audience behind me and a hundred and twenty feet away, while Ariadne jumps up and down on me and chippers angrily in a spirit of criticism that such an old master as I am should be treated in so undignified a fashion. For my part, if they want to film me mother-naked, let them.

The throne upon which I seat myself is at least supposed to be private. The throne-room is at least small and I cannot see any videotape recorders in it. The big studio may have had dozens of them, hidden about to get action shots, but here perhaps not. However, since when I am working in the studio, it becomes my skull and what work there is is in my brain, it is as if some diabolical doctors have put electrodes in my cranium—and the way I feel, maybe they have—so that they can tap me even in here. That must be fantasy, but I shall suppose, since it is peaceful here, that it is not fantasy and that what I am thinking will go onto a long spool of tape while some tiny camera is focused on my noble and powerful face because, after the first moment—if long shots in shit houses are practical at all—the camera can hardly move around registering my crouch to crap indefinitely. I shall think, therefore, if Ariadne does not steal the scene, of something to say to the world, which they would not get any other way, or from any other convenience, public or private, about what I am. That is what they want, isn't it?

Well, I was born, in 1891, of Italian parents in the village of Paestum, once called Poseidonia, which was without tourism in those days and undug, largely, by archaeologists. Its three still standing temples, which are the greatest, the most complete and the most beautiful anywhere outside Greece, were built by Greek colonists perhaps from Sybaris, around about 540 B.C. or maybe 450 B.C. or some time in between, I forget. In the fields, a little to the northeast, near the mouth of the river Sele, and buried a few metres underground, there lay the metopes from other temples, which you can now see in the museum but couldn't then because there was no museum and they hadn't been found. Beyond, there was the sea. And Paestum is where I went to school and perhaps became what I am by means of supernatural memory and strange inner vision or, more accurately, an osmosis or something. The sculptor, as I became, dredged what I am up out of the earth straight from its womb which had not given secondary birth to its contents in those days, but still hid its past under the muddy skin of the estuary of the Sele.

The first seventeen years of my life were uneventful. I worked. No, that won't do, scrub that. My father, a simple peasant early learned the craft of forging antique sculptures so that when we moved to Rome in 1907 . . . No, that is simply a lie. If I can't do better than that I may as well shit. I am not taking myself seriously. What is true then? That I felt the Greeks in the ground? That I felt that I belonged to them, driven by that sensation? But I am a modern artist, aren't I? I am a great innovator, a vital contributor to contemporary art? The truth is that I am not. I am the tail-end of the ongoing, the last straw. What is admired most in me is what everyone can understand, because vaguely they too remember parts of it from somewhere. What is the best in me no one understands since it is what everybody has ceased to look for now, except Estelle who has no brain but holds the pomegranate instead, and perhaps Addle, who perhaps knows. Jeannot, what will he do? But none of that is to the purpose.

My secret is that I invented nothing, but was invented—an aphorism. Who invented me? Memory ploughed deeper into the past than anyone could readily discern, therefore new. The function of a true artist is to understand what is further back than anyone is concerned to look and to make the present from it. Bringing that to the surface is one of the great confidence tricks because the so-called art-loving public has just enough memory buried in it to stumble towards the narrow bridge and over to its own remote past and then find itself strangely and inexplicably at home there. This semi-conscious trip is learnedly confirmed, being explained, reverentially but with the context possibly wrong, by art historians like the precious mosquito, bless her innocent heart and her American youth. For example, children, what of Giacometti? A forger of archaic Sardinian bronzes, paperclipped to pre-dynastic Egypt and galvanised by a touch of Etruscan hysteria. And what of young Moore, with Chakmool from Yucatan and the whole British Museum up his jumper? And what of Rodin, with his carefully contrived museum fragments cobbled together, so that the best is an assemblage of spare parts got from mining Michelangelo and you do the work with your semi-cultured recollection of what was smashed by the Vandals and is now served up deliciously destroyed? Try to use your loaves, aesthetes, as well as your little wet fishes.

And what of Brancusi, the Roumanian with the power-lathe and all so simple that he may seem truly to have invented the egg? This is becoming rhetorical, but it is not out of place. I have produced, in this very moment, a long and notable egg myself, dispensable but notable. This is the haptic egg, laid most beautifully compacted, as is sculpture made by blind children, which is also the sculpture of the gut itself and should not be lost to sight in the part played by sculpture as it forms the human psyche. This is a morning message for fart critics everywhere. It is however rhetorical, so let it be. I shall not do so for I shall flush it away because it is not intricate and intricacy is an absolute requirement of sculpture if you are not to find yourself with an Arp. Intricacy must be so integrated in the forms that they look simple. But of course they must not be simple, else you will lose control of the spectator, your victim, who can shit as well as you can and, let us hope, regularly does. Now when the gods fashioned men out of mud and women from spare-ribs, there was a trick to it. That trick is to twist the forms so that they come alive by contesting the inertness of the mud against the spring in the rib and hope to yourself that the gods will pop a crumb of the divine into the mix, since the result is being offered to them.

So, given the human frame, with its exact limitations of function, as your armature, what is the trick? The trick is to put it under a certain kind of interior strain beyond nature, but without losing the invariable and obvious counterpoise of taut against slack which you can find in those dispositions of your own flesh and bones that you wear so self-consciously. Furthermore, let me tell you, you must not fail to abut blunt to sharp, as you wrestle forms out of quiescence, for if you neglect the sharp you will have no bite and if you neglect the blunt, your arse won't keep you on the seat, will it?

Well, dears, what do you think that Michelangelo's slaves, those that he kept locked in the stone, were struggling to do, toss themselves off? Were they trying to get back into the matrix where it had been peaceful? If he hadn't known every transition, every interlock and every articulation so that he could contain their energy, those slaves would have burst out in all directions like the squits, or like the time I got locked in this historically notable jakes and had to break the door down, or like that idiotic Laocoön group which is an exercise in rhetorical marble farting. Not, mind you, that there is no place for rhetoric, which has often played its part in breaking the wind of change, but of its nature sculpture is perfectly still. It is a vessel for energy, not an overspill. It does not jump about unless it is bad sculpture. It is for you, children, to jump about and for sculpture to hold still and try to contain itself.

Or am I making it too difficult for you as I set here invisibly clenching and straining the muscles of my thorax to produce a downward motion for my continuing health and personal satisfaction? The intricacy of my actions has produced several simple forms, which have only in the last few decades engaged the enthusiasm of critics but, purely as sculpture, it is the marvellous muscles and twisting entrails of my belly itself which are interesting to contemplate, not its by-products. So I shall, as I put on my shorts, turn my attention to the Greeks who were not very fashionable when I was young but who could, in their best times, make sculpture which contains a musculature as vigorous and as controlled as the athletes they were so proud of, but for all the strenuous action that their centaurs show in taking the piss out of their lapiths, that action is strangely invisible. It is suspended in a stasis where you read in the forms what happened and what will happen next in a stillness like silence. In such sculpture there is a noble constipation, a rhythmic straining inwards, which is the reverse of the stone squitters of the Pergamon altar or of the High Baroque. You see what I mean? Sculpture must clench inside itself.

I am now finished in here but this erstwhile oubliette of the Duke's is maybe forty feet high, if otherwise a small box, and as usual Ariadne has perched on the cistern by running up the chain as soon as I pulled it and is up there now, shrieking abuse at me, the way no critic would any more. No critic, indeed no creature of its weight and size in nature, can scream like a marmoset and so my next period of creative endeavour will be taken up with getting her down.

III

Rough Assembly

Even into the best-regulated shooting schedules events can intrude and, whilst the great Capo is trying to distract his screaming marmoset and get her down from there, Addle is sitting on the great stone terrace, in an elegant white silk suit and with a panama hat on his head to protect it from the full sun, talking urbanely to Hansi Schlegel and Moustique Whitaker, both of whom are markedly more relaxed than they were last night, if still overdressed. It is an art-historical conference.

Meanwhile, as those concerned start to think about editing all this footage and getting some shape into the product, Estelle is giving Lens a little whisky-soda in the dining-room and seeking to calm her and Lens is apologising, while Nella who, having glimpsed the Master stark naked, has come to feel quite relaxed and at home, is wandering round the *piano nobile,* valuing the works of art, not from any sense of cupidity, but because she has a highly developed sense of values. As for me, and you will recognise from the familiar tone of voice that I have the narration again—never mind what the director said about piss and wind—who is he anyhow, ex-RAI and now CBS, does that make him somebody? As for me, I have the narration but I can feel it being cut, even as I speak, and I only have the narration because the director cannot think how else they can cobble the thing together and keep any continuity. So while the camera dollies about over all the acres of smooth marble flooring in the hall and the crew is at pains not to cannon into any of the art objects with which this hall is haphazardly set about, since people keep giving Capo things and Capo keeps making things and leaving them around and getting hold of things which may come in handy or be an inspiration like the sperm-whale's skull, which takes up quite a bit of space, and the Minoan terracottas which take up practically none. Among the hazards are the Chola bronzes and the Shang ritual vessels, the inevitable African carvings and the canvases stacked against the walls. The stuffed fighting bull from Pablo takes up considerable room and so do the packing-cases which will some time get unpacked, if anyone thinks they require something that may be in one of them. What with the etching-press, which is supposed to be in the room with the two other presses but has not got there yet, progress with filming gets very breathless. In any case all the rooms in the building, if they are not filled with relatives whose names Capo cannot quite remember, or members of his entourage, whose names I cannot remember, are filled with things that may be important and often with animals which have wandered in from Capo's zoo in the garden or have been quarantined by Estelle because she thinks they may be coming down with obscure complaints. These creatures include cats, mastiffs, owls, ducks, a very old leopard and several unusual goats in which the leopard is too lazy and too well fed to be interested. There are also porcupines and various monkeys, all called after museum directors with the exception of a hamadryad baboon named Theseus. There is also a very dishevelled group of parakeets, in a large cage, all called after distinguished journalists. Then, too, there is a noble and very menacing moufflon ram, with great curling horns, who has the run of the place.

The noise in certain parts of the castello is formidable and the assistant director who runs about calling "Quiet" gets no response. Fortunately at Capo's end of the building, where the good Duke held audience and condemned felons to dire punishments, there is now a very sacred quiet and the assistant director who calls "Quiet" there has the director telling him to be quiet.

So action, and the director himself has an 8mm hand-held camera and is squirting it more or less at random. And it is round about now that the verbal consequences start, which is Round Two. While Capo is still out of shot, although his voice may be heard alternately pleading with and abusing his marmoset, three players are on the terrace, and three more are seated on a large couch in the anteroom where once the Duke's petitioners waited upon him. This room, which is furnished as if the removal men were due, has in the centre of it an island of tranquillity which Estelle creates wherever she sits down. And there she is, knitting something in red wool with red needles and listening to Lens, or very nearly, when Nella, who has made a very exhaustive inspection of the movables, joins them.

78

Lens is giving an account of her early life in Detroit, Michigan, and telling Estelle how her father, who was a failure, used to behave to her, even when she was no more than a little kid and about her mother who was a bigot and a puritan and only cared what the neighbours thought. She is describing how both of them had this terrible guilt. The great weight of guilt which midwest, grass-roots Americans carry with them always is a subject Lens often touches upon in mid-afternoon. Estelle is very sympathetic, just as she was when Lens told her, last time she came on a visit, all about what it had been like to be the only child of an automotive engineer during the depression years in Detroit, Michigan, who hadn't made it and had only got by because his wife had all the strength that came from her pioneer stock which had driven her to see Lens through Wayne State University where, God knows, she had found it difficult to identify with her peer group. At this point Nella, who is bemused, asks what a peer group might be and is further puzzled to learn that it is a class of people who share a common cultural and educational background. "But we all do," says Nella, "in different classes. I meant that I grew up with people who are just like me in this. At the convent and also in Switzerland to finish, there were the Gaetani and the Doria and the Buonfigli and all girls who are sharing this background except that some of us are much older than some others."

"Older?"

"Older families. Otherwise some are rich but most are not absolutely rich and some are new-rich, which my mother does not like and some very rich which my mother says was not as it should have been because trade is not something admirable, but something essentially *milanese*."

"What did your father say?"

"He does not say anything about that and he talks only with his 'peer group' at the *Circolo,* where we are not let in, but where they talk about land and horses, of course, and perhaps women and naturally about the communists who are corrupting the *contadini*. It is only since I am married to Hansi that I learn about business which I find rather dull."

"You're a nice kid, Nella, but for Pete's sake . . ."

"I am not a child. It is simply that I was brought up in a certain way. I am old-fashioned and think that money is not something to speak about. I do not hear Signor Capisco speaking of money." Nella is piqued.

"Capo never speaks of money," says Estelle, "but he keeps a great many banknotes in a trunk under the bed in his studio. He says he might suddenly need to buy something or alternatively the bottom might fall out of the market for pictures and sculptures and such-like as bad as the ones Addle sells."

"But Signor Capisco must be of the very rich."

"I don't think your mother would approve of him," says Estelle.

Lens is at once intrigued and suspicious of Nella, who may be taking the mickey. "Capo is not rich. He is simply beyond money. With Cap, who needs a cheque book?"

"Addle," says Estelle, firmly.

"No but listen, I mean with Cap, he can do a couple of gouaches or maybe a batch of drawings in a morning and, sight unseen, they're worth more than their weight in gold. What about that? Getty, Rockefeller, they need money. Cap pays restaurant bills with a signature on the tablecloth. I guess nobody knows what Cap makes in a given year."

"He makes sculpture, Lens." Estelle is wary of this familiar line of far from oblique admiration for Cap. She stops knitting.

Nella is frankly shocked but, being well brought up, is tactful. "Do you have children, Signora Lodge?"

"No . . . and what's it to you?"

"Lens, darling," says Estelle, "let us walk in the garden."

"What gets to this Nella, she wants to know do I have kids?"

"Lens, the garden is very pleasant in the afternoon, at this time of the year."

"Don't try to soften me up, Estelle. This Contessa is getting to me. Kids, no, I don't have kids. When did I have time for kids? I had schedules. I had to work my guts out on assignments since I graduated and I had men who didn't get together with me for home and motherhood, believe me. Kids. Capo has kids. He has kids like trophies over his mantel; gold-plated kids, golden kids by golden girls. Get me out of here, Estelle."

Estelle puts down the ball of wool and the knitting on the couch,

saying "Come, Lens," imperiously gentle. "Lens has been overwork-
ing. She is very tired."

"Yeah, I'm tired, I guess," says Lens, being led away.

"Troia," Nella whispers very precisely to herself, when they have
gone out. It is not a word of which her mother would have
approved, but having voiced it she joins them on the terrace.

This maybe terminates the first consequence of bringing members
of Capo's court into a social relationship at a time when the Master
himself is still having his problems with Ariadne of the golden pelt,
who is at last down from the cistern but is leaping from bronze to
bronze until Capo, breathless, opens the door of the great hall of
audience and peers out at the mid-afternoon, his early morning, at
which Ariadne of the lovely locks, using his bald pate as a spring-
board, catapults into the anteroom and lights on Estelle's ball of red
wool. This, like a minute Atlas, Ariadne takes upon her head before
clasping it to her belly and going up the ornate overmantel, perhaps
by Primaticcio, which one of the first Duke's modish descendants in-
stalled in 1552, feeling the need for a touch of Fontainebleau at
home.

The terrace wears a bourgeois look. The gentry are seated in
deckchairs or are promenading up and down in dappled sunlight. It
could be by Vuillard, but the trio of ladies are wearing costumes
dissonant enough to raise the key to Bonnard's pitch. Estelle is lavish in a housecoat with a vast pattern of orange and gold flowers on
it, Lens is striking in a trouser suit of shocking pink, and Nella is
perfection so far as pale violet silk can make her so. "Matisse," says
Capo to himself, staring out into the sunlight at them and he is
reminded of a story that Matisse used to tell of his visit to Renoir in
old age, at Cagnes. "Young man," said Renoir to Matisse, "I cannot really stand your painting; I am too old to understand it and I
would dismiss it as rubbish but you seem able to hold down the
black. That is difficult to do, so difficult that I think you cannot be
absolutely bad." "And there," thinks Capo, "is the black held down
against the yellows and greens of the garden with sudden dark blue
shadows and with Lens's pink, grating and clashing in the teeth of
Estelle's gold and orange whilst the light, splashing about in the
shallows of Nella's little cobalt violet sugared almond of a dress, is
singing like a throstle. The harmonies," says Capo to himself, "are

the property of the late Matisse and no one else's and the blacks of Estelle's hair, which has grey in it and of Nella's, which has not, are held down. Renoir could not have done it. Furthermore, I couldn't do it myself, although as sculptors neither of those old men had much, whereas, as a painter I have what I need."

Raising his eyes slightly to get a splinter of cerulean sky into the composition, the man, not quite so old as Matisse would now be, fails to notice that Ariadne has moved down from the mantelpiece, wound a coil of red wool round Capo's legs and darted through the long window and onto the terrace where, in a series of leaps and scutters, she has wound up Lens and Nella and bound Estelle, in whose arms this marmoset now rests, as triumphant as a gladiator who has netted an opponent and is ready with the trident.

This of course is great material for the 8mm hand-held camera and the tape is running on Capo's expletives, the conjoined cries of Nella, the husky ejaculations of Lens and Ariadne's own sharp chippering; a charming sequence symbolising, for a mass audience, the home life of the most glamorous sculptor of our time. I myself am enchanted. It occurs to me that Ariadne in her immediate future progress could tie Addle, Hansi and Moustique in knots, for they are only a few yards further up the terrace. Then all that would be needed would be a coil or two round me and a few round Kir, who must be somewhere about, and back on to Capo's head in a single bound to tie us together as tightly in fact as Capo has us tied together in other ways with the red, red thread of a coil of consequences, some of them going back for years, if not for decades.

I am not surprised, although Nella is terrified, when Theseus makes his entrance from among the bushes. What else could happen when Ariadne is running round with a red thread?

Theseus is the size of a mastiff, but much heavier, and since he is maned like a lion, has an arse like a Turner sunset and two-inch incisors in his dog-face, he is formidable. Theseus is very dangerous and in no way to do with settings by Vuillard, or the singing harmonies of old Matisse. Theseus is no bourgeois either, but a baboon lordly as Cerberus and the subject of a whole group of Capo's most urgent, recent small bronzes. It is a moment of increasing symbolic significance, as I see it, for it gets Nella into a sudden desperate clinch with Hansi, who flies to the rescue but it also has the less edifying effect of netting the other ladies still entangled in the red wool into a clinch of their own and pulling Capo stumbling out and in amongst them, to his vast enjoyment. It drives Ariadne wild, I may say, for she has reason to dislike Theseus, as everyone knows. So Ariadne leaves, taking her ball of wool with her, back to the overmantel by perhaps Primaticcio. "Cut," shouts the director, who is running out of film, but no one can and it is only gradually borne in on the panic-stricken Schlegels that Theseus is secured by a long chain on an even longer wire along which the chain runs with a sinister sliding and rattling sound. This pulls him up short to strain snarling like a raging ancestor at his trivial descendants the hominids, just above him on the terrace.

Moustique is laughing with what is, from her, an improbable volume of sound and Capo is full of child-like delight. Addle is not much amused. Estelle produces gardening scissors from somewhere about her, and cuts the red thread of Ariadne, thus preventing Theseus from entering the labyrinth of Capo's castello in any legendary fashion, quite apart from the chain which fortunately is not mythical and holds him off.

"It is very dramatic here," says Capo. "You see it is the lair of more than one monster."

Estelle, for her part, having disengaged Lens and Nella with dextrous snips of her scissors, goes in to answer the telephone.

"I do not like tame animals much," says Capo, looking sideways at the company. "I like them fierce. Not like Dali, who walks about with ocelots from whom the claws have been removed. Unless," he adds vaguely, "it is the other way round . . . I forget."

There is, as I have tried to point out to members of the unit, an ever-present element of farce in keeping company with men of genius who are as legendary as Capisco. The pratfall is always in the offing. So I can congratulate the director on having got so remarkable a sequence in the can, but the Schlegels are still pretty shaken. It is Lens who, familiar with such sudden shocks and starts in her profession, restores order with tact and soothing words, which come as almost as great a surprise to Nella as the advent of Theseus himself. "Don't take on so, baby," Lens tells her, encircling the Contessa with a comforting arm. "That's nothing but a little old monkey, or maybe a relative of Capo's." At which Capo, in high good humour, goes through the dignified motions and sober grimaces of a mountain gorilla, feeling them to be some sort of contribution to the restoration of order. I am, I sometimes think, a visitor to, if not inhabitant of, a remarkable menagerie.

We now cut to Kir, who has come in through the building by way of the path which leads directly from our cottage, over the hill, to the back door of Capo's ancient monument or camping site. Kir is in obvious distress but it is not to me, but to the amateur gorilla that she goes.

"Capo, it is too much."

"What is?" The mighty anthropoid is, on the instant eclipsed by the humane grandfather, all warmth and incomprehension.

"Our cottage is filled with tourists."

"Rather premature, I should have thought."

"No, honestly, Cap. It is."

"What are they doing?"

"They are being conducted round by Poitevin, who is charging them for seeing your picture. He says that in future there will be frequent parties coming at weekends. He has advertised locally, he says."

"What picture?"

"Oh, Capo, the big drawing you did for us. The huge one on the studio wall."

"Oh that. Yes, it's not bad."

"But, Cap, they're tramping about all over the house. Do pay attention. What are we to do?"

"Who let them in?"

"Poitevin, he has a key."

"Why?"

"He is the landlord."

Capo is clearly surprised. Landlords have not played any part in Capo's life since World War I. As for me, the facts are clear and I suppose not surprising. Capo's feather-light touch has made our house uninhabitable.

"Kir," Capo is commanding, claws extended and no surrealist's tame ocelot. "You will send that little tradesman to me. Tell him I will see him at once, or anyway after lunch."

"It is after lunch. What shall I say?"

"Tell him that unless he leaves you in peace I shall destroy the present."

This, metaphorically at least, brings a strangled cry from me and I am a past master of strangled cries. In Capo's company one is bound to be. The drawing is, after all, a Capisco and morally at least it belongs first to Kir and to me and afterwards, doubtless, to the world. What is also apparent is that, with the exception of Capo himself, all the art lovers grouped on the terrace are evidently planning to make up their own party, at once, to go and look at the thing. The private life of the Choiseuls has, suddenly, become a centre for tourism and it is not Amphitryon who will benefit, nor even Zeus disguised as Amphitryon, but Isidore Poitevin, the local high-priest of culture and gastronomy, who will be collecting the tribute, without any suggestion of a rent rebate.

Kir is looking helpless. "They will steal things," is all she can think of to say.

"What?" asks Capo, genuinely interested.

"Our things, Jeannot's paintings, everything."

At this gratuitous opening, Capo favours me with his ironical-satyr face, all grin and wrinkles. "Jeannot's paintings?" His voice is very silky. I lead with my chin.

"They will probably think those are your work, too." What else can I say when I know what's coming?

"And aren't they?"

"They are not," says Addle sharply, bless his heart. "They are quite other." He could mean that as praise, but one couldn't tell from his expression. Capo snorts.

"Well, go and tell the Poitevin to present himself." He becomes the seigneur, having lost the round. And Kir goes, absentmindedly collecting Ariadne of the scarlet thread who leaps onto her shoulder as she passes and thus the house of Capisco is joined to the house of Choiseul by a long red cord. The hand-held camera misses nothing of this. I have a presentiment about today. It is going to be very symbolic and sewn up by marmosets and baboons, in allegorical guise, winding chains and red threads round it. I have a feeling that it will all end badly.

"For God's sake," says Lens.

"Scarcely," says Addle, and Nella, who responds dramatically to drama, is saying that everything to her has become quite unreal and everyone is mad, but utterly mad.

"It is quite real, Signora Contessa," says Moustique. "It is simply that Monsieur Capisco heightens reality. We are in the company of genius."

"You can say that again." Lens has her little Leica in action now and is irked at having missed the telling shots of Ariadne's woolmazing. Absently, she snaps Theseus who by now is sitting back on his haunches, erect in the hieratic pose adopted by baboons; long hands on knees and very lordly in the ancient Egyptian manner.

Nella, thinking, doubtless, of her private view of Capo in his studio, giggles. Moustique is very pink from wishing she had sounded less sententious.

"What is real here is for me to decide," says Capo, re-establishing his rôle. "In a sense you are right."

Addle looks warily at Theseus. "There is no doubt, my old friend, that you make quite sure to be the determining factor, when you are present. It can be strenuous. Why you should need a zoo when you have such a variety of other toys responding to your whims, I cannot imagine." Theseus barks and then yawns cavernously. This silences everyone and the silence is sufficiently prolonged for all present to consider just what is real to each and every one of them.

"Psychoanalytic insights in distorted forms," says Addle abruptly, "have become so general nowadays that one can watch persons having them." The Arri on the dolly-whip pans off Cap and on to Addle, but the director is still squirting at Cap with his little 8mm and Cap is looking sour.

"Ah," he says, "the Friend of Freud."

Addle ignores this jibe. Nella, Hansi and Moustique, who have all been having psychological insights of various kinds since kingly Theseus yawned, look rather guilty. Lens does not. "My analyst would have a field-day here," she remarks brightly, stating a norm.

"Your analyst would not get past the gate," says Cap tartly.

"Why?" Lens is genuinely puzzled.

"Because I do not welcome exponents of unscientific, non-proven and ill-founded theories of behaviour—especially my behaviour."

"But, Cap . . ."

"What do they know about us, about me, even about Jeannot?

They think of us as case-histories. They think a sculptor is a neurotic busily reacting to some deprivation in his childhood; that sculpture is a symptom of neurosis."

"But Jeezus, Cap, your behaviour can be pretty neurotic."

"I am not in the least neurotic. I do not work to heal my wounds. I work to celebrate. What I do is not to be judged by Wienerschnitzels saying, 'Ah, ha, vee know vat you *really* mean.' They are a joke."

Addle is smiling broadly. "My friend Freud, as you call him, suggested that the genesis of a work of art and of a joke are analogous."

"Your friend Freud made a fool of himself over Leonardo."

"But not over Michelangelo."

"The truth is that your Freud and his followers are bigots and puritans. They think that they know what is real and that what we make are substitutes for reality. They cannot define any reality beyond their own pragmatic diagnoses. They think they are scientists when they are merely limited to their narrow definition of what they think is real, and if they had their way they would cure every painter, writer, sculptor or musician of his talent."

So serious an accusation against a contemporary dogma as Cap has made seems improbable to the others, who do not expect such judgments from him. But Capo has lost interest. He is looking abstracted in the particular way that he looks when he has started to work. It is a strangely blind expression that he wears for a man whose sight is so concentrated, but in fact it is Theseus who has his attention because Theseus has an erection like a blazing knitting-needle. "Knitting-needle," says Cap absently.

"*Pazzo*," Nella whispers to Hansi who does not respond, except to frown. It is a curious moment. No one but Cap and I were looking towards Theseus just then and until his chain rattled as he moved off into the bushes Cap had had the floor. By now, Theseus had his fierce flaming arse towards all of us and is striding off as one well satisfied with the comments on psychiatry expressed.

I'd better go and see what's happening to Kir.

Moustique and Addle are moving out of shot with Addle ultra-Viennese and saying, "Ah, ha, ve know vat zis means," which for once, I don't think he does.

Lens is on her way back indoors where the whisky-soda is and the Schlegels are waiting for me to take them on a little excursion up the hill to see Amphitryon where Alcmene should, at this moment, be issuing Cap's ukase to honest Poitevin upon pain of being bound for ever to a stove with a *langouste à l'américaine* gnawing at his liver.

Looking in through the glass door leading from the terrace, I see that Cap is removing one of the red needles from the ruin of Estelle's knitting. I know what this means. It means that Cap has his point of departure for the life-sized version of Theseus. It needs just such a simple object to start him on a major work and all those little baboon models which have been standing and crouching on his workshop window-sill, already cast weeks ago in bronze, will now serve their long-term purpose. Capo, with the needle, is gone into his workroom and has shut the door.

"We'll break," shouts the director happily. He has plenty in the can for now anyway and he knows that Cap is safely back in the good Duke's hall of audience with all the hidden videotapes running on. "Half an hour."

The set-ups for the opening sequences after the break will be much as before and are intended to continue the action as soon as the crew has eaten its sandwiches. The director and his unit, being refreshed by the absence of the cast and the presence of comparatively peaceful coffee and snacks, discuss getting a "to camera" sequence from Cap with me as the tactful interviewer and con-man, or perhaps better with Addle. The director opens the bidding in this dubious auction by tapping tactfully on Cap's closed workroom door and he does not deserve what he gets because pat on the moment Cap comes thundering through it screaming like Theseus and the director takes the brunt on the nose, because the door opens outwards. There being no biz like show biz, this is as funny as it used to be when Stan Laurel repeatedly did it to Oliver Hardy and hilarity is general, which enrages Capo further, never mind the director.

Estelle enters from the prompt corner bringing grave news gravely and for one irreverent moment I see that she can, by her noble nature, closely resemble Margaret Dumont in *Duck Soup*.

"Where are the maquettes?" Cap in a rage is galvanic. "Where are the maquettes for my baboon? Who has dared to move my Theseus models from the window-sill? Who is the thief?" And he looks fiercely at the crew, his obsidian eyes awe-inspiring.

"Capo, darling." Estelle is as unshaken as usual by the roaring of the ram, which is no sheep's bleat. "That was Madeleine."

"How could it be? Of course it wasn't. She is in Paris and in any case would not touch my maquettes."

"No, darling . . . she was on the telephone."

"Then how could she have stolen my maquettes?"

"No, darling, she was on the telephone, ringing from Poitevin's. She says Pier-Francesco is also here."

"Where?"

"Here."

"Never mind that, who has stolen . . ." and then Cap stops. His attention has been captured. "You say Piero is here?"

"Yes, darling, he is in the village with friends."

"Then he should be here, visiting me and not at bloody Poitevin's."

"I imagine he is on his way. And besides it is not Piero but Madeleine who is at Poitevin's."

"Who then is with Piero and where is he?" asks Cap, looking grimly at me who, being much of an age with bloody Piero, am obviously a conspirator. In a sense I am. Only Estelle and I, of the present company, know about Piero and also why the subject of the missing maquettes has so suddenly been dropped.

"Madeleine didn't say who," says Estelle, "but I expect he has his usual friends, you know. Or perhaps new ones."

That comment, in my view, will not help. Piero's choice of friends is wide and various but the variations are not, to Estelle, agreeable. Capo is looking very disturbed.

"He is with his mother?"

"Madeleine only said he was in the village. She herself is at Poitevin's. I would be surprised if Piero was with his mother."

I can see Capo putting two and two together and deciding that what he thinks, or immediately thought, could not make four. He is, I suspect, wrong. At any rate he turns on the director very sternly. Those piercing eyes make no obvious impression on the director, who is tenderly feeling his nose and inadvertently weeping, as one does when suddenly clouted in that area.

"Put your face down," says Capo, *maestoso,* "and tell me if you, or any of your group, has moved or tampered with the little bronzes of Theseus which were on the window-sill in there." But he is asking *pro forma* and I doubt if Estelle is any more surprised than I am when the director looks blank and shakes his head, without putting down his nose. The crew all shrug and shake their heads with great solemnity.

Capo looks piteously at Estelle. "Oh God," he says and goes back into his workroom, closing the door.

I take Estelle by the arm and together we walk out on to the terrace, hoping against hope that no bugging devices or videotapes are beamed on us. Estelle says nothing except to remind me that Capo hates anyone to refer to his son as "Cappellino" which is of course the term all of us, who know him, apply to the son and heir even when he is not being gratuitously offensive, which is rare.

"I expect he will turn up at Poitevin's this evening with his cohort, rout, or in-group."

"Oh God." Even Estelle has been known to voice apprehension, under stress, but this chink in her armour she quickly closes. "Capo will become anxious if he doesn't come. He is devoted to Pier-Francesco."

And so he is. He idolises this coral-snake of a son, the one he had in wedlock. He is not consistent but, let me tell you, or, while I think about it, let me put you in the picture about Pier-Francesco Capisco, the heir-apparent to the great man who is so unconventional, except where, apparently, he is not. Cappellino is a personage whose head is too swollen for a little hat or cap and who should have been prevented from being conceived, any deep-seated pun notwithstanding. They should have put him back and fucked for him again. However he was engendered and his father loves him, if not now, in any way, the mother who bore him.

Only Estelle would not have repeated the pious exhortation. She does not say "Oh God" twice. She is thinking, I assume, about how to ransom the maquettes of Theseus and whether to ask Addle to see about it. And it is now that Addle returns with the rest of the party who have, as I expected, paid a visit to my studio and seen

Cap's present to us blazoning itself on our studio wall. Addle looks so thoughtful because he thinks it is by Cap in his top form and I suspect that he has become as puzzled as Kir and I are about how to arrange to excise a masterpiece from the ancient plaster of a rented cottage. Not that the problem is serious technically. It is done, as well Addle knows, by getting an expert to attach linen to the surface of the work with a water-based glue, cutting into the wall round the picture, rolling the art-work up like a large *crêpe*, so that it comes cleanly off the laths in the wall and then unrolling it on to a strong canvas and gluing it back down. If you are dealing with a Florentine *fresco puro* of the early fifteenth century you will find that all will be well. If you are dealing with *Zeus, Amphitryon and Alcmene* by Capisco, heir to the *quattrocento*, you had better enquire of him what media he used, in the hope that he will remember. Otherwise the work itself may be water-miscible and will all come off in the rolled pancake. It's a risk and so of course is Poitevin the, at least, part-owner. I myself believe I know, after careful study, just what combination of charcoal, emulsion, ink, oil-paint and whatever was handy Capo used, since I know what the typhoon left of my working materials after its passage. Distemper in both senses played its part and I would advise, if asked, a thin spraying of the surface with epoxy resin before trying to move the thing. For Poitevin, a little strychnine should be enough.

So Addle enters full of bounce and takes off his panama. *"Ach,"* he doesn't say to Estelle, or to me either I suppose, "is en edvence" or "very interestink." He says, for once, "Is incredible," a phrase I've never heard from him before. "Ach, Gott," he says, making that one more example of today's comment in all circumstances. "One has never before understood how much Capisco has read. It is not to one apparent that he has so much read. The *Amphitruo* of Plautus even. What is present in that drawing, if it is to be called exactly a drawing, is not only the protagonists, which naturally are Zeus-Amphitryon of course, and Amphitryon naturally, and naturally Alcmene, but also the other doubles where is Mercury doubling also with the slave Sosias, no less than Amphitryon doubled by Zeus, as we know."

This is news to me. What is not, of course, news is the little figure I had recognised as Pancho, the chauffeur, with no little wings on his feet, but up in the top left-hand corner, above the scene, holding a thing with snakes twirled round it and therefore obviously Hermes or Mercury. I thought that had been some wild afterthought of Cap's, when, drunk with battle fatigue he needed something in that eighth of the composition. I should have known better.

Moustique attends this disquisition of Addle's as if she were in audience with the Pope. She, too, of course, and Nella naturally, and naturally Hansi, have all been up to our house, but not as tourists. Tourists are simply ignorant, out of town rubbernecks not to be confused with the cream of European culture knowledgeably rubber-necking. I wonder if they even glanced at the other works of what I hope is art, hung on the other walls, up there. I suspect not. Oh God. All are now back and all agog, but it is only Nella who addresses me personally, in my capacity as *pro tem* tenant and curator of this now new museum of Capo's. "You are so fortunate. To be allowed to work always in the presence of such a *chef d'oeuvre*. It must be *too* inspiring." And this benison she gives me in a whisper from under her eyelashes.

Too inspiring is so accurate an assessment, that I am not sure for a moment whether this is a gush of eloquence or a genuine perception. "I looked," she confides, "at other things in your house as well."

I am flattered but wary. "I shall speak earnestly with Hansi about them when he is less distracted by the Capisco." She smiles conspiratorially and I smile idiotically back. She looks very attractive indeed in pale violet. I am surprised at myself, I lie, but I am very cheered.

Meanwhile Hansi and Addle and Moustique are playing consequences as a team, or rather as a ball game, one winning on critical points, one on stylistic analysis and one, poor Hansi, keeps throwing the topic back into the arena to keep all in play. None of them will have looked at anything but *Zeus and Alcmene,* chez Choiseul. "Such marvellous protraits of our friends," breathes Hansi, from behind all his buttons.

"That is not the least of Monsieur Capisco's gifts," comes from the mosquito.

"Who is this Plautus?" Nella wants to know, still directing her attention to me.

"A Latin playwright."

"Is he amusing?"

"Not to me, at the moment."

"You have read his plays? I have not, although," she adds defensively, "I am not uneducated. I am just ignorant of Plautus."

I take the point since I am in a similar, if reversed, situation. I am not ignorant of Plautus, just uneducated. And I confess that I haven't read Plautus either although I am discovering more about him than I wanted to know.

Lens and Estelle are woefully uneducated but Estelle, at least, is aware of all plots, Plautine or otherwise, in which Capo may be playing the lead. And now we are back on the set, all of us excepting the Master who is sulking in his tent and the crew who are tearing about, sparks, grips, lighting cameraman and all, in that familiar turmoil which will lead to several minutes of film and the repeated cries of "Quiet please" and "Could we have quiet?" from the assistant director, who is the only person present who is making any great noise.

"I'd like a straight 'to camera' sequence between Cap and Addle now," says the director to Estelle who shows, fleetingly, an evident distaste for these familiarities. "Monsieur Capisco is working," she says, freezingly, "and his son has arrived and may visit us at any moment."

"Great, great, great," says the director, "we'll have a great scene —father and son meeting here in the castello—kind of a bonus."

"Cappellino is here?" Addle is aghast. Estelle is loyally displeased.

"Do not call Pier-Francesco by that name. You should know better."

"What's with the name?" the director is puzzled. "What kind of kid is he?"

"I have heard his father call him a vacuum-cleaner." I shouldn't have said that. Estelle's displeasure now extends to me.

"He is not here now at the castello. Doubtless you will see him this evening. Jeannot, you seem overwrought and I do not think you should any more 'to camera,' whatever that means, at this time. Why don't you go and look for your wife?"

She is right. My attendance on Addle now to be interviewing

Cap, contrary to the schedule, is best postponed until I feel more awe-inspired and less awful. Also it is possible that bloody Cappellino and his horrible mates are up at the cottage tormenting Kir or worse, making themselves agreeable by offering her poisoned chocolates, or snow or something. Nella smiles at me. Moustique smiles at Estelle, for her consideration towards me. Addle is fanning himself with his panama and Hansi is looking uneasily at Nella. So, given the director who is simply looking blank, that makes a half dozen of them who can play out their own consequences very well without me and I go in through the house and follow the red thread on up the hill and so to my very own personal, private place of work and our bridal suite as it once was.

No Cappellino do I find there and none of his grotesques, but Kir and a quite different set of visitors. However, I am now out of shot. What goes forward, down on the terrace, I shall doubtless hear on play-back. Meanwhile, you, the audience, may have watched and heard the rough assembly of this probably award-winning documentary.

Two Cables:

OKAY RESTAURANT UPSCREW STOP RUSHES OKAY BUT GET
CHATPIECE NO BOYWONDER STOP RUMOURED MASTERPIECE
HIDDEN GARDEN SHED STOP COVER STOP REACTIONS THIS END
UNTHINK BUDGET RETHINK PRESS ON REGARDS

JANOS

CAP CAPTIOUS ASSPAIN HAS MASTERCAP HIS PAD HENCE
SOFTSOAP STOP CASTELLO GREAT ZOO GREAT APES SCENESTEALERS

LANDK
SANDY

IV
Master Positive Reel II

I know perfectly well that even locked in here I am not safe from the little video boxes. They may be anywhere and so far I've only found one and that was stuck sideways between the cistern and the wall in the lavatory. It must have registered the back of my head and my powerful (so they tell me) shoulders and I suppose the fine electronic thoughts I had in that small sanctuary this morning. They, at least, were for publication. But the other boxes could be anywhere. At least I am not now physically naked and have taken absurd pleasure in hitting the box in the bog with a hammer.

Listening to the unit and the little man giving the orders to it, out on the terrace, I heard odd phrases which, so far as my English permits, I understood to be technical terms used in making films. What, I wonder, are "kickers?" Some of the jargon even I can understand, such as "mid-shots," but "wowing" which seems to be something to do with the speed of sound and "flick zooms," what are they? To me "lens flare" is something I encounter personally, from time to time, when she is drunk, but what do such phrases mean to the unit? Do they think they can find something in me that is not perfectly in evidence from my work, by means of kickers and wowings? That I love my friends and my women and my animals and that I do what I want to do is the whole story. Do the public that film people serve perhaps envy that and enjoy this "documentary" evidence that film makers provide as to what bizarre kind of a creature the artist is? I give nothing away, I hope, or do I? Are they milking me of some stimulant they need? They are welcome. I do not despise the public for giving me so much response. It would be churlish. On the other hand, what is the public to me? Strangely little. I do not care much nowadays about its responses, except when they are malignantly obtuse and even then I find myself absurd to notice. Yet I should not like to have no public. I have needed success at times, but almost for as long as I can remember I

99

have had it. I should, I think, notice the public only if it were absent.

I suppose I must admit to watching my prices in the saleroom, which seem when they make records, to me, as to so many people, crazy. If they began to drop, perhaps I should worry about the noughts and yet I get no thrill from them any more, as they rise and rise. I do not find my work thus validated. It is too late.

It was said by Degas, when a picture of his fetched so many thousand gold francs at auction, that he felt "like a horse that had won the Grand Prix" but it is inevitable that as one's early work gets earlier and earlier, as it must, it gets more and more prodigiously expensive. A time comes when people get some sort of kick from the fact that one's hand has touched, actually touched, the material and done so all that time ago; that one made marks on paper which are called drawings in the remote past before World War I. Paradoxically, the fact that one's early work is admired most conveys the impression not that one has gone off, but that one is still ahead of taste.

Since I am made more than usually public by these technical devices, by the video boxes which only go to augment the reproductions, the art books and speculations of my learned admirers, there is no longer much purpose in my expressed hope for privacy. That, too, is too late and no one's fault but my own and perhaps Addle's and yours. I have, one way and another, long exposed myself in public, a misdemeanour as the police would probably say. So I will not now hold back from any of you my thoughts and actions, nor bash any more little black boxes. It was childish of me to break the one I did.

It is here then, in this long, untidy workshop that I work to find out what I am doing and therefore who I am. Does that content you, viewers and voyeurs? This is the practical enlargement of my skull into which you can see. Does that content you? It is here that I model wax and have gained some expertise in handling it, knowing for instance where definition may be in danger of being lost when molten metal replaces burnt-out wax in the negative mould of the investment. And "investment" here is a technical term which has nothing to do with finance. It means covering a wax model with fireproof material and it is done by slopping handfuls of wet plaster mixed with granite chippings all over the thing.

Now to make investment work, children, you must attach to your model tubes of wax which will allow the metal to flow freely into and through the negative which has been left empty when the wax in the fire-proof investment has been burned in smoke, in the kiln. Are you with me? Now if we lived in ancient times, I would do all that myself, but nowadays the foundrymen are very expert and much of this work may be left to them except, let us say, when I have made a little figure whose hands show the fingers splayed. If I have done that, it is wise for me to put my own wax runners in between the fingers and insist that I cut the metal away between them, once the work is cast, rather than risk losing the fingertips. This is simply because bronze founders are not absolutely called upon to know the appearance of the articulation of the fingers, but only how to use their own with skill.

I do not wish you to think me patronising, but I do not know if you are genuinely interested in this shop-talk. You may want only to invest in prestige baubles if you have money in your grasp, rather than grasp the implications of investment as one of the technicalities of my trade. I do not know if you care any more about "investment," "core," "runners and risers," "piece moulds," "chasing," "water blasting" and what-all than I do about the "jump cuts" and "strobing" and "bounce lights" which film men talk about. But they are the catchwords of crafts and honourable jargons.

I will tell you a personal secret to liven things up for you. I will make a confession, before I begin to work on the plaster of my baboon, Theseus, upon whose leonine and yet partially canine and partially human shape I am at this time concentrated beneath this blather that I am soliloquising for your benefit. It has come into my head because I must make some drawings now to clarify Theseus for me and make his joints join right when he himself is out of sight, but not out of mind. That is how I work. If he were in front of me now, scratching or screaming, I should have multiple impressions of him, whereas he is outside and the re-inventing of him is what I must manage, inside.

So, drawings and the secret: I abhor the vacuum of blank paper!

I am frightened of it. It may be ambiguous but in my alarm, I must always commit myself to the destruction of the sheet and I am always momentarily horrified to defile it.

You too must feel this, if you are over the age of twelve and no matter how many blank sheets of paper you daily despoil. It is this ancient memory, I suspect, of the sanctity of the virgin surface which makes you *sketch*, which makes you, when called upon to demonstrate on paper how a thing is shaped, nervously start to make short, hesitant marks, each overlapping one another to extend the contour. And you do this not for fear of spoiling the image you seek to make, but for fear of spoiling the paper. Is it not a fact that the only sure marks you make, when you are not writing down what you mean, is when you are not meaning what marks you make?

Is it possible that this is an ancient memory dating from times when paper even more than vellum was so expensive that only monks and clerks could mark it, or when Leonardo covered every spare inch of both sides of every sheet he had?

To make a mark on paper deliberately and seriously, and this new-found notion of mine, which has been true all my life although I have only just thought of it, has nothing to do with the squalid use of paper for writing on, or printing newspapers or other nonsense; to make a drawn line deliberately, requires nerves of steel and the ability to hold one's breath while a line lasts. The touch, of course, can be light but the aim must be to aim for certainty. People, and there are some, who feel no deep-seated need to draw, except at conferences and such-like, only achieve certainty of line when they are not thinking what they are doing, which is called doodling. Do not be alarmed by this. There may be no need for you to draw, or to think either, but to those afflicted, the two processes are identical.

I remember being agonisingly conscious, when I began to make prints, that it was the litho stone or the etching plate which frightened me, because I was not then absurdly rich as I now am, but was facing the fearful expense of these costly materials that in a moment I might irreparably damage by marking their surfaces wrongly. I was fearful of the awful commitment of chalk to laboriously ground stone, or needle to laboriously polished and grounded copperplate. Also I was thinking of the dreadful cost of printing an edition. The results were feeble then and they look feeble now except to dealers and their victims. They are feeble because my fear shines through them. How then could Michelangelo burn all those of his drawings he could lay hands on at one time? Was it fear of so much paper accusing him of violation? It is a thought to conjure with if not, perhaps, much.

No such problem exists for stone-carvers whose vanity is inevitably Michelangelesque. Who else would dare, except of course persons of divine facility and repellent genius, like Bernini? Everything except drawing and stone-carving can be rectified, even etching and lithography, given the money, or the confidence, or the patience.

When Pablo was making prints at Lacourière's during the last war because it was warmer at Lacourière's than anywhere else, he had men about him whose time was costly, but not as costly as a Picasso print. They stood round him like satraps at the court of Alexander, waiting for his precious marks; the simple, often silly, scribble Pablo would make. And then they would lovingly proof the thing, or burnish or polish it out, or regrind it thereafter if he demanded it. It was only sometimes *after the silly scribble*, when Pablo had the image like a woman under him and mastered, that the scribble burgeoned. It was only then that the image would build and frantically pile herself up like a nine-minute pregnancy bulging under his fingers and then she would sing out and old Pablo would seem to conduct a brass band with his needle, or his brushful of acid, or whatever came to hand to orchestrate the sum of his marks. The fear had left him and the vainglory with it. There is no vanity needed when the image itself truly burgeons.

I think Pablo taught himself early to conquer the fear of blank space. Alberto never did. The strength of Alberto's work is all in his fear of space. Perhaps that is why he died so young, at only sixty or so. Perhaps he had to get his feverish pencil and his nerve-racked thumbs and fingers on to a space and a clay beyond what we have available here. Or is that fanciful? Giacometti is perfectly the right name for him, little Giacomo who was not small but who looked like Chico Marx and never stopped talking and tried so hard to make a fat sculpture, which fear of where the form might lie always corroded. I am wandering. And I am, I know, on display. I am not so frightened as Alberto was of the first marks on the paper, or the first fistful of clay, or spoonful of plaster. He had the virtue, or perhaps it was the strength, when his nerve failed, to leave the fragment or shadow of the image out there in the middle of the sheet all alone and he would retreat and begin again. But both Pablo and, in his way, Alberto at least came up, gasping often, when they couldn't breathe any longer under the pencil's weight or the brush stroke. I am more hampered. I cannot leave these mudholes and come up for breath. My drawings are beaten to death and, each time, I with them.

So that is for your private ear, children, as I sit here, wrestling with the image of Theseus.

Now that you have had your lecture, you shall see the *practical* as I believe it is called in the classroom. Watch what I am actually doing in the way of holding together the unwieldy mass of rough plaster which is the first move towards shaping the head of Theseus, eponymous hero and baboon. It is based, as you may have noticed, on a small upended wicker wastepaper basket which I dug out as I began my soliloquy and have somewhat cut down. I have laid plaster-soaked scrim on this, is a thin mix with much water, and slopped thick spoonfuls of plaster over that, which is why I am slowly becoming white with the stuff myself. I throw nothing useless away, which is why I live in some confusion, but how else would I have at hand a child's wooden pencil-box when I need it as I need one now? What I need is a monkey's muzzle and where would I find a better armature? So I thrust the box into the still soft plaster pudding on the basket and strap it on with more plaster-impregnated scrim. Whether, in the end, this particular head will crown the final Theseus I am not yet sure. I may have to start the whole thing again when I get the irons up as armature for building the whole figure. In that case this object will become a study for the Head of Theseus. Waste not, want not. That is providing I can find another pencil-box or some equivalent ideal for building monkey muzzles. But can I? I shall worry about that later.

It looks a mess to you, this head? It is. But, while it is still fairly soft, I cut into it. I am paraphrasing under the knife the skull of an anthropoid and taking into account the mane of long fur that rises over the temples in dense tufts as thick as yard-brooms. These whiskers spring up the sides of the low skull to the little plates of ears, widely spaced and well back. Now the face of this anthropoid is like a coffin for a rat or small bird and it juts forward from under the low overhand of brow to end in a long snout with nostrils aligned like the muzzles of a double-barrelled pistol. Below this a long jaw like a lifeboat is suspended and hinged to open like a trap and scream. The mask is strung with sinews interleaved and moving counter to one another as striations under the thickness of the skin which can wrinkle with rage but looks in repose, as smooth as alabaster. Above this muzzle, the brow stands like a short turret pierced for eyes set close and as frontal as deep gun-ports lowering from a bar of bone from which spread wide and plated cheekbones which —let me tell you—embody the zygomatic arches, or eyesockets to you. This whole head is a fortress to be built, so watch the sockets and the snout as I come at the thing in the near-dry plaster because luck is attached to the next stage and it must be forced wrong to feel right. If not it will stay tame and be wrong.

Who but a grand old man like me could make something so serious and so monumental out of the image of a randy ape? I ask you; you who are so solemn and so impressed by art. The little Moustique, who is so moved and so reverent in the presence of drawing and who was reduced to silence by my monumental *blague* of a *Zeus-Amphitryon,* can at once remove under the local anaesthetic called, paradoxically, "aesthetics," the whole gut-hauling, joke-motivated, arm-wheeling fart of fun or cry of pain from what she would call "the creative act." She understands in her sensitive way only the cool shadow that dehydration by time and historical fatigue leaves behind for cultural analysis in the stain of the wet dream left on the sheet. No, that is unfair. She is only drowsy from the poppy of appreciation and vulnerable, oh yes, vulnerable to the shadow which lies aslant the expert and shows the act to have taken place in the sun beyond. Thus is Addle drowsy in the hum of the market-place where values, which are not what were once called "tonal values," touch truth only where his creative act rears something out of the dunghill by getting a record, and therefore to be venerated, price for it. But to be just to my old friend and victim, Addle has no veneration for prices, although they do, on aggregate, convince him that he was right all along the line. This helps.

Meanwhile, as you can see I have this red knitting-needle as pointer and the head in rough on its basket is on the turntable. Theseus, or rather just his erection, is standing hero-mythic all on its own in my hand and no balls or pelvis or hump and weight of shoulders nor as yet much of his head are there to thrust it home, until I gather wire and wood and plaster and whatever bones, bits of palm tree, old baskets and metaphor-proposing bits of driftwood I can find to guide me towards him through my pile of props which is my palette made from bones. Mud and spare-rib was all it took in the first place, to make male and female on a Friday or Saturday, Jew or Gentile, at the birth of the world. But I need the wrack from the seashore and the forms that do not lose their individual identity simply because I combine them in the guise of large baboon, but hold their own in him as we hold, in each of us, the flotsam rigidities of memory, separate and independent, in the context and matrix of forms.

My son is here and of course you, who are sophisticated viewers and listeners at the box, have cottoned at once to the fact that he has not been established by way of the subtle mechanism planted to expose me to you, but has come on his own as part of the rich tapestry of vicarious life upon which, friends, you feed like the grubs of clothes-moths.

What shall I think of him for you? That I love him? But we all love our children. Are they not our hostages to fortune, or immortality? Is it less than that for me because the critics and auction houses would make me independently immortal by butchering my brains to make an ad-man's holiday? I will be frank with you. I fear and love my son; of several sons he more than the others. What atavism is this then? Pier-Francesco, who early gave himself to motor-cycles and contempt for my reputation which, understandably, he resented, is not to most people, lovable. He could be called spoiled by his mother, whom I can now see so clearly and who lured me in fancy-dress into the *beau monde*. She is not lovable. Madeleine and her child are now among us. To be more exact, they will be among me this evening and knowing what she is and who he is, I shall feel, as before, disgust with her where, if I were able to be rational, I should see him as disgusting. He will disgust and defeat me, the golden boy with his tarnished friends and I shall come back here once again, as usual, and work on with my Theseus, who has no concern with gold, but only with his red knitting-needle and his great dignity. Mythologically that is ironical.

Can you hear me? Can you see me? Am I coming through clear to you? Theseus was a hero and a killer who deserted Ariadne, dishonoured the queen of the Amazons, drove his wife Phaedra to suicide by his inadequacy, betrayed his father to his death and comes to me as an anthropoid in majesty, flame-arsed and needle-pricked, because he is not golden; because of his bestial innocence.

Whatever break in the continuity may result, I am now going to piss. This I think I can do safely because I have bashed the box in there.

I thought, while I was in there, that you were entitled to my political opinions as part of the package you are getting and this was because, still thinking of Theseus while I was pissing, it occurred to me that the baboon in the garden and the protobaboon in the legend were probably ruthlessly akin, neither having any developed ethical sense.

The ancient Theseus did, however, achieve a widespread reputation as a by-product of Athenian politics, as has often been the case with heroes and indeed with Athenians. Nothing complicated about that. But then you would not expect anything complicated about politics from me, but rather the expression of some unworldly views, stated briefly enough to make me sound as simpleminded as visual artists are comfortingly thought and hoped to be.

It is important only to the young, like Pablo, that anyone should be committed to political concepts, but it is satisfying to the middle-aged that old men's views should be sufficiently banal to allow practical men of affairs to smile at them since practical middle-aged men who are ageing are those who conduct political affairs. This they do largely because they crave power and have complex notions about holding it by circumventing ideas. That's simple enough for a start, isn't it? Politicians need power. On the other hand, I have power. I have it over inert substances and, as a result of manipulating these materials as others manipulate men and women, I also have some power over the human imagination including perhaps yours. This power has doubtless corrupted me, but less than power over people corrupts. Mine is the preferable power, as almost all the major political and military protagonists who were responsible for

World War II managed to demonstrate. They were failed painters, or poets or writers of one sort or another from Hitler to Churchill, by way of Goebbels, Mussolini and even Stalin. Tick them off on your fingers. It was their hopeless failure in such serious endeavours which corrupted them into politics and since success in politics depends upon the manipulation of the human failure to understand human failure, only failures can succeed, whilst those who succeed as human beings fail in politics.

Certain incorruptible concepts are embedded in politics and these ideas politicians nose round resentfully because they are notions which so interfere with the conduct of practical matters that they may sometimes even escape control. The admiration these notions enjoy is called sentimental because they are moral and both the young and the old are regarded as the victims of sentiment, the one for lack of maturity and the other for having passed it. I subscribe to these ideas, which have to do with justice and equity. Have I given you an old man's maundering to patronise? It is politically expedient to assume that people like me are simple-minded, otherwise how could we be envied and despised in equal measure? Let me put it this way. The artist is distrusted if he attempts to communicate anything complicated and especially if, in surmounting a complex of difficulties, a certain weight of thought subtends the images he makes. He is trusted only if he can so disguise the evidence of his mind that he seems to be doing something very simple. If he manages this, he is a confidence trickster and no simpleton, but it is comforting to regard him as simple. With politics the reverse is true. Politicians are assumed to be astute in surmounting simple problems with apparent difficulty. If they were not, who would accept their manipulations since no one envies them nor finds them superior? Could it be that it is politicians who yearn for love and beauty while artists pursue power?

That should give you enough to be going on with. I can only hope that, because I play with paradox, you will not find me clever. Paradoxes, like paraphrases, are among the tools of my trade. I am really a simple, candid old man and I am a man of the left because I am not cynical enough to forgo humanity for the sake of *Realpolitik* and I have nerve enough left to prefer the simplicity of the adherents of the left to the knowing baboons, with their simple answers to complex questions, on the right. So much for that.

I interrupt this broadcast to divulge what I have been doing while I was thinking and telling you my thoughts, because the thinking and the doing are not quite the same things. It may be that you have been listening so reverently that you forgot to watch. Many people cannot both look and listen at the same time, and many of you are, I am sure, abysmally stupid as well. Never mind. What I have been doing is to balance the weight against the thrust and the soft against the hard in the conjoined and braced-up elements of Theseus' front and top, his bone head and blatant visage and the heaped and leaping forest of his hairy temples laid down the ridge of his low and cunning skull. The time is coming when I shall build his neck back from this mask and pile up the great cape of fur he wears on his shoulders, which strikes out sideways as if sprung. And the various laths, bits of iron and chickenwire which you see I have assembled here and have rather insecurely wired together can be partly bricked under for support and partly hung from the pulley. It can all be brought to hold together by the scrim, with the binding agency of great gouts of plaster. For that, wait.

It may have struck you, if you have not been asleep, that I have begun a vast sculpture as compared with the going dimensions for your average baboon. A real baboon is much the size, at maturity, of a large dog, as you saw when mine came out of the bushes beyond the terrace. I am making a hero-baboon. It will be seven feet high. Let that content you. I am making a political baboon, an ape statesman, a presidential field marshal, ruthless and dedicated to the very simple but pitiless requirements of his calling. And he will make me bleed, for as you can see from my knuckles, which are scarred and invariably sore, the contact between the plaster surface and my poor flesh is endless in the act of defeating and eventually smoothing the harsh and dry lime which forms the ape and scrapes my skin. And also, if you didn't notice, the damned material hardens off so fierce and often, that half my working life is spent in scraping out bowls of dead plaster and mixing up in water the bowls of the living.

Now that I have pissed my wisdom on you and shown you some

mysteries, I shall deny you nothing, you who are greedy to know my secrets and why I am so young for my age and so well, all things considered, preserved. I will tell you that my reminiscences will be of less consequence than you might hope, because I do not in fact feel nostalgic, at least at this time in the afternoon. Also my memory is enfeebled by self-indulgence and celebrity and longevity.

I do not look back on the old days as a golden age. I rather think my own golden age, recent as it is, may be waning, except in simple terms among the unsophisticated or "art-lovers" because I do not have much effect any more. Nor does Pablo, nor any of the big cheeses of the first half of the twentieth century, except maybe Matisse and he is exempt from fashion, once having become fashionable, because the lyrical use of bright colours remains absolutely fascinating in itself to children of all ages. Everyone truly loves colour and many people insist upon confessing it, unless of course they feel it sounds vulgar to say so.

I do not much miss Matisse.

However I remember with affection a story Gertrude used to tell of Matisse at Clamart, where he lived with Madame Matisse in great pomp, owning a garden and a conservatory where they grew exotic blooms including begonias which Gertrude swore got smaller and smaller. Anyway, Gertrude visited the Matisses one morning for bourgeois lunch and found them staring into a packing-case in which lay a huge laurel wreath garnished with a red ribbon and a card which read "Henri Matisse triumphant" or some such, sent by an admirer. Matisse said he was not dead yet, whereas Madame Matisse said the wreath was of excellent bay which would go well in soup, whilst the ribbon would do to tie up Margot's hair. That was in 1912 or 1913 and doubtless the wreath would have entered the still-lifes of Matisse, had it not gone into soup, and there in a still-life it would have acted as a foil to the diminishing begonias. The Matisses wasted nothing. Where was I? Yes, I do not really miss Matisse, having known him, because he tells one all one needs to know of him with his *bouquet garni,* which is permanent.

It is the ones who kept something back that I miss, especially those I missed.

I am desolate not to have known Degas. I miss him because I

missed him and he was more profound and moving as a sculptor and acerbic and unpleasant as an old gentleman than I like to feel I have missed. I would have liked to know Velasquez for his humane solemnity and Poussin for his sternly balanced seriousness and Ingres for his immense and, for him, soul-saving pomposity of which he made a sculptural virtue no sculptor of his age could match. And then of course I would like to spend my declining youth with those whom Estelle calls my "revered and corpsed contemporaries" who were at Pisa and Arezzo long before me and in Florence, before it got so noisy and then earlier and earlier and less and less easy to meet because of the layers and layers of time which muffle their voices and cloak one's view of them.

I do not have Pablo's vendetta with the dead, but then I am in so much less of a hurry than Pablo is to get them to match up to me. He is a great bully, Pablo, shoving Velasquez and Delacroix and even slippery young Manet about. He is a veritable sergeant-major making them all tuck their chins in and straighten up and square off from the right and fuck on the word of command, you, Rembrandt, or else. Or else cubism, when you come down to it, and Cézanne-bashing, except for that peerless line of his that comes down his arm all the way from between his ears and jets, right to the tip, like the needle of Theseus. You have to admire the vast waste of paper that Pablo has had the courage to achieve, selling some with marks on it only to buy more; a laying waste in his frequently justified belief that sowing salt and dragon's teeth on the sheet will produce what he can produce when he is lucky.

This kind of aphoristic comment on my contemporaries is what you expect from me, isn't it? Well, on some of the others I have known, some of whose works, now of great price, I have absent-mindedly come to own, I shall be mercilessly brief. Modi, for example, died tragically fast and young and spared no one trouble about his doing so. There he was, a young fellow and sickly, but able to bring Duccio madonnas absolutely up to date, swan necks and all. Much my age, Modi would be if he were alive now, and with just the one outlet of a notion; to marry African sculpture, which he did not understand, with Sienese *trecento* saints, which, being born thereabouts, he was born to. Modi had a keen perception of timing as to death, but no time to become a sculptor, poor child.

I missed the *Douanier* by pure chance. I could have met him and maybe attended the famous banquet Picasso so cruelly gave him in Spanish honour and humour, but I didn't. I think I should have liked being bored by old Rousseau and would not have been disposed to take the mickey out of him to point up his marvellous simplicity, as were so many; nor yet find him so great as they do nowadays. I was reading the other day that some museum had paid God knows how many million dollars, or francs, or whatever, for a painting of a tiger in a rain forest which Rousseau had painted from memories of the *Jardin des Plantes* and I also read of an angry nature-lover who wrote to the papers saying that the money would have been better spent on saving real tigers from extinction. And I thought then that Rousseau would surely have agreed with him and, had he not been so gentle, would have taken great pains to have had Christians thrown to the picture in the velodrome, while playing his fiddle. I miss him, but not really very much, except as an idea, now over-plagiarised.

What more can I tell you? Is the secret of how to make sculpture what you want? Then I will give you part of it. You must invent or believe in a recipient for your work. And I do not mean anything banal in saying this. A sculpture is an object made to be offered but neither to a museum nor a collector should it be offered. Neither should be a worthy shrine for it. Make what you like of that.

I am become gnomic and oracular. A sculpture is made from the capacity to recall and combine an assembly of interlocking memories and the ability to make a decoction of what is remembered by grinding all the memories into a paste and then making a model from that paste which wastes only what you can afford to neglect. What do you make of that? A sculpture is a retort to my previous question and the setting of my next one.

A sculpture, blast the thing, is frustrated by spilling the plaster, as I have just done, all over the floor, by dropping tools and by bleeding from self-inflicted wounds. It is frustrated by finding that the armature is wrong, under the mass, because you have changed your mind and cannot remember where you are going to find impervious irons in there, or wire netting just where there should be none. A sculpture is luck and never allowing the tension to get slack except where there must be slack, or there will be no tension. A sculpture is a mess, as this is now, unless I can pull it out of the mess. A sculpture is no fucking good, for no obvious reason. I shall stop and look at it and pray and deliberate on whether I shall smash the whole thing with this hammer or whether I can win. A sculpture is a contest in which the weapons are steel implements, and the wounds are first in the mass and then in you. Your opponents are hardness and the stupidity of your own errors, failure of observation and failure of retention in the mind's eye. A sculpture is an act of conquest, as fierce as the myth of Theseus, which ends in harsh caresses and the slow smoothing away of scars.

But you don't want this stuff, do you, just because it may be true? It has no savour; it is the shop-talk of the private mind and, after all, I am public here. You think, don't you, that you can watch me and I can do what I do and I can think about my son, at the same time? This would encourage you on both counts. It would give you the experience of watching me perform and the spice of listening to what I am thinking, because, curiously perhaps, they will not seem exactly to conjoin. You are right in a way. The battle is with the raw materials, the pushing, pulling, building, cutting away, underpropping, mixing, smearing on and the calculating it will involve. But this will all go forward in an area of decision quite remote from my ongoing indecision about Pier-Francesco. Does that seem strange? It is not. The actual making is camouflaged, even to me, by a cloud of seemingly idle fancies, scraps of songs, repeated rubrics, immemorabilia and vague appetites. Cézanne, they say, used to sing a little song at his work. It went: *"La peinture à l'huile est bien difficile Mais beaucoup plus beau que la peinture à l'eau."* He repeated it endlessly and I am not sure whether he even believed it. Underneath the level of the proposal, the contest with the difficulties went forward and out came the little apples, praise be to God.

You may now just as well cut the sound-track and just watch, if you have a mind, because what you will hear will be antic ramblings off the top of my bald old head while I work. There will be no more insights revealed into the deep experience of making just one more plaster for a large bronze. I wish that bloody boy had not sneaked in here and collared my maquettes. Why does he have to do that? He perfectly well knows that I would have given him the money, the market price, if he had asked Estelle for it. He won't get that much from his dealing friends either. I could use those fucking models at this minute . . . although of course . . . I shall not need them for very long . . . The trouble with plaster is that it dries faster, you cannot relax as you can do with wax.

V

Processing

With Capo locked in his workshop, thinking heavy thoughts and confiding them with a considerable lack, I daresay, of remote control, there is nothing on the floor for Sandy and his unit to do, since Cap's scheduled "to camera" interview with Addle shows no sign of taking place until Cap gets good and ready, which could be never. So, predictably, the director trundles up the hill to our place to get some footage of Cap's most recent *magnum opus*, of which Kir and I are the worried curators and which dominates the largest wall of our pad.

Equally predictably there is Kir guarding our lair, like a small tigress, against Poitevin's second service of art-loving tourists and I have arrived, of course, having climbed in through the bathroom window. This situation gives the unit a buckshee crowd scene because there is our so-called garden, which Kir cherishes, now being trampled underfoot by a public assembly which is milling restlessly around the fat Poitevin who is hammering on our door and demanding what he calls his right. All good material for farce but not conducive to the flowering of my genius in the tranquil atmosphere I need to nurture that sturdy but vulnerable plant.

Kir has barricaded herself behind our door, with all our available movables piled up against it and there is an impasse in every sense of the word.

Imagine, then, the scene, you who have not yet had the opportunity to view all this merry footage on your television screens. To Poitevin's paying public there is added the crew with all their equipment and the vans they carry it in and the director's jeep, all confronting the picturesque studio-cottage we temporarily call home and where we seek peace from the hurly-burly of Castello Capisco. It is here on other days that I try to work to rival him eventually, given time and encouragement. The featured player in this scene is honest Poitevin disguised, as is his custom, as the financial editor of *La Dépêche de Toulouse*. He wears a sober suit with watchchain, a stiff collar, an artistic bow-tie and a black straw hat shaped like a fedora. He is angry. He is breathless. He brandishes the pince-nez hanging from him on a black ribbon. He gesticulates. He implores and demands entrance. Kir, standing behind the door and armed *cap-à-pied* with a broom, traditional weapon of the outraged housewife, looks splendidly enraged.

"Thank God," she says, when she sees me sneak in, "thank God you have come."

Strong drama here, as of Liberty confronting the Forces of Tyranny. All she needs is the Phrygian cap and cockade to be a veritable Delacroix.

"Oh, Jeannot, what shall we do?"

"All is not lost."

The rumble of the invading force beyond the door adds to the effect of a larger thunder muttering in the hills. A storm appears imminent from the clouds building up. All we need is hurry-music to make it an epic sequence, with the weather lowering and the crowd lowing.

"Courage," I add, to create confidence, "courage, I am here."

"What good will that do?"

"We stand together. We shall not fail."

"Oh, Jeannot, do stop it."

The visitors are now peering, like the trapped inmates of an asylum, through the large window which admits my working light and at other times gives me a panorama of the sweep of the bay and a view of the back of the Universe and Liberia. The front rank of the mob is trying to look sideways at the Capo which is on the wall angled to the window above the place where our bed would be if it were not playing its part at the barricades. They can't see *Zeus, Amphitryon and Alcmene* without pressing their faces sideways against the glass, thus forming a tight frieze of compressed noses, goggle eyes and open mouths.

Since all these avid spectators have their hands pressed to their brows to cut out reflected light from the window glass, I am much struck by the effect.

"I shall call the cops," I say comfortingly to Kir and the truth is that it seems a shame not to build the event even more by adding a touch of uniformed confusion to it, including two more hard-boiled eggs, if they have them.

"Do you think they will go away?" asks the figure of Liberty, now slightly dishevelled, if neo-classical in pose.

"Give them time."

"Time for what? They will tear the place down."

"Don't fire until you see the yolks of their eyes."

"Oh, Jeannot, what shall we do?"

"Hold out to the last man."

"Dammit, Jeannot, stop the bloody jokes."

"Well, what would you do?"

"I could unbarricade the door, open it and suddenly hit that Poitevin with this broom as he comes in."

"Risky. People might trample him and we owe him money."

"Bourgeois," she snarls. I think snarls is the *mot juste*.

"Shall I summon the forces of law and order if that's what I am? Bourgeois is as bourgeois does."

"Why don't you *do* something?"

"What?"

"Call the police."

The window is bulging ominously inward under the pressure of those greedy for cultural experience. I dial the gendarmerie, but naturally, in the middle of the afternoon, there is no reply.

"No reply."

"Then prop something against the window."

"What shall I prop?"

"Anything."

"Seems a pity. They look so curious, with all their noses squashed."

"Oh, Jeannot."

Wishing to help, I take my largest available painting, eight foot by six no less, and prop it on the window-sill. It occurs to me that members of the crowd may derive an unexpected benefit from this. If I keep swapping pictures, I shall have my own one-man exhibition, with captive spectators. Maybe one, at least one, art lover, preferably well-heeled, will recognise talent when he or she sees it.

There is an unquestionable lack of reverent hush outside, despite the quality of the large and important example of my work that I now elevate before the public. I take it down and try another and then another. No improvement. No gasp of awe. The sheep only want Capo. I hear them screaming for blood. Well, let them have Capo. It's all his fault. I phone the castello hoping to get Estelle. I get Lens and explain the situation.

"Great," she says, "I'll be right up," and she rings off. That is what you get from dedicated newswomen with expensive cameras.

I write with charcoal on a big canvas, in capital letters, the message NO ONE AT HOME and hold it up to the window. Kir says that will make them angry. I rub it off and write again.

"What have you written?" Kir asks.

"OUT TO LUNCH."

"It's the middle of the afternoon, you fool."

"Late lunch."

"Ring Estelle, you clown."

I phone Estelle and get her. I explain our predicament. I tell her we have our own Dien Bien Phu up here.

"Who?"

"Hanoi."

"That must be a joke in bad taste, Jeannot. Please make yourself clear and please be quick. The film people have been using the phone all day and I have calls to make."

"Hold on," I say and prop my best big nude against the window. As I get back to the phone, I see this masterpiece fall off the sill. I suppose you could call this a happening. The crowd seems to be rounding on Poitevin who has stopped pounding on the door and now appears to be explaining, with histrionic gestures, why there may be some impediment to the public gaining access to Capo's new masterpiece. I think he is being asked to give money back, judging from his expression.

"Estelle," I cry, "help us. This place is a disaster area. A lynch mob is breaking into our house. Rogue elephants in musth."

"Explain," she says calmly and Kir takes the phone from me giving me the broom.

"Estelle, it's me. There's a crowd outside trying to get in to see Cap's picture. And Jeannot is clowning and won't help."

"Then I should let it in. That would be best." I can hear Estelle's bell-like tones come through the apparatus, cool as spring water.

"But they will wreck the place," says Kir piteously.

"Nonsense."

I take the phone from Kir. "Estelle," I say, with matching calm, "what we have surrounding our premises is Cap's public and they are mad with hunger for culture."

"No one is."

Maybe she has a point there. They are not, I think, responding to my big nude, which Kir has now repropped on the window-sill with the aid of the broom. And it is one of my most successful recent pictures.

"Why don't you just leave, my dears, and come down here? I think they will probably go away. It is going to rain."

"I am not sure the defences will hold until then."

"Of course they will. Cap's admirers are always excellently behaved. Besides it will be a heavy shower."

"You think?"

"Certainly. Also I shall send Pancho to speak with Poitevin." And she rings off.

So Kir and I climb out of the bathroom window and go round behind the crowd and get a reverse-angle shot where the unit is having a field day with *vox pop* interviews: the many wanting to comment on Capisco with ignorance and in nauseating homage while walking on Kir's fuchsias, or whatever they are in the border. A matron spots us and raises what might easily have become the hunt, but on the moment Zeus Taranis, god of storms, shakes his aegis over us and comes to our rescue, with lightning and vast thunder. The wall of black cloud which has built up over the mountain behind the house seems to pause in mid-sky so that half the area is partially eclipsed, while the other half is sun-beaten; a brazen glare coming off the rocks and the sea. The landscape holds its breath and then whistles up a harsh, cold wind which effectively silences even Poitevin. A curious, instant desperation welds the whole teeming group in our garden into one apprehensive clutch and there they all are, struck motionless and overlit like waxworks. You would think they were expecting the day of wrath, although all it is is a thunderstorm even if unusual hereabouts, before high summer. Big drops begin to fall.

I watch, with Kir, this bubble of alarm hold the company petrified for an instant and it explodes and all break for cover, of which there is none nearer than the Universe and Liberia. However this efflorescence of promising custom homing in on his other premises gets Poitevin moving like an athlete and he is off, leading the field down the hill, while the unit are jamming themselves into the van and struggling to get the hood up on the jeep. All that are left in situ seem at first to be Kir and me and the rain hasn't really started. The sun is still fighting back, but clearly losing. Over beyond the wall, in the dying convulsion of the light, is a curious group consisting apparently of a girl like a lamp-post, a seedy all-in wrestler in jeans and T-shirt, a dwarfish mechanic in overalls, a male model in leather and a figure who, in this light, appears to be made entirely of gold. All are leering except the lamp-post girl who wears no expression. She never does and I can tell you this because I know her. I also know the others. The golden figure, becoming tarnished as the sun is covered by the now dense cloudbank, is Cappellino. He is rare, among gold objects, to be able to tarnish. It is a gift.

The reason why he seemed so suddenly golden was a transitory effect of light, of course, such as impressionists probably used to catch. Doubtless it is also because he is Capisco's son. Also it is because he favours yellows; chrome yellow slacks, ochre yellow shirt, lemon yellow neckerchief, gold ornaments and bright golden, but golden, hair. He is holding, on a length of yellow twine, Capisco's ram, whose great curling horns also seem golden and that, I see, is because someone has fancifully gilded them. It all makes a rare pagan spectacle, lacking only vine leaves and panthers.

"Oh God," Kir says, "Cappellino."

"My father doesn't like people to call me that, you know," says the son and heir, with his charming smile as he moves languidly towards us, his satyrs thick behind him and the lamp-post nymph trailing along behind them.

"Jeannot," says Cappellino affectionately, "how good to see you. Kir, you look radiant." And he offers us his long gold, gold-ringed hand in turn, and in turn we limply take it.

He really is beautiful, is Pier-Francesco, beautiful as Nijinsky must have looked in *L'Après-midi* and not in the least like Capo. Kir has gone cold and remote.

"How popular you have become, Jeannot. Were those all clients, beating at your door with their cheque-books? Why didn't you let them in and conduct them through your studio, modestly nodding at each extravagant compliment and letting Kir conduct the sordid negotiations?"

The friends have now bunched themselves in a pack, carefully grouped according to height and weight. They seek to look charming, echoing the mood or following the lead of their master, but charm they do not have. Cappellino likes heavy contrast in the effect he makes and he likes to point himself up by exercising control over sinister companions. So he gathers sinister companions whom I think he rents to Fellini when he isn't using the whole group.

"You know Petronella," he murmurs, indicating the lamp-post, who gazes blankly past Kir. "And of course Aldo, who looks after me so marvellously." That is the muscle in the T-shirt, who creases up his face like a rubber toy. "And Gordon Bleu?" Gordon Bleu, who took his name from a signboard outside an Italian restaurant, bobs at us. He is the dwarfish mechanic.

"Do you know Niki? But of course you do." Niki is the dark beauty swanning around in leather from head to foot. A very haughty, silent creature is Niki. He cannot pass a mirror without a long pause and he, too, is a figure to contrast with Cappellino, being so handsome in such a different way. "And you've met my poor uncle?" This enquiry accompanies a slight tightening on the twine which holds the ram in check. The ram makes no sound, but rolls an eye. The twine is at least visible, while those other strings which Cappellino holds so easily in the same hand, each of silk or gold wire, are not. Each one runs, however, to the neck of one of his companions and it needs no pressure of his fingers to draw them along with him.

"It's starting to rain," I growl, "we'd better go in."

"How can we do that?" asks Kir. "The furniture is piled against the door."

"Privacy is so important. One has to go to such lengths. But I'm sure Aldo and Gordon will climb in and open up." The fingers flick and the puppets dart off for the bathroom window. The rain comes down suddenly now in great, widely spaced spears. The sky and sea are now both black. Cappellino and the ram process, Niki in train and Petronella straggling, towards our long-suffering door and we follow to shelter in what there is of a porch.

"That's Cap's ram," says Kir.

"A relative," replies Cappellino. "We are renewing our acquaintance with Uncle and have made him look spick and span, don't you think? Presently, when the rain stops, we shall garland him."

"Is anyone else here with you?"

"Mother is down at Poitevin's and of course Ambrose is somewhere about with his little secretary. They look after bills and things."

I know what that means. Ambrose is a runner in the trade and I think his secretary is a dab hand at writing *vrai* on the backs of photographs, with a variety of signatures to validate such statements.

"Why are you all here, Cappellino?"

"You really must *not* call me that in Father's hearing. He hates it so."

"Well, why?"

"Duty, Jeannot, duty. Family duty."

Gordon Bleu opens our door from inside and bows us all in. Kir has nothing to say, nor have I. The storm is now furious and it is pouring with rain.

"How splendid," says Cappellino, and it would seem appropriate if Theseus were heard to bark, or howl menacingly from down the hill, but he doesn't. The ram is restive for a moment but then docile again. I find that odd. It can't be the company he's in.

Silence as they say is golden, but I have never known it gold-plated before. Kir and I move the furniture back into place while Cappellino and his henchmen contemplate Capo's mural with various degrees of attention. Petronella doesn't give it a glance, being on another voyage somewhere, but the others look, each according to his attention span and capacity to register, with nudgings and elbowings, the meaty content of the picture, allegorically conveyed to those receptive of it. Cappellino, who will miss no implication and subjects the work to prolonged contemplation, utters a high-pitched little giggle. All the others, except Petronella, laugh dutifully and I find my guts gyrating. Few guardians of a twentieth-century masterpiece have, I realise suddenly, to endure quite such an emotional charge as part of their duties as keepers. If art is a distillation of life, then this is an illicit still producing, if only for me, a jar of rot-gut.

My ambivalent response to Cappellino's light laugh is remarkable. I am at once enraged by such a response to the drawing as a work of art and the contempt expressed but at the same time, discreditably, I immediately hate the thing itself with an iconoclastic loathing for its betrayal of me, myself and its savagely irresponsible mockery. I do not think that I have ever felt so violent a response to an image. It strips my skin off. Looking at it now is like receiving an anonymous letter, filthy and malicious. Yet at the same time, instinct prompts me to champion the thing for what it is, a drawing, in the face of the pop-cretins who are gaping at it.

Kir is looking desperately vulnerable and quite grey. No one speaks. It is the ram who causes the necessary diversion, by impatiently pulling forward on his string and knocking over a chair.

"Aldo," says Cappellino easily, "has the prognathous jawbone of an ass. I use it for smiting the Philistine. Pick up the chair, Aldo, and pull in your chin."

This sally gives great amusement to Gordon Bleu, who laughs immoderately.

Cappellino frowns. "Hold the ram, Gordon, and be quiet. What is his name, by the way? Jason, I suppose, to keep everything classical. We should spray his fleece golden, don't you think, as well as his horns?"

"Wild, man," is Niki's comment. Niki has a grating voice which he has long been grinding down to the minimum to augment his cool. He has filed off all pronouns, verbs except in the imperative and nouns of more than two syllables. He is content with adjectives as affirmations. Gordon Bleu, on the other hand, whispers and squeaks endlessly to Aldo, like something behind the woodwork, except when silenced by his master. Aldo never replies, but adjusts his rubber face appropriately where the bone formation allows. Does that give you the picture? That and the little Gordon struggling with his charge?

"Father is so obvious," says Cappellino, curving himself into a

125

chair. "Never a cliché missed. But as a caricature portraitist, quite exceptional. The likeness is never lost under the conventional pastiche he makes of his own earlier work. No?"

"No." I have found my voice, under the saliva washing round my mouth as a prelude to vomiting. "No, that is absurd."

"So loyal, Jeannot, dear heart, and so long-suffering in your loyalty."

Kir has gone Kir-coloured.

"But he is quite omnivorous, is Papa, is he not? So many lumps in the porridge. You find a gobbet of Attic vase painting, some unmoulded Klee and the detritus of all those little thefts from old Pablo cobbled on to memories of the *quattrocento*. It is really rather repulsive as a mélange. He is so astute too. So many dried vegetables in the package soup that the liquid is quite strained away. So dense with little shared experiences that no one can find anything obscure in the taste. And the taste is like expensive fish jam. Caviar, I would say, for the generality. Even the composition is divided up like one of those compartmented trays people eat from while watching television."

He has his back to the picture while delivering this critique and we are all ranged in front of him like schoolchildren at assembly.

"Perhaps you find my views harsh, but then I do not find Father's work stimulating, you see. Only useful."

"I suppose sons do find the weight of their fathers hard to carry, when those sons are comparatively insignificant."

Schoolboy bad manners and pompous too. It's the effect Cappellino always has on me. I am invariably boorish to him, to my invariable disadvantage.

"Ah, how true that is; I am only the little hat, am I not? Nicknamed after the little cap my mother should have worn had she not been a Catholic. To think nowadays that I should be prevented, precluded from a rich and fascinating life, by something even simpler. I am a living advertisement for the pill, but how cruel of you to imply it, Jeannot, my dear."

I am silenced of course.

"I cannot think why you are so unforgiving, Jeannot, and so ungenerous when I admire you so. I always have. I feel your work is so much more fulfilling than Father's. I can see from here several pictures of yours, all incomparably richer and more complex than those dreadfully banal lumps he calls his sculpture. I feel I derive enduring pleasure from your pictures. If I owned one, I would find more and more in it every time I looked. I should hang it on the wall opposite my bed."

Petronella has mooned across to the ram and is communing with him. She has folded up like a piece of trellis and is gazing into his eyes and caressing his muzzle. He does not favour this and backs away between Gordon's legs. Gordon clucks and chatters sibilantly.

"It is curious, isn't it, how little we recognise our mainsprings nowadays?" says Cappellino, brooding on his grouped acolytes. "We no longer live by shared rituals. Sacrifice has been depraved to the level of Manson, mindless in California, with Polanski not quite getting his own drift; so unsavoury I think. When one considers the *Bacchae* and poor Pentheus trying so hard, you know, and the divine *acceptance* of Agave, not understanding the situation at all, but intuitively knowing what was expected of her, I begin to think that there are things to be set right. It is a contribution I could make to our times."

It has stopped raining and the whole landscape is glittering outside. There doesn't seem any reason for Kir or for me to say anything; I, of course, being disarmed and weaponless in the net of this gilt *retiarius* with his trident. There is no purpose to be served by talking to this cobra but, God, he is hypnotic.

And now Theseus does bark and does howl from down the hill and Cappellino smiles like a faun. "Such timing," he says, as if talking, for a change, to himself, "if there is one thing I have to hand to my dear father, it is his capacity to contrive the anthropomorphic. He remains the ringmaster of his own circus."

Cappellino has what I dislike to call charisma. He has an animal magnetism, or a glamour at once insupportable but compelling which he habitually works at. I can't find how to fight it and he makes me feel like a hayseed, a compound of cereals, or some sort of laxative breakfast food compressed from husks. So now we have two protagonists, Cappellino and me, facing each other in an arena with an invisible blood-crazed crowd waiting for a kill, and I am losing unless Cappellino's attention has been drawn back, by the cry of Theseus, to his real opponent who is, as always, his dad. And his dad is in the royal box, far from the blood and sand but gazing at the combat maybe through a cubist-cut cabochon emerald, while I am leaden with loyalty and loathing and wearing a gladiator's kit, with one half of me naked and open to the trident and the other all armoured by my vocation as so-called creative artist and my solidarity with the old monster who spends his energies on horse-laughs at my expense, spread all over my wall. I can feel the weight of my huge helmet which I hope to heaven masks my face from the wide eyes of this pastiche Peter O'Toole, with his mirror-blank irises which are gold as a stater.

"Should we have coffee?" asks Kir, in there pulling the bull away from the gutted horse and flopping her cape.

"How delicious," says Cappellino, and now comes a knocking at the door and for a moment I feel relief at the thought that Poitevin is back with his cultural group and we may be saved by a rush of extras. Not so, it is Pancho, sent by Estelle.

"Pancho," says Kir, throwing wide the door. And Pancho, who is one of those Von Stroheim types, as in *Sunset Boulevard,* clipped and fanatical, butts into the room, head high and nostrils aquiver at the feral stink of Cappellino's people.

"Madame sent me."

"Ah, the Figaro," says Cappellino amiably, "and how is Madame? Well, I trust."

"She is well, sir." Pancho is sizing up Aldo for weight and speed.

"My mother will be so pleased."

"Yes, Signor Piero."

"They've gone," I confide to Pancho, "the rain did it."

"Madame assumed so." Pancho's eyes roll like the ram's, but he is very correct.

"Tell her we shall all dine at Poitevin's, a family reunion."

"She expects to do so, Signor Piero." Pancho bows like a robot, heavy with bone, but agile.

"*Olé,*" I find I have said.

I forget whether it is a *paso doble* or a *sardana* that is played while the heralds ride across the ring to salute the president and prepare for the Carmen bit, where the *cuadrillas* march in, but the music will go on to the track and that is not, for the moment, any business of mine. I wonder too if Sandy has got his video gimmicks hidden on this set so that we are all taped, but I don't quite know how.

Cappellino uncoils from the chair as if boneless, and the sun, coming through our lately beleaguered window, glints on the lacquered peroxide wizardry that holds his cap of golden hair so set in place and I hope against hope that the scene is now shot and we can break, but no. In the doorway behind Pancho is Moustique with her notebook, come all scholarly to analyse and record the Capo on the wall for posterity.

"Gee," she says, "I hope I'm not deetrop."

"We are just going to have coffee," says our hostess, with visible, but I think premature, relief.

"Why, that would be just wonderful."

"Introduce us, Jeannot," demands Cappellino, flashing his irresistible charm in the form of more teeth than there are in the human head.

"This is Miss Whitaker, Pier-Francesco Capisco." And dot, dot, dot on the transcript, because the snake and the mouse act is instantaneous. Cappellino eels across the room, hooded like a hamadryad to take the, what-they-call, nerveless hand of Capo's speechless celebrant and dedicated archivist, only to find that Petronella has eased in between them with an expression which is the first she has yet registered round here. "Oh, you are lovely," says Petronella.

"Why, thank you." Moustique is in some amazement.

"Coffee," says Kir, and makes for the kitchen.

"Pancho, my old," Cappellino switches over. "Is all well? Father is in good spirits? And the menagerie?" He hangs an arm round the hump of Pancho's shoulders which twitch noticeably in this embrace.

"He is well, Signore."

"And the animals?"

"Well."

"The evening is becoming quite beautiful." Cappellino looks lyrically out to sea. "Wild," says Niki abruptly. "Not quite yet," Cappellino purrs. Gordon chirrups and Aldo contorts the gutta-percha over his neanderthal brows. Social relations are becoming smooth. We are all friends here, except that Moustique seems to have gone into a trance. Those penetrating eyes, which can distinguish immediately between the states of an etching, are glazed in contemplation of the golden calf around whom, lacking a Moses, the children dance, careless of the law. If I only had the tablets I would brandish the commandments like Charlton Heston, and my cotton-wool beard would bristle and grow miraculously. But I don't have them and I see no way to prevent the coils of the serpent from winding round Eve and pressing an apple into her little, frozen hand. De Mille is not here to direct and my biblical metaphors are getting as convoluted as Cappellino's intentions.

It is a relief when Petronella begins to stroke Moustique, without regard to the proprieties, and what transpires is an odd, oriental sort of dance, comprised of Moustique's embarrassment, Cappellino weaving with irritation, Petronella's oblivious writhing, and a cast of what seems like thousands dressing the set. I have watched too many old movies. What is needed now is an iris out on the doves, as the moving finger writes *"Mene, Mene—Tekel Upharsin"* and Babylon comes to grief. What we need is Griffith and he is dead. What we get is coffee.

So we all sit stiffly down, except Pancho who stands rigid and Gordon who is trying to hold down the ram and is twitching about upstage, whispering to it. So Kir pours out and silence falls again.

Cappellino is fixed on Moustique and Moustique is staring at him like the victim of the basilisk and Petronella is slowly manipulating Moustique's breasts of which, seemingly, Moustique is quite unaware. What time the sun is striking through the window like sounding brass and tinkling cymbal and glinting on the goldwork which is all of Cappellino and the horns of the ram who is called Alexander and not Jason, but may yet stand in for the fleece hung on the protected tree beyond Colchis, up for grabs. And there is still distant thunder, as if the storm had paused, but had not passed.

On the wall is my portrait, in Capo's parody of Greek armour, arriving like a twit outside a tent which is cut away to show me in bed with Kir and at it, me bigger because it is Zeus disguised as me and tupping my faithful wife, with Pancho winging about in the sky on a small scale, doubling up for Sosias, they tell me, who is Mercury or Hermes. The sun on that shows just what Cappellino denies. It shows that bloody Cap can draw and draw and draw and there is no justice.

But the sun, which seems to have remained suspended, as legend would have it, for several days, over this fuck-up is now actually sinking in the West and the light is actually dying and the social event of Cappellino's visit to our humble home is as dead as a flounder on a slab. Everything feels like a still-life or *nature morte* and framed. Someone has to move and it is Pancho, who nods courteously to us all and exits, which rather inexplicably breaks up the gathering. They leave, all of them, seeming to process as before with the ram like a regimental mascot going ahead and then the rout following and then Cappellino moving like liquid and finally the maenads, high as kites for different reasons, Petronella and Moustique, dazed as heifers and lowing for the sacrifice. It would not surprise me to see Cappellino pause in our battered garden to gather vines, branches of pine trees and other appropriate vegetation, to drape and garland his company. Taking his time, he does just that.

So Kir and I are left, sitting there with the empty coffee-cups. And Kir doesn't cry, as I would have expected, but simply stares at me and I can see that she is very, very angry. I am very angry myself and revolted and undeniably defeated.

"I am not going to go on here," she says, flatly.

"I don't think I am either."

"You don't seem to understand."

"How do you mean?" I can't see why it should be me she is furious with.

"I mean I don't like you. I love you, I think, but I don't like you."

"For Christ's sake, why me? It's not my fault. It's Cap's."

"Do you think you can hold the old man responsible for everything? Can't you grow up?"

"Kir!"

"No, it's no use. You make me ashamed. You and your bloody vanity. I could have crawled into a hole, watching you drink in Cappellino's poison, not ten minutes ago. You know perfectly well he was buttering you up to get the knife into his father and yet you couldn't resist it, could you? Any flattery, any attention you can get yourself; even when it's got arsenic on it, you eat it. Cap humiliating you and feeling me up gives you a terrific kick, doesn't it? Just hanging about, waiting under the table for scraps is enough for you, if Cap will give you a pat on the head, once a month, and you can troop round carrying Estelle's knitting for her. I think you even married me to please them, down at the castello. I think your most developed organ is the tail you wag and I can't take any more." And still she doesn't cry and there's no cassis mixing with the sharp white wine.

I had expected this, just now, and I haven't got a reply. It doesn't seem much good to fight back. Put that way the answer to most of Kir's accusations could very well be yes, if I am honest. And I dislike being honest as much as everyone else. I don't speak, I get some pernod from the cupboard.

I sit down and begin to examine the case against me and I do not find the defence is holding up too well.

It's true I can't resist flattery any more than Cap ever has, or any more than any painter, or poet or any piano-player, or sodding actor or, in the event, any fucking woman can. We all live on it and gobble it down to assure ourselves we truly exist and aren't some sort of gloss on proper life as lived by people who think they're real people, in the down to earth, face up to it, what's art for anyway, labour versus management and vice versa, honourable establishment and/or panthers, party card-holders, dispossessed, stateless, my-little-girl-could-do-better-than-that, committed victims, enemies and heroes.

Why am I blustering away to myself like this? Because anyone who has that many home-truths thrown at him, and by a loved one, in one burst, is bound to bluster away to stop rocking about on his heels. On the other hand, of course, I can try to be honest and admit that living round Cap is as perpetual a feast as having a dirty mind. But I've already got a dirty mind. And I have talent and all I need is . . . and all that. I wonder about Nella, becoming calmly disloyal without any change of emphasis. Why not? I don't have to justify myself. I wander up and down the room, moving with feline grace, lord of the jungle. I shall have another drink. I may go to Milan.

Meanwhile from Kir, nothing except the close shot on the hands, where the knuckles show white through the skin. She is just sitting there, looking carefully composed and looking at bloody Cap's pic.

I didn't marry to please anyone but Kir, did I? She is overstating her case. And of course I would carry Estelle's knitting and so would she. Anyone would. But then it's true, I have got used to playing the courtier; initiate in the precinct, privileged fool to the monarch, I suppose. But that's how to learn one's trade. Kir knows that. Or does she think I've learned it? I wonder why I don't grow up. I know why I don't grow up. I am too young, and too able, and too handsome to have to grow up yet. No, I can't buy that. No one could buy that.

"Kir," I say. "Yes."

"Yes, what?"

"Yes, what you say is mostly true."

"Then let's get the hell out of here."

"You mean now?"

"More or less now. I can't sleep under that picture much longer. You might come to me all randy and looking like Cap in a tin hat."

"What'll we do about it?"

"Leave it. Do one yourself, somewhere else."

"Leave it for Poitevin? You're joking."

"Tell him to stuff it."

"Capo *farci*."

"Yes."

"Okay."

"So, okay. So let's tell Cap and let him work it out."

"He won't like it."

"Oh, I don't know. I daresay it's served its purpose for him."

"And Cappellino's?"

"Screw Cappellino."

"Your language is becoming very vigorous."

"I am quite a young and vigorous woman."

"How would you feel if I wagged my tail at you? It's the only organ you say I've got. Would it make you feel young and even more vigorous?"

"Well, it's a lovely handful."

"Certainly it is. It is the envy of thousands."

"Not Cap."

"Cap too, by now."

"Yes."

And so with the conscious, calculated cruelty of the young and vigorous I move, thinking of Cap with envy and laughter, and I wag my tail for Kir who may come to accept me and come, too, while she bites through my golden chains and cuts the Gordian knot and performs within the context of the myth.

Halfway down the path towards the castello, as we went forth to tell them how we were going out to seek our fortune in the wide world, we saw Pancho performing a stately dance. In a series of slow, not quite classical *enchaînements,* he was cavorting rhythmically to and fro, where the path is overhung with foliage.

"This is a very odd day," Kir said.

"Anything could happen."

But what Pancho is doing is gathering and rewinding Estelle's red wool from where Ariadne, in her flight from terrors on the terrace, had draped the trees and bushes with her prize. Capriciously looped and tangled along the way, the navel cord with which she linked the castello with our cottage is being rewound by patient Pancho, whose genuflections towards the scrub and leaps towards the lower branches of the trees are being conducted with an easy grace surprising in so compact and sturdy a figure as Pancho's. So we follow at a decent distance and in time we arrive among the good Duke's pantries and butteries and so through the winding passages of the castello, to the antechamber of the chamber of audience where everyone waits and where Pancho completes his red ball and passes Estelle's one remaining knitting-needle through it before laying it on the table next to Lens's whisky-soda. He then makes his usual silent and dignified exit.

By her whisky-soda and at ease sits Lens, looking her best and nodding affably towards us.

"How was it up there?"

"They pulled out."

"Poitevin's lot?"

"Them, first."

"We were pretty good in there today," says Kir, entering into the spirit of Hemingway, who often has Lens's dialogue in his grip, albeit in French, his work losing so much in the original.

"I went up," she says, "but I couldn't get in there. What the hell, I thought, just a crowd scene, so I came back down."

"We were pretty good in there," I echo Kir.

"No pasaran?"

"Sure, go on and kid us. But listen while I tell you something. We were pretty good in there, today."

"Good at what?"

"We held the pillbox."

"Against the Poitevin?"

"Sure."

"And Cappellino?" Lens reaches for her glass.

"Guns jammed, outnumbered, what could we do?"

"Chicken."

"You could say that."

"You been out here too long."

"No, it ain't just that. We feel like hell."

"You been out here too long. That's all."

"Oh, Poppa," says Kir.

One of the things about Lens is that she can pick up the thread and run on with it in any vernacular.

"You tried the red?"

"No, I ain't tried it."

"You better try it."

She picks up Estelle's ball of red wool and tosses it to Kir. It's strange what a gift Lens has for reducing tension. It must be part of her tense profession. Kir is smiling and I am smiling. Lens pours large whiskies from the handy bottle and gives us each one.

"You see his girl?" she says. She must have "Today is Friday" by heart as, oddly enough, Kir and I have.

"Wasn't I standing right by her?"

"She used to have a lot of stuff. He never brought her no luck."

"Petronella," Kir muses, "Petronella, superstar."

"That's not Hemingway country," says Lens.

"Cappellino never brought no one no luck."

"True."

"What's the score then?"

"Cappellino and, I suppose, Madeleine and God knows who else will be at Poitevin's for dinner."

"Jesus Christ."

"You're a regular Christer, big boy."

"Oh, enough, enough of Poppa," says Kir giggling, but we are somehow back to normal, at least for a moment.

Estelle sails in with the Schlegels in tow and Hansi looks fat with joy. I suppose Capo has relaxed and let him see some new things after all and Hansi is already starry-eyed with book plans.

"Madeleine has been." I could have told that from Estelle's rigid pose.

"That's bad," Lens says.

"She does upset Cap, but perhaps she is well-intentioned."

"Estelle, she is Pier-Francesco's mother and a barracuda."

"It cannot have been easy for her."

"Everything is easy for barracudas. They live by biting pieces out of the living flesh. That is not difficult if you are built to bite."

Kir is a little high. "And women like that part which, like the lamprey, hath never a bone in it."

Estelle looks quite blank, because Kir has suddenly spoken in English, but Lens is on to it as fast as usual.

"Ain't we the culture kids," she says, "Duchess of Malfi still."

"I do not understand English," Estelle remarks, "but I try to think there is good in Madeleine."

"And Pier-Francesco?"

"I shall go and try to get Capo to put some clothes on and see that he takes his pills."

But here is Sandy, the director, nose a bit swollen, but bright as a button and agog for gifts from the gods. He has had a rich afternoon filled with improbable experiences, useful cutaways and the sense of unexpected developments continually coming to his voracious little 8mm camera, which he waves about as if censing the flock. What he wants to know now, of course, is how to get Cappellino and his glamorous mates in the can and when will the first Madame Capisco be available. He is your true documentary man, ready for any improvisation.

"*Les sanglots longs des violons de l'automne blessent mon coeur d'une langueur monotone,*" Lens puts in with melancholy relish, being now overflowing with literary offerings.

"Huh?" Sandy is a documentary and not a literary man.

"Madame Capisco is a pain in the ass, a drag."

"Really, Lens darling, you should not speak like that."

"But, Estelle sweetie, it's true. Madeleine has three rows of teeth, all set backwards. She will end up gaffed."

"Huh?" says Sandy again, looking keenly at Lens who is by now thinking about the old days and Poppa if not Verlaine for whom, by more than half a century, she is too young. But Verlaine comes up again: *"Tout suffocant et blême, quand sonne l'heure, je me souviens des jours anciens et je pleure,"* Kir murmurs and Lens begins to weep benignly as Estelle moves towards giving Capo his pills and getting at least some trousers on him.

Kir and I, looking at one another, mutely agree that this is not the time to tell anyone that we plan to cut the navel cord and depart from the omphalos and get the hell out.

"Ah, kids," says Lens, "it is all so sad. Life is so sad."

"I think it is rather comic," says Kir. And I think so too and Sandy has no clue as to why, with Lens weeping for the snows of yesteryear or Kilimanjaro, we are laughing like crazy and Estelle is very stiff and proud.

"Kooks," says Sandy, unguardedly and we are convulsed by the accuracy of this designation. Even Lens cannot cry for laughing. Only the Schlegels, who have contributed nothing to this educated dialogue, look bemused and really only Nella, because Hansi is caught up in his dreams of *éditions de tête* on *papier d'Arches*, signed and numbered.

"Tutti pazzi," says Nella astringently to herself.

"Pazzi cake, pazzi cake, baker's man," mutters Lens, dreamily adrift in her childhood and happy.

But suddenly I realise that we are all invited to dinner at Poitevin's for retakes and unavoidably, I am pretty sure, for additional dialogue from Cappellino and the chill of the storm has not exactly lifted despite the pernod and now the scotch that I have put away. *"Et je m'en vais au vent mauvais,"* you might say. And it is getting dark and Theseus does not bark.

How the next sequence got put together I am not sure. Either it was still rolling on the hidden videotapes in Cap's workshop or Sandy crept like a shadow in Estelle's wake through the doors which, earlier in the day, had laid waste his long, inquisitive nose. Once in, he could have taken cover readily enough by crawling into a plaster bin or something. Anyway, he doesn't seem to have been noticed and the rest of the reel in his hand-held may have been developed and cut in, but Kir and I were not present, being jovially engaged with Lens and her memories while bringing Hansi gently out of his trance. The long, wobbly track-in which bridges the gap between our cultural chat-show and Capo's shop now brings the action back to Capo. This must be Sandy moving close on Estelle's track and into the master's vast den. Because there is Cap, in the dying light of late afternoon, hunched on his truckle bed and as white with plaster as a half-finished wedding cake. In front of him, in the rough, is the plaster spectre of Theseus to come. It is some six foot high even in the crouch and combines iron, wood, chicken wire and scrim with a large wicker basket playing thorax. Inside this unsteady structure, propped as it is on bricks and partly suspended from Cap's yellow crane, which he calls *caro* by way of endearment, breathes the malevolent, bony spirit of a twice-life-sized baboon, twisting at the chicken wire and silently screaming to be fleshed. Cap holds the hatchet which he customarily uses to subdue recalcitrant sculpture in the early stages.

"I doubt if you can see any more, Capo darling. Why don't you put on some lights?"

"Because I don't want Theseus to see me just now. I don't trust him."

"He looks quite calm, with no arms."

"Little do you know."

"Well, it is time for your pills and to dress."

"Why?"

"Because you must take a bath and then we shall have drinks and then go down to Poitevin's."

"Let us do that another day. Better still let us not do it ever."

"The film people say they must do retakes and besides Pier-Francesco will be there."

"Why can't he come up here?"

"He has been, darling, you remember."

"Yes," says Cap. "Yes, I do remember. I needed those maquettes today, too."

"I shall get them back for you this evening. I think Ambrose must have them."

"Who, in the name of *art-nouveau,* is Ambrose? Ambrose. What sort of a camp item is Ambrose?"

"He is Piero's dealer friend."

"That abortion, that homunculus of Addle's?"

"Addle will have nothing to do with Ambrose. He says he is a thief."

"Poncing for Cappellino and fencing my work."

"I thought you did not like anyone to call Piero Cappellino."

"I can call him anything I like. He is my son."

"Yes, Capo darling."

"Anyway, I'm past needing the maquettes now. I now know perfectly what Theseus looks like."

"Yes, Cap."

"So go away and let us stare at one another in the dark. We are measuring each other. We are both nocturnal, at least at night."

But Estelle switches on the big floods and the strips and there in the mess of plaster fragments and dust, the bits of wood and thrown-down tools, crouches the partial ghost of Theseus, blank white and staring, as only plaster stares. And there is Capo mostly white and staring at Theseus, half-made in plaster, as only Capo stares. After a passage of time long enough to establish the grievousness of the interruption, Capo resigns, rolls on his back and closes his eyes—a sure sign that Estelle has won. He opens his mouth wide and Estelle drops pills into it, as if making a wish with each. She hands him water in a cup, forcing him by this shift to surface. "Come along, darling," she says.

"This," says Cap, "is what Pygmalion must have endured, once he had got himself stuck with Galatea." But he allows himself to be dragged protesting out of shot. Estelle kills the lights, but there are the lumps of half-made Theseus, rising in the rough and baleful with the irons of his armature showing black where his arms will come to be when Capo gets back to fight with him.

Some of us walk and some are driven down to Poitevin's. The crew take their van and Sandy takes Kir with Lens in the jeep and the Schlegels are in their car with Addle and presently we are all back on the jetty of the Universe and the boys are setting up. Poitevin and his jackals are circling and slavering in the restaurant, the lights are on and the staff is scurrying.

Word having got around, quite a crowd of people have booked tables, so that Capo's usual one is almost the only one empty and all is potentially festive. And everyone waits, as everyone waits and waits during any filming, while the assistant director tries to set the scene for retakes, although it is not clear to me, not having seen the rushes, why these should be necessary.

We are nearly all met, except Capo and Estelle who now arrive, driven by straight-backed Pancho, and seeing the general turmoil they stay in their car. Only Moustique is absent and she, now I come to think of it, has not been seen since she left our place with the Rite of Spring and his kinky lot. I suddenly don't like that and I can see that Kir doesn't either.

Nella comes over to us dressed as on the previous evening which we all are, by request, so as to make both evenings into one dinner party, on film. "Jeannot, *caro,*" she whispers. "I do not like it."

"What don't you like?"

"I do not like the feel."

"What feel?" But I know what she means. It is darker than it was last night, because the storm clouds although broken now are still heavy and how they will match up to put the clock back to last night, I cannot imagine. It is different in other ways.

"Kir," asks Nella, "doesn't he sense anything?"

"Yes, he does," says Kir.

"It has changed."

"Yes. And we are leaving."

"Leaving?"

"Leaving here."

"That is wise," says Nella gnomically.

"The gipsy's warning," I put in, frivolous to the last.

They ignore me and Nella removes her elegant little paw from my arm and gravitates to Kir whom she very understandably finds more comprehending than I am trying not to be. It is curiously cold.

Sandy goes over to Cap's car and taps on the window which Estelle winds down. From what I can hear, he wants Cap to go back among the junk in the vacant lot by the hotel, and look searching. Out of the van, someone takes the perambulator with all that Cap collected in it last night carefully reassembled—the brass bugle-thing on top. Cap doesn't look too pleased with this trespass, but equably seems prepared to go through the motions again.

"He will get his feet wet," I can hear Estelle object.

No one can find Cap's straw topee: a lapse in continuity. They send for it and the assistant director drives wildly off in the jeep to find it, up at the castello. And so we wait some more.

"Where is What's-her-name?" asks Lens.

"Miss Whitaker?" Addle too is puzzled.

"Mouche, or whatever," says Lens.

"Moustique."

"Yes."

"Well, where is she?"

No one has an answer.

"Where do they go in the winter-time?" Lens is chilled.

"Into the print room." This is not well received from me.

"Shut up, Jeannot," Kir says.

Cap and Estelle haven't left their car. They are waiting for Capo's hat. Pancho hasn't moved either. There is an impatient rustle from the nobility and gentry who in this production are the extras out on the jetty. The fairy lights go on. "Kill those," shouts Sandy, and they go off again. A sort of generalised movement now takes place as people shift their weight from one leg to another, or one buttock to another and cigarettes get lit.

It is getting very dark for retakes. They will never match. Sandy looks worried. The sea is not the placid silver shield of last evening, but moves like ruffled lead. Nella looks pinched and Kir has her white-wine look. Addle and Hansi have drawn together in what is perhaps some business discussion, seeing that Hansi is voluble, with tight little movements and Addle is hunched, peering warily out of his shell. Lens has sat down and is calling for a little restorative, which she gets and I could use.

Then the jeep with the hat comes tearing back and action stations are called and Cap is helped out of the car by Pancho to go and get his feet wet and he is given his pram and wanders off. Sandy gets set to shoot and Sparks tries to get some light on the *Maestro* who is not looking very hard for *objets trouvés* and is not enjoying himself because the paths are waterlogged and the bram-

141

bles are dripping on his knees. He is not looking searching. He is grumbling.

"Okay," says Sandy, "cut. We'll have to leave it."

And he goes off, getting his feet wet, to bring Cap back and I can see that no warm friendship is developing between them out there, while Sandy carries the pram and Capo tells him of the shortcomings of the film industry. Both of them go into the Universe and Liberia to dry off. And we all wait some more. The wind is now coming, biting, off the sea.

Hansi and Addle join us and a desultory conversation proceeds about how remarkable Capo's recent drawings are. Hansi is the only one present who wants to talk about how remarkable Cap is and he is also the only one who is blandly unaware that Nella and Lens and Kir and even Addle and I do not want to discuss how remarkable Cap is just now, because if he were not, we could all be elsewhere.

"It is important, Herr Schlegel," says Addle, "to realise that Capisco does not consider himself unique. His strength lies in his sense of being a part of a larger whole, an ancient and continuing tradition to which he is an heir. He is really a modest man."

"Bushwah," says Lens, crisply.

"What is bushwah?"

Lens tells him and I must say that of all today's contributions to Cap's laurel wreath, this bay of Addle's seems the one most likely to be used for soup. Kir, Lens and even Hansi do not look persuaded of Addle's hypothesis and Nella is openly amazed.

"*Ma . . . !*" she says.

"What Capo has," says Addle, not to be put down, "is a profound sense of reverence for his forerunners in an age when such a sense of the past is fostered by many people, but not by the *avant-garde*. The sense of history in their view is restricted to those who relish it nostalgically and discuss it academically but can find nothing else to do with it. 'Garbage' is the *avant-garde*'s name for it.

"Those who wish to be up to date in the visual arts still find the past embarrassing. It interferes with modernity and our young contemporaries are vain as to their own iconoclasm. Their sense of their own importance is greater to them than any sense of the importance of the arts they serve. They are like prospectors participating in a

142

gold rush who know no more about mining than to seek for nuggets, broken away from the lode, which they hope to beat into simple shapes which will prove to be new inventions. They cannot smelt the ore; they can only make beads of what they find lying on the mainstream bed. By what digging they do, they merely break up the matrix and the stones they excavate they burn for lime, which in turn they use to whitewash their inadequacy. I am mixing my metaphors, I fear."

"I don't follow," Nella admits, plaintively.

"Forgive me that I express myself with so much heat, but I tell you that Capo is one of very few who understands his matrix. The work is not capricious, only Capo's behaviour may sometimes seem to be and it is not new that an artist should protect his work by interposing his life-style as a mask. Capo seems capricious . . ."

"You can say that again." Lens can only take so much exegesis.

"I had not intended to say it again."

"But surely Capisco is extraordinary. He is an original. He is a true inventor," breathes the reverent Hansi.

"Herr Schlegel," says Addle, sternly, "there are very few inventions to be made in any age, in any art . . . not so?"

"But . . ."

"There are discoveries, but they reveal what was always there. Inventions are another thing. The ballpoint pen is an invention. It makes the performance of note-taking more rapid, but does it improve the handwriting, or the style, or add to the significant content of what is written? The computer is an invention, the internal combustion engine is an invention, the steam engine was the invention of Hero of Alexandria, but this utility was of no value at the time. Inventions are facilities appropriate to their time, just as originality is the means to draw sudden attention to appropriate discovery and is not discovery itself."

"But, Herr Ritterbaum, it is Capisco's originality which makes his greatness. This is his gift above all."

"He would deny it. He maintains not entirely ironically that he copies."

"Copies! It is not possible. It is unthinkable!"

"On the contrary. He copies any work of art, of any period, which is useful to him. Naturally the process produces something other than a copy but that is true of all good art. The history of art is a history of imitation. You may follow the image of Giorgione's *Dresden Venus* through Titian and Rubens and down history to Manet's *Olympia* and beyond. It is the additive which determines distinctions between these separate acts of homage, each in its own time. Each draws attention in turn to Giorgione's rediscovery of a Greek original and each exists in its own right."

"An original artist," I put in, dutifully quoting Cocteau, *"cannot copy. So he has only to copy to be original."*

Addle nods approvingly.

"Perhaps," says Nella, with sophistical innocence, "art is generally becoming a little overdone, nowadays. I mean Hansi is so bound up with it, that I sometimes wonder if he should not take more time off to enjoy himself."

This rather floors Addle, who has never failed to enjoy himself in being bound up. Hansi is silent. He has never thought of enjoying himself, except in the line of duty. Nella, protectively and because she is surprised at herself for wandering on to Tom Tiddler's ground, links arms with her husband, to show solidarity. And Kir links arms with Addle to make him feel comfortable, after so determined a lecture. As for Addle, he draws his neck into his collar and, as for me, I review my own work in the light of Addle's analysis of the contemporary scene and slightly restructure my opinions to accommodate what I do in the way of painting. Does it pass, or am I at work with my little pick and shovel on the incomprehensibly great ruins of the past as reproduced in the glossy art journals; not building but placer mining, like the rest of us young people? Not waving, drowning?

"There is a guy in the office," Lens puts in ruminatively, "called Leverkühn. We call him 'Breakthrough,' because everything cute that comes up on the art scene he calls a breakthrough. He has this Armenian kid he's mad for who puts out these blank canvases with tape recorders at the back and the tape recorders say what could be on the front of the canvas, including the working time and the costing and next to each canvas on exhibit is a printed sheet which says that if you pick up the telephone below the canvas the artist will be heard telling you what is new. And he tells you to ignore the tape recorder on account of the information it gives is no longer accurate, time having passed, because of price rises and new inspirational concepts and that you should go out to Utah and look, from the air, at the work he is now doing with a bulldozer. He also tells you where to book the plane."

Addle looks contained, if a little blank. "What is this called?" he asks.

"A breakthrough," says Lens.

"Ach."

"Magari . . ." says Nella, and suddenly all the little bulbs come alight on the jetty and Cap and Sandy come steaming out of the restaurant, arguing.

"Places, please," shouts the assistant director and we all go and sit at the table and are back as we were for the opening sequence of this production, except that Moustique has not turned up. "Lights" comes the cry and up they go.

The assistant director, who now has an electric megaphone which should have been denied to him, is bawling anxiously, but with a vicarious authority, for Miss Whitaker. Otherwise we are all set for dinner and Cap has put on his hat again to preside at the top end of the table and is having another go at sounding his horn. He seems quite cheerful. Estelle has lost her bag as usual and everyone gropes for it, except Cap.

We eat and it tastes like sawdust. We drink and it could be damson juice. Cap, I suppose, puts his hand back on Kir's thigh, but she is thinking about something else. Lens has a whisky-soda to dress the scene and the continuity girl is bustling, with her nice little hips rotating, to get all set up to comply with what it looked like last night and doesn't feel like any more. She finds Estelle's bag and returns it. Even the little slips of paper and the pencils have been supplied, by thoughtful Poitevin, still in hope of souvenirs, for the consequences which have already taken place. And the consequence is . . . what else could it be? Cappellino with Capo's ram, Alexander; his horns gilded and trailing vine leaves, arrives, as before linked to Cappellino, who has put on a gold lamé jacket.

"Cut," shouts Sandy. "Who, for fuck's sake, are you?"

"I am Pier-Francesco Capisco," says Cappellino, "and this is my uncle Alexander."

"Who is?"

"The ram. He is sacred."

"Well, get him the hell out of shot."

"Oh, you don't understand," says Cappellino. "I am the star of this sequence. After the commercial break, you know."

"Piero," says Cap, putting Kir down and standing to embrace his son. "Look at this trumpet."

"The man with the golden horn," says Cappellino, and bends to accommodate his father who comes up to his shoulder and could not otherwise reach to kiss him.

It makes a remarkable shot which Sandy doesn't miss. There is the greatest sculptor of the Western world, locked in an Italianate embrace with his very own, great big boy and with a large moufflon ram locked uncomfortably between them. It is the ram who determines the length of the take.

"Figlio mio," says Cap.

"E poi?" says Nella to me *sotto voce.*

"Ma . . ." is all I can think of to reply.

"Where is Madeleine?" asks Estelle.

"She is not well," Cappellino replies.

"Good," says Capo.

"Capo!" Estelle looks severe.

"Well?"

"You should not speak so about Piero's mother."

"Pfui."

This makes Cappellino laugh and Alexander moves impatiently.

"What are you doing with Alexander?" Cap looks unsure of this theatrical element.

"He asked to come."

"Ah."

And Alexander muzzles Cap's crotch, which reseats the master a little abruptly.

"Where is Moustique?" I ask in the momentary quiet that ensues.

"Oh, the little historian," says Cappellino vaguely, "a charming person and very knowledgeable."

"Yes."

"She is somewhere about. She took a shine to Niki. Indeed I think she is interested in all of us."

Kir is looking hard at me.

"We need Miss Whitaker for the next sequence," Sandy says.

"Then let me try to light her for you," Cappellino replies courteously and he gracefully turns to swing a flood, which catches and blinds the extras on the jetty and darts its beam out on to the shore behind them. Slowly Cappellino pans the lamp, scanning across the beach. What it picks up is Moustique and the familiar group of Cappellino's playfellows. What it brings is a sharp intake of breath and the absolute momentary rigidity of everyone who has followed the light.

Down on the beach is Moustique, kneeling, as if devoutly towards Mecca, her forehead in the sand. On her is Gordon Bleu, riding her arse like a dirt-track motor-cyclist, pushing for the finish. Without pausing in his urgent motion, he gives us all a jaunty wave. Petronella is there, smiling. Aldo is there sweating and hauling up his jeans. Niki is buckled up in his leather, except where his improbably modest prick rears out of it as he prepares for the next entry.

"They must be taking turns," Cappellino remarks gently and swings the flood off them and blindingly back on to us.

VI
Cutting Copy

It is Pancho who moves first and fast from behind Capo's chair, and it is then me. The going across the soft sand is nightmarish, because it sucks at the feet and with the blinding light gone we are blind. Pancho reaches the group and although I can't see what is happening I can hear it. When I get there, Gordon is yards away, on his back, and Pancho has caught Aldo with his pants down. I hear the blow, which must have caught Aldo in the gut, because he is wheezing painfully. Niki I can't see but he connects with the side of my head and he puts the boot in when I go down. My mouth is full of sand and the pain in my belly is terrible. Pancho must have got to Niki by the sound of it and then the flood swings on to us again because I can see, when I get to my knees, that the men have all gone, running silently, footsteps muffled by the sand, but audibly grunting and panting in the dark middle distance. Moustique is still there and hasn't budged. Nor has Petronella, until she leans over and takes Moustique's skirt between a thumb and fingertip, moving like a sleepwalker and smiling vacantly. She tweaks the skirt back into place and pats Moustique's upraised bottom as if it were a well-laid table. After that she just stands there. As for me, I vomit. Someone on the jetty laughs.

People are now milling about, picking Moustique up, while ignoring Petronella. Someone gives me a hand and, by God, it is Poitevin. I am dazed, as if I had been thrown by a horse as, in a sense, I have. Poitevin is brushing me down with a table napkin and giving me more help than I can take. When I get back to the jetty most of the crowd on set is still sitting where it sat, but now whispering busily. A couple of journalists are making for the phone and various flashes indicate the presence of photographers at their trade. Not Lens, however, whose camera, for once, lies on the table.

Estelle hasn't moved, nor has Capo. Nor have the lesser stars, not even Kir, although now she makes for me and I tell her no bones broken, hoping there aren't. She moves on towards the crowd around Moustique and then Estelle follows and together they support Moustique into the hotel.

Back at the table, a waiter gives me brandy while I try to get the sand out of my eyes and stop retching.

"This is monstrous." Hansi's reflexes are slow. His sense of outrage is just surfacing. *"Ja,"* says Addle, grimly.

"Rather an elegant little experiment," says Cappellino, "didn't you think?"

"To what end?" Addle's head snakes forward as he asks the question.

"To point up the comedy." Cappellino is languid. "And to bring a little irony to the artist's quarter."

"Irony? Is this violence to you irony? This brutish thing?" Hansi is caught on the horns of expressing his disgust while equating the event with its administrator, Capisco's own son. He looks round piteously for support, for shared revulsion, for protest. He is swelling with indignation, but he is waiting for Capo's reaction, to know exactly what is expected. There is no obvious reaction from Capo. He doesn't move. He doesn't look at Cappellino.

Nella has no such hesitation. "You are filth," she says.

"Golden filth, Madame," is Cappellino's equable reply. "I feel I owe it to my father. Something acrid to perfume this homogenised milk and all the little slices of bread which float in it."

A long, well-modulated, varied and imaginative stream of Italian abuse comes from Nella and it is clear that Hansi has never realised she even knew all those words. He is now outraged on this count, too. It is all very confusing for him.

"Clearly, Madame, you live in a less rarefied atmosphere than our other friends here," says Cappellino. "For the rest of them, there is nothing much to be said. And really nothing to be said to them either. I therefore address myself to you and, of course, to my father for whose personal benefit this charade is being staged, on this my birthday. I assume that it is being recorded. Such a waste if not."

It is being recorded all right and two cameras are churning and Sandy is not going to stop them before they run out of film. I can see him dimly, over towards the railing, wearing the expression of one who has found the end of the rainbow and the payola that goes with it. It's nice that someone is happy. He will be zooming in and out and cannot be blamed for once. This is no moment to change the set-up if a documentary is to document. Doing my own personal zoom-in on Cap, I try to read his expression and I can tell nothing from his bronze-hard mask.

"Let me explain a further dimension of this happening." Cappellino now slides carefully into a vacant chair while stroking Alexander's fleece to calm him. "Apart from enlivening the evening a little, I have paid a metaphorical tribute to Marcel Duchamp."

"Who is he?" asks Nella.

"The only artist of my father's generation who can now be taken seriously, since he was never serious."

"Duchamp? I do not understand," says Hansi, who thinks he knows all about Duchamp.

"What you have been privileged to watch, friend, was a demonstration, a retransposition from glass into flesh of Duchamp's masterpiece. You have seen his *Great Glass* melt back into sand which after all is the matrix of glass itself. You have witnessed what he called 'a glass delay.'" The group round the table, including me, is seemingly hypnotised by this hermetic little discourse. "For Jeezus' sake . . ." Lens breaks across it. "Is this a put-on?"

"Perhaps a toss-off rather . . . an alchemic orgasm, a gas. You see, where Duchamp insisted that it is better to project into machines than to take it out on people, I incline towards the opposite approach. One must not plagiarise."

Nella and Hansi are looking baffled, as well they might. Capo's eyes are fixed on his son not as if seeing him for the first time but not giving anything to the glance either. As for me, educated fellow that I am, I get the drift. Cappellino is brazenly paraphrasing with a squalid gang-bang a famous art object and such is the conditioning of all those present except Lens, and perhaps even Lens, that we are being somehow conned into a calm response to an outrage by this transposition. It is weird. Even Capo is listening, at least I think he is.

"I have shown you a metaphorical steam-engine if not in this instance on a masonry pediment; the bachelor machine all grease and lubricity. My friends, the tormented cogs, give birth to the part of the machine which manifests desire. You recognise the quotation of course, Addle, or rather the paraphrase."

Addle, looking sick and avoiding looking astonished, but perhaps unavoidably impressed by Cappellino in this oddly ceremonial role, nods.

"In general this bride motor," Cappellino continues, "must, as Duchamp says, appear as an apotheosis of virginity. And of course, as you know, she was, and she did, didn't she? 'Ignorant desire, white desire with a point of malice' is the phrase. Rather a triumph, as an event, wouldn't you say?"

"*Lieber Gott,*" Addle whispers, "*La Mariée mise à nu par ses Celibataires, même.*"

"Or, *M'aime,*" Cappellino is benignly explicatory, "to give the pun its flavour. I thought you might find this excursion into art history, by way of a virginal art historian, instructive and perhaps stimulating." And he gives us all that feline smile of his.

"Trash." Lens is spitting with rage.

"Such a fabulous movie, so casual." This last, drawled out with extreme urbanity by Pier-Francesco Capisco, breaks the spell.

"Take me home, Hansi," Nella appeals to her husband who now appears to be semi-cataleptic. "I feel sick." But Hansi makes no move. At this point Camera 1 and then Camera 2 run out of film, one after the other, and Cappellino orders a glass of Vichy water. No one on set seems capable of restoring the disorder that all feel to be the natural outcome of the situation.

For the life of me I cannot see what Sandy is going to do with this material. Naturally he couldn't resist shooting it. Naturally if he could use it, this modest documentary, intended for late showing when children and all but the intelligentsia are presumed to be in bed, would gross a million on circuit and cause every counter-permissive element in Western society to file injunctions, including all those present at Capo's table who are in a less permissive mood than at any other time in their lives. Sandy's dilemma is pitiably in evidence from his expression.

Here is a situation where a prodigal son has smeared the gravy of a fatted calf all over his dad and damaged to hold the company at table in thrall with a bizarre and obscure metaphor so timed as to short-circuit their revulsion and yet underline it. I feel reluctantly that he is entitled to his smirk. And so presumably does Sandy, because with cameras reloaded and clapper-board clapped, he is shooting again, while, from the separate tables much confused muttering goes forward as to who or what is this Duchamp, and are the police coming, and, equally, where are the drinks. Only Poitevin's waiters are in movement and Alexander, who is thrusting hard to get from the indolent Cappellino to the comfort of Capo where perhaps a ram may find solace.

This urgency of Alexander incommodes Cappellino who is certainly not used to having any of the strings he holds in his hand pulled by anyone else. It prevents him from sipping his Vichy water with the studied ease he had intended to show and indeed he spills it. The pull on the thread jerks him away from a wider audience to face his real target. Unwilling to release his grip on Alexander, or on the limelight, it looks as if he may direct his immediate firepower on his still mute father, which perhaps his sense of timing tells him would be premature. He will wait for that until the Master's female allies return from ministering to Moustique, in the hotel. I also suspect that he is waiting for his own accessories to steal in from the shadows. Hauled off balance by Alexander's sharp struggle, Cappellino is briefly at a disadvantage.

It is a miscalculation, even if it does not seem much to disturb him. I sense, however, that Capo, whose expression does not change, is aware that the match will not be quite so unequal as it may now look. His stillness and his untypical silence could be a makeshift shield behind which he is hiding anguish, humiliation, perhaps guilt and maybe clay feet. It could be a slow power build-up to a battle station and I passionately hope so. Capo, if I can judge by the bleak gaze he has now fastened on Cappellino, is not showing any weakness, whereas Cappellino, if not disconcerted, has lost a little of his cool from the inadvertent movement that Alexander forced on him. I do not think that Cappellino expected this absolute stillness from Capo. I think he expected to be the one whose stillness would contrast with some blatant reflex from his father and, if so, he is not getting the response he was hoping for. He is getting no response at all.

This spectacle of Capo motionless, whether or not at bay, is some distance from the amiable exchange of bland reminiscences between Capo and Addle for which Sandy had been angling. It is raw and it is going to get more so. The climax is still some time off and I think

Capo is aware of it. I cease to wonder why Capo hasn't just broken up the party. All he had to do was get up and leave for this elaborate audience-participation show to fall apart, but he's not going to do that. It is not in Cap to get knocked off at a crossroads on the road to Thebes by a son who knows perfectly well who he is. And as for young Oedipus, he seems to me to be already married to his mother, or what would be the point of this elaborate performance which now has to move forward if Pier-Francesco is to meet his private production schedule?

I look round at the others and there is Lens very white, and Hansi very pink and Nella not looking, after her outburst, and there is Addle who is sizing Cappellino up and who, I have the uneasy feeling, is going to ride out on to this improbable tilt-yard and break a lance to keep Capo intact, as if that were needed by jousting at a windmill which is pretty well bound to unseat him, despite the fact that it is no Rosinante that Addle rides, but as sleek a sumpter mule as ever bore up a Medici.

Cappellino is all composure again and is lighting a cigarette with his right hand. He sees Addle in the lists and turns to meet him by reeling in Alexander which brings the ram's gilded horns up and stops him dead. Cappellino's left arm must have a lot of iron in it.

"Metaphor," Cappellino remarks, "is the very stuff of art and in particular of allegory and whist allegory may have become rather cumbersome after the Renaissance, you would surely admit that it is now in short supply. My revered father is almost alone in making blatant allegorical metaphors into what you all consider to be sculpture, but in my view the means he employs are threadbare."

The smile is there and the manner composed and it seems to me something of a feat to produce a lecture of the kind that Cappellino is in the process of delivering to an aghast audience whose attention has just been drawn to a rape. And it must be particularly taxing to maintain an aura of ineffable calm while holding an anxious adult ram on a string.

"Now where my father and I differ," Cappellino muses, "is in the means by which we each express ourselves. He, poor old man, has spent a lifetime in making objects which depend upon the Addles of this world to peddle them. I make events upon which no price can quite be calculated. Both of us, you could say, perform rituals but mine exist only at the climax while his, once performed, lie about like so many merchandisable fossils, as inert as the battered stones which his beloved Greeks left around when they were finished. His rituals crumble into museums as soon as they are made and the reverent assembly seated at this table is a party to the profitable dodge."

Addle, who feels that it is now up to him to ride out, blinks. He had not expected such a calculated discourse to fall from the lips of the boy whom he had once dandled on his knee and if he is enraged, he is also nonplussed. "You should speak so as if you had your father's talent! You speak so about the Greeks? You speak so in front of your father, who has given you everything and who is a great artist?" Addle, I fear, is unhorsed at the first exchange.

Cappellino's smile is unwavering. It could have been carved by one of those old Greeks he so despises. "What do you think my father has given me, reflected glory? Of course he has and I am here to repay what my father has given me. That is why I came on my birthday, to make my particular homage and surely I have begun well. I have given him a metaphor, derived from Duchamp admittedly, but that was to acknowledge with delicacy the essential absurdity of art history. However, like all good metaphors it is open to several interpretations. It was a new version of a ritual which once gratified old father Zeus. Smoke from the burning thighs of cattle rising from the altar, you know. Surely apropos. But, to continue before I am further interrupted, and because there will be no time, I'm afraid, for questions afterwards: what is interesting to you all about my father is not what he does or has done, but the fact that you know he has done it. What he has, and I share it with him, is star quality. But, unlike my father, I do not need to leave a lot of clutter about the place. I mean the second-hand artifacts that he could get done for him if he were not so obsessed with his own fingerprints. It is out of courtesy, dear friends and Father dear, that I am staging this little pageant for you. It is quite real. Reality is whether you can get it up and how far up it gets. Who needs a metaphor for what is already metaphorical, or a paraphrase for an empty phrase come pat, when we have pataphysics? Take our little art historian, the bride who so graciously participated in the scene. She had room for Aldo and Gordon and Niki too, if that ape hadn't sapped him, in her card index—if I may put it so. At the other end what has she got? Catalogue entries? Who needs them? My father's work bores him as it does everyone who is not too square to admit it. His 'art' is a desperate confession of inadequate means to avoid boredom. Even his impulses are reduced to boredom in becoming 'art.' He is a toymaker. Surely my toys have better works and better-greased machinery?"

"What in hell is Cappellino on about?" Lens asks of the company in general.

"You must not call me that. My father does not like it, but I will tell you, dear Lens. I am giving you and all these highly trained and talented film-technicians an event which should reach more people than ever strained their dutiful necks to glimpse the Sistine Chapel ceiling. I am also giving you a picture-story for the arts funny-papers. I am giving life to art for a change and this is my narration to go with it."

"I don't get it," says Lens, but she does and her hands are near her Leica.

"My father is a monument, wouldn't you say? He is a household word, an international celebrity. I am celebrating him and so is Uncle Alexander here. We plan to make the evening memorable, Alexander and I, by mixing a draught of life and death together in honour of the great Capisco."

"It is some horrible joke." Hansi is trying to come to terms with the celebration and it is moving rather fast for him.

"Oh no, sir, it is not a joke, it is a solemn ceremony."

"What is meant by this?"

"Take me home, Hansi," says Nella, who is as properly alarmed as I am and perhaps less morbid or less hypnotised. She clearly wants out.

"No. I wish to know what is meant."

"Consider then the nature of tragedy," Cappellino turns to Hansi. "It is the song of the goat, is it not? And, lacking a goat to sing, Alexander has bravely volunteered to stand in. Then again tragedy is born of the implacability and capriciousness of gods and the destruction of great men and, in another sense, it arises from heroic flaws. I have, I confess, several heroic flaws, a certain capriciousness and perhaps implacability, while my father, wouldn't you say, is a great man?

"But tragedy is also a mere dramatic form, in which those cunning Greeks had all the action take place off stage with those ridiculous messengers popping in to describe what had happened somewhere else. Very economical but that won't wash any more. The Greeks, in my view, had less appetite for tragedy than the Romans, who at least required a little real blood to convince them that life and death is a game that all the family can play; a laugh in every line. But all of them are dead as antique doorknobs now, aren't they? All that stuff is down the drain. Only educators and museum men and suchlike, only Addle who can turn into cash tomorrow's regrets, care about all that. Do you think I do? Or does Aldo, or Niki, or Petronella, or little Gordon, give a damn for art-loving? Art is not life to us, my dears, it is far too slow and too empty of sensation."

"Such a little Nero to burn Rome," says the partly recovered Addle.

"Think of me as Petronius at Trimalchio's banquet." Cappellino returns the ball across the net with a smooth backhand. "I have the poise and all of you have the vulgarity."

"My God, but you're a bore." Lens is piqued, although her highly tuned sense of journalism denies the comment. She wants more but just for the moment she isn't going to get it.

"Cut," shouts Sandy, and a lanky young man who combines the functions of loader, clapper-boy and dogsbody runs about like a gnu. He is called Barnett something.

"Let us say nothing for the moment," Cappellino advises. "We don't want anything off the record." But Capisco has walked off the set and into the hotel and suddenly we are all bit players except Pier-Francesco who is stroking Alexander to subdue him and waiting as if Make-up would come and give them both a touch of face powder.

"Okay," says Sandy, not having noticed that Capo is missing, and Barnett Thing chalks "Shot 290: Take 1" on his clapper-board and stands ready.

"Hold it, please," says Cappellino. "I think some of the supporting players are off set."

"Okay, hold it," says Sandy obediently and the assistant director runs into the hotel. We wait.

"Who does this little sod think he is?" Sandy asks rhetorically.

"Today," replies Cappellino urbanely, "and in some ways tomorrow." And Alexander heaves away from Capisco's golden boy and pulls hard on his string. Like Nella, he wants out. Unlike Nella, he is a heavyweight.

The characters at the other tables are a little restive, but none of them shows any sign of leaving. They move, rustling and clucking, but they wait. The waiters also wait.

Addle suddenly smiles. "This silly boy," he says, "does not understand anything about time."

And he's right. The strain is coming on young Pier-Francesco to hold out against the anticlimax which Capo has contrived by simply going off. I don't underrate Cappellino. He has another trick or two for sure in the reticule of his hatred, but if the continuity breaks here, he'll never get his show back on the road.

"Time," Addle says, "is simply a product of the control of memory. What your father can do is to make time as memory work for him and so for all of us. I do not think you can. I think you can do no more than contrive the odd moment which only we here shall not quickly forget. You are ephemeral. I think your life will land on the—how do you say—cutting-room floor."

"But he will come back," says Cappellino calmly. "He has no alternative. And he has been changed."

"For sure," Addle looks like a monitor lizard, "he will come back." And of course Cap does, but not quite yet.

Nella, who is sitting next to me, just as she was last night, is feeling very isolated. Cap's chair on her right is empty and so would Kir's be, opposite her, except that Cappellino is sitting in it. Nella is looking round desperately, having got no support from Hansi and feeling strongly that this episode has no part in her life. She wants to leave now and I don't blame her. This is no sort of dinner-party for a sheltered contessa, even if anyone believes what she will have to tell around the salons and at the hairdresser's when she is back in Milan. Until they see Sandy's TV movie that is, diffused and rediffused, as doubtless they all will, even in Milan. She touches my hand and, Kir still being absent on her mission of mercy, I return the gesture by letting mine slide comfortingly along her aristocratic thigh, which is hard up against mine. After all, I never know when I might be in Milan, one way and another. But she is not looking at me. She is looking out over my shoulder.

"*Vedete i Mafiosi, dunque.*"

And when I look round there they all are, of course, Cappellino's pack, sidling back with Gordon Bleu doing a little double shuffle, all bumps and grinds, while shaking two tins like maracas. Why he has the tins, which, from the clicking noises they make, must be aerosols, I don't know. Next comes Petronella, who has pulled her singlet off one shoulder to reveal one undistinguished tit and is swaying slowly off the beat to Gordon's rhythm, and then Aldo, lumbering, and Niki all braced back into the black leather and trotting as if he were in training. They look as blank a group of groupies as ever went on a trip, like a trip to Disneyland, man, where life is real and plastic and no one knows anyone else, but no one. And that's wild and groovy.

Gordon sets down the tins on the table by Cappellino and jigs off to where the group has formed up behind their leader, and Hansi gets up and goes into conference with Sandy, whom he feels might have the authority to clear the riff-raff out and leave the area free for persons of rank and quality like our lot and even, I suppose, Pier-Francesco who is, despite his friends, Capisco's son. Sandy shrugs. He's an old enough hand with wild-life shorts to know that if you want to film lions in safari you must accept hyenas, jackals and vultures as part of the entourage round the kill. He's not going to direct. He's going to get whatever footage he can and then edit. So Hansi returns discomforted and muttering, and sits down very stiff, declining the glass of whisky which Cappellino generously offers him from Lens's bottle.

So there we are, waiting; the table arranged as it was last night except that Estelle and Kir and Moustique are not in their places and I suppose Moustique isn't likely to reappear. Otherwise there are just the Dead End Kids weaving about and dressing the scene by vaguely shuffling around behind Cappellino, and there is Alexander, who has got his string round several chair-legs and thus restlessly has imprisoned himself.

Suddenly Alexander begins to struggle and Cappellino is making soothing noises which are not helping. Alexander doubtless senses that things are not going the way a respectable ram wants them to nowadays, and that there is something impending which belongs to other times and other rams. I share the feeling and so, I think, does Nella whose thigh is now tense along mine. Cappellino has Alexander held but trembling and he picks up one of the tins and shakes it, so that the little tumbler clicks inside it. And when I look up, I can see Capo coming out of the hotel with, to my amazement, Moustique, her skirt hanging smoothly cylindrical as Duchamp's symbol in the glass. Estelle and Kir are following, and then Poitevin, and a phalanx of pilot-fish waiters are swimming and circling.

Nobody says a word. Capo takes Moustique to her seat and Estelle to hers, very formally, and Kir goes over to Cappellino and stares at him. Cappellino stares back, but he doesn't move to get up and no doubt any such courteous gesture would be difficult in view of Alexander's anxiety and the need to string him along. Poitevin brings a chair for Kir who signals him to put it between Nella and me. She misses very little, does Kir.

"Roll them," Sandy says, the cameras start purring, Barny Whatnot claps the board and Sandy calls "Action."

"Action," says Cappellino, "we shall now have. We are going to dress Alexander in a fashion suitable to this important occasion. He has the vine leaves already as you will have noticed, but now . . ." And he starts spraying from his paint tin. Alexander's fleece begins to turn golden and nobody moves to stop it or says a word. "Instant argonautica," says Cappellino, spraying from the tail. He moves the spray up the flanks and along Alexander's back in a cloud and stink of cellulose and Alexander is glittering in seconds. When he gets it in the muzzle, he bleats like a rusty hinge and pulls back and up with a strength which brings his forefeet on to the table next to Capo. He glares down at Cap, eyes bulging and, so far as a ram can scream, he screams. Capo jerks back, his chair going over and now he is standing and looking close into his son's face as if their horns had locked. But Pier-Francesco's eyes are shut and his face is blind, ecstatic. He has Alexander tight on the string, now, pulling with all his strength. The paint tin is back on the table so Cappellino has one free hand and is fighting Alexander with the other.

And there, in a frozen frame, there is a sort of crazy updated Poussin. A golden ram, vine-garlanded, is rearing towards an old man; and a golden boy, at grips with it, dominates the centre. Behind this motif, the rout is still mechanically dancing, and in the middle distance a mass of indeterminate figures against the night sky is swaying and craning forward towards the action. On the track, Pier-Francesco's voice is thin and high. "This is for you, Father," he shrills, and then, as the frame unfreezes, his hand goes up with a knife in it.

One brief neo-classical tableau and the baroque breaks in. Alexander, turning against the twine, throws Cappellino sideways and brings that gleaming forehead with its curling horns into play; the full ferocity of this action catches the hero of the event straight in the balls. Cappellino goes down across the table, knife-hand outthrust and that hand gets broken. Capisco, striking like a leopard, brings the paint tin down on it and it must be more than luck that he has his thumb on the spray when it hits and he holds it there, because suddenly Cappellino's face is as gilded as Alexander's horns and the gold spray is round his head in a cloud.

"Cut" comes from Sandy, in a sharp gasp. And then the table collapses and the rest is black slapstick. Hansi is overset with his legs in the air. Cappellino is writhing on the ground with his hands in his crotch and Capo is standing back with one hand on his hip, as if waiting to receive Cappellino's ears and tail. Alexander has left, like a bullet.

"Well, for heaven's sake," says Lens, who in some extraordinary way has escaped unscathed, the table being in two sections with her end left standing. She reaches for her whisky-soda. "What in hell was all that?" she asks Estelle fretfully. The only other sound is of Moustique laughing. Pity they didn't get any of that last little sequence on camera.

VII
Print

The waiters come and pick up Hansi and dust him off and they put another table where the broken one was and they put a new cloth on it and Poitevin is adding up what he can charge. No one disturbs Cappellino, who is lying on the ground in a foetal position because of his knackers and his hand and the unexpected curtain on scene two of his pageant. The rest of those present you might say sit stunned, except for the members of the press who are off again to the one telephone in the hotel, and the photographers who are clicking and this time Lens, who is very, very plastered, takes a desultory snap of Cappellino under the table and one of Cap still standing at the end of where it was. And this doubtless turns out to be the best photo of the year of Capo and will win awards.

It is Capo who picks his son up, very tenderly, and puts him on a chair where he sits bent over for a while and then very slowly and painfully straightens up. His face is entirely metallic, bright and glossy and, with his yellow hair and clothes, he looks like an effigy.

It occurs to me that it was the bang in the balls and the cracked fingers that kept his hands from his face, because the quick drying spray would have smeared if he had touched it, and it hasn't. His eyes were shut so perhaps it didn't sting them. Anyway the lacquer is a quite perfect covering.

"A case of gilding the lily," Moustique suddenly says, quite merrily, "or could it be gelding?" And Cappellino's eyes come open like a mechanical doll, the metal lids sliding up like shutters.

"Consider the lilies of the field," Moustique goes on, "they toil not, neither do they spin. But let me tell you, Pier-Francesco Capisco, Solomon J. Solomon in all his glory never had your gear." And she starts to laugh again and goes on laughing, pitched very high, while Estelle makes soothing noises.

"Let me see your hand," Capisco says to Cappellino, and those are the first words he's spoken since the end of dinner.

His son looks round at him but without expression. Then he looks back at Moustique and his face cracks open like a comedian in gold face, if you follow me. His right hand is so swollen as to resemble the paw of a lion.

"You mother-fucking bastard," is Moustique's response to this glance, so Cappellino makes an effort, still wearing that rictus grin. "I don't think you've met Madeleine," he says.

"I have." Estelle has also not spoken since dinner. "Although I did not know her very well, until now."

"I withdraw the remark," Moustique says with a sort of hysterical sobriety, "you are not a mother-fucker, at least not any more," and then she looks surprised at herself. "Moustique," Estelle says, "Moustique," as if she were quietening a frightened pony. Moustique gets up and goes round Addle and kneels by Estelle.

"I'm sorry," she says. "I'm sorry, sorry, sorry." And then she is in tears. "I've been raped, you see."

"Yes, darling."

"Raped."

"Yes."

"Not by that thing over there. Not by that metal thing. He didn't. He couldn't. He had to have it done for him and he wanted me to be a virgin. He said I was. You all thought I was. You didn't know I wasn't."

Cappellino's grin is gone.

"Poitevin," Estelle tells him very quietly, "you will send for the police."

"But, Madame . . ." Poitevin is agitated. "The scandal."

"Poitevin," Estelle repeats and he goes obediently into the hotel.

Cappellino's wolf-pack is edging away now except for Petronella, who has covered her unattractive tit and just stands there. Niki has her arm and leads her towards the road. She goes without a word, sucking her thumb. Aldo has gone and Gordon Bleu. They are all grouped briefly on the road, in the light from the hotel, and then they are not. And now a lot of the extras are settling their bills and I can hear cars starting up. The Schlegels are moving to leave, he with little bows and token hand-kissing motions for Estelle, she without gestures. She just touches my hand and offers hers to Capo, who takes it and then they are gone. Lens is asleep. So that leaves Estelle, who is holding Moustique to her, and Addle who is watching Cap and Cap who is watching Cappellino and Kir of course who is sitting next to me, and me.

"It hurt," Moustique says into Estelle's bosom, "but it didn't touch me."

"No, darling. It hasn't touched you."

"He made me eat something, you see—and then we just talked for a while and I should have known, but I didn't, that it wasn't just sugar. I mean it was. They were all just sort of munching and being friendly, at least I thought so and he was; well, he said I was beautiful and that his father must have seen that and why hadn't he and—no, I mean drawn me. And then we were sitting round on the shore in the dusk and then it got dark and peaceful and he said not to hurry away to get changed for dinner and if I was hungry, he had some sugar which was great for energy and asked how was it in college and . . ." And during this broken monologue, which gradually goes up and up beyond the range of the human ear, Estelle strokes Moustique's hair. And all the time Cappellino and Capo are staring at one another. Nobody else says anything. After a while, the lights die and Sandy is whispering and the crew are packing up.

"We'll call it a day, Signor Capisco," Sandy calls.

"Is that what you would call it?" says Capisco, not looking up.

Moustique is quiet now.

"Get a doctor," Cap says to me, and I go into the hotel to find the phone.

In there, Poitevin is shouting into the instrument and banging the thing up and down. But it is quite dead, he says, with eloquent shrugs.

"Did you get the police?"

"How could I, Monsieur, the apparatus does not function."

"Leave it then and send someone for a doctor. Monsieur Capisco's son has hurt himself."

"I will send at once." And he is all drive and urgency in his relief at not having to have the cops nosing around in his Universe and Liberia. "Thank you indeed, Monsieur. I shall inform Madame Capisco at once and I shall send Gaston for Doctor Gachet, who is only a thousand metres towards the village. At once, Monsieur," and he is off bawling for Gaston.

Doctor Gachet; every generation needs a Doctor Gachet to take care of schizoid artists, I suppose. At least, Cappellino still has both ears.

I had forgotten that Madeleine was in the hotel. Now there would be two invalids upstairs, because at that moment Cappellino comes past me, nursing his hand and limping. He doesn't look at me.

"You need a cellulose solvent, like amyl-acetate," I tell him, "to remove the make-up. Nail-varnish remover, if your mother has enough." I always like to be helpful. But he doesn't acknowledge this practical hint. He walks past me and starts to go upstairs.

"No flics," I tell him, "the phone's dead." At this he turns balefully and stands very disdainfully looking down at me.

"The bachelors grind their chocolate themselves," he says and that is more Duchamp quote and more than enough; what with one hand on his cods and the other hung out chest high and swollen, he looks like a bronze lion who could be holding a scroll with *Venezia* written on it.

"I came and they came with me. She came with them, but they didn't come and she didn't come with them."

"Well, now the flics won't come and you're lucky," is all I can think of to reply to this ritually hermetic utterance, but I suppose it is possible that the event we have witnessed was less seminal than we thought. He goes on up the stairs to Mother and I go back to our table and tell Estelle about the phone. She nods and thanks me and says she would be obliged if I would summon Poitevin.

So back goes the messenger whose business is to describe the offstage action to the audience and I find Poitevin again.

"I have sent for Doctor Gachet," Poitevin says.

"I think you should come out now and bring the bill," I advise him.

"The bill? But Monsieur Capisco runs an account."

"Well I should add it all up and bring it."

"Very well, Monsieur."

When I get back to the jetty, everything is as before except that Moustique is composed and has gone back to her seat.

There is not much light now. Just the 40-watt bulbs of the Universe and the full moon shining down on Poitevin's clean tablecloth and Capo's bald head. The rest of the company are only dimly to be seen and for Moustique's sake I am glad of it.

"Is Poitevin coming?" Estelle asks.

"I told him to bring the bill."

"You were right," Capo says, "I shall pay it. I shall pay now for the whole thing."

And we wait. Presently Pancho comes and picks up Lens very gently and carries her to Capo's car.

"I have told Capo that you are leaving and taking Kir," Estelle tells me. "He is desolate."

I don't quite believe that. But I assume, perhaps, that we have been useful and Kir perhaps more. At any rate it seems to have been all decided without consulting me and I am too tired to argue.

"Find my bag for me, Jeannot darling, I think it is under Capo's chair."

Why should Estelle's bag always be under Capo's chair? Still, she is right; it is. I retrieve it and Estelle takes from it a wad of bank-notes which would make up into a double-bedspread. Capo has his head on his chest and his hands for once are not moving.

Poitevin comes out in a flurry of bows and subservient gyrations, with a plate of papers pressed to his large belly. These he presents to Capo with that contortion they call a flourish. Capo picks the bills up and peers at them.

"You forgot to put the cottage on it."

"The cottage, Monsieur?"

"Yes, the children's cottage. Put it on the bill."

"But the picture . . . ?"

"If you don't put that hutch on the bill, I shall paint out the picture and you can have the cottage back in the condition 'as found' when you leased it. That, Isidore, is how the lawyers would put it."

"But, Monsieur . . ."

"Do as Signor Capisco says," Estelle speaks sharply. "And I know the market value of the property and also the terms of the contract."

"I must go back inside and see what should be done. I must consider, you understand, Monsieur. Forgive me."

"Put it on the bill and send me a waiter with a torch," Capo says.

"A torch? Of course, Monsieur."

Poitevin goes in, and out comes a waiter with a huge battery lamp.

"Hold it for me, Jeannot, and shine it down on the cloth." Capo is peremptory. He gets up and starts turning out his pockets. The contents pile up on the table, cigarettes, matches, a pocket knife, one of Estelle's lipsticks, a seashell, partly broken, a little plaster head of Theseus in bits, some string, a piece of aluminum wire and a handkerchief, very dirty. The growing heap seems inexhaustible and there, crumpled up, are the consequences, those little folded drawings we all made last night, whenever that could have been. I can see my head of Capo with the horns where the ass's ears were and Capo's head of Kir which he made, left-handed, while he was feeling her up, and Hansi's head which is remarkably not bad and shows a lean, smiling, archaic sort of head garlanded with vine leaves, which is very strange, considering.

Capo finds what he wanted, a stick of black litho-chalk, and he crouches over the table like an old wrestler and begins to draw. On to the until now white cloth, by the light of the big torch and some help from the moon, Alexander begins to take shape, life-sized. And Capo is hammering him out of the white ground, with the chalk breaking. He picks up the bits and goes on working with every fragment and with his thumbs and he spits on the chalk marks to mass the blacks and rubs them in with the side of his hand. The vine leaves are there, wound round the great curling horns and Alexander's eyes are rolled forward, staring. His hoofs are splayed and his whole body is twisted sideways in panic and Capo is hitting his eyes and open mouth with Estelle's lipstick and then spraying, spraying with what remains of the gold paint in the tin.

There is something demoniacal about the act. Capo is tranced with fighting the image and his eyes are staring as Alexander's did just before he hit Cappellino in the cods. And then it is over. Where the tablecloth was is a Capisco. And the paper consequences have blown off the other table in the sudden wind and are flying and scattering about on the beach below the jetty. They are lost in the dark and maybe they are now in the sea. Not even the one waiter left, the one who brought the torch, makes a dive for them.

Poitevin is back with more papers and explanations and excuses and then in front of him is the Capisco which is, well, table-sized. It

172

is a very large drawing and a coloured one too, gilded and therefore gilt-edged.

"This," Capo says, majestically, "will settle the bill, but bring me a thousand francs in hundreds. I need change." This Poitevin does, knowing the exact extortionate going rate for studio cottages in the locality and no less the price of Capiscos *au bourse,* but he is not looking happy. Capo distributes the hundred-franc notes among the writers who have all eeled back and are grouped respectfully. Having discharged this transaction, he puts all the bits and pieces back into his pockets, retrieves his straw solar-topee and slowly pushes his little perambulator filled with junk towards Pancho and the car. The moon gleams on the brass bombard, riding unsteadily because one wheel of the pram is buckled.

Estelle kisses Kir and then me, and Addle pats me on the shoulder and then takes one of Moustique's arms, and Estelle takes the other, and together they follow Capo across the road to where Pancho has opened the car door and is putting Capo's pram and the found-objects in the boot.

All the lights are out now and the restaurant which is at once the Universe, including even Liberia, has put up its shutters. Kir and I sit on the jetty, looking out at the building-site and the sea and presently we'll go up the hill to our place, which now belongs to Capo, and we'll sleep under the Jeannot mortal and the Jeannot who is not and Alcmene, who is Kir as Capo would have it, in the big drawing which now also belongs to Capo again, I suppose. The moon is going down, but the storm clouds have been torn apart by the wind so that the sky is full of stars. But it is cold.

VIII
Post-Synching

It seemed to me, on the way up to the castello, that I, Capo, had been screwed during the course of the evening. Moustique was not the only one to be done. There I was in the car with Estelle radiating disapproval, with Lens out like a light and the little mosquito doused with insecticide, and so with no view but the back of Pancho's neck, rigid with emotion recollected in tranquillity. And they were right. I have been far too permissive. It is time I broke the bad habit of letting the machinery get up my arse. It is time I became a recluse, before I get to be an old man. It is time I stopped letting rubber-necks neck me and become a mysterious figure, which is why you are now going to get the last public bit of me. From now on it will be long shots of the wrought-iron gates and clips from old movies of me with Stravinsky or Cocteau or some such dear departed, if there are any such, and interviews with torch singers who learnedly sing of knowing me, for want of any other viable activity.

All the way up here Addle carried the torch. He talked very learnedly on and on. It is a habit he has, when he is disturbed, providing no customers are present, and I daresay it did not matter much to him that I was not listening nor Estelle much, either. He talked about the collective unconscious and touched, I expect, on the *anima* or the *id* and on archetypes of which he insists that I am one, being in my absentminded parental capacity a primordial image of the most undesirable kind.

I remember two bits of what he said which memorably stuck out of his monologue. One was a story about a picture by Francis Bacon which had reached a record price at auction, despite the fact that Bacon himself had discarded it and given the canvas to a friend of his to paint over. The friend had turned the canvas and painted on the back, because that was the primed side which he liked, whereas Bacon always painted on the unprimed side at that time. So now there were two hundred and seventy thousand francs changing hands for a picture that the painter thought was no good and his friend thought was no good, but which, because the friend liked to paint on primed canvas, he had not painted over but turned over. "That," Addle said, "is what is called a financial turnover, or bringing home the 'bacon,'" and he was very pleased with this, his very own *English* pun, and cackled immoderately.

The other thing he said was that the artistic innovator was regarded as abnormal because society accorded itself the luxury of believing he did not concern it and that he did not put in question, by the mere fact of his existence, any accepted social, or moral, or intellectual order.

I was rather struck by this. "Who said that?" I asked.

"Lévi-Strauss," said Addle.

"That's very good for a man who wrote all those waltzes."

"Not Johann, Lévi," replied Addle testily, "the anthropologist."

"I thought he was Richard," I said, which dried up Addle, briefly, but then he went back on to Pier-Francesco again and referred to my son's "horsedrawn phrases" and "silky" or maybe "sickly" pedantry. I didn't quite hear.

"That's well put," I said, which cheered him up again. Wanting to keep Addle cheerful, since he was the only one, I thought it would please him if I said something profound. So I said, "Piero is an enigma and an enigma is as intriguing as a metamorphosis is intriguing, or an anamorphosis, come to that. Ambiguity is the very stuff of sculpture, where it lies beyond the formal."

"What do you mean?" Addle asked warily. But then I think I may have nodded off.

We stopped, of course, at the gates where old Tancredi, who is Ernesto's grandfather, I think, very slowly unlocked them for us and took off the chains, which are there either to keep me in or the public out, or the animals from devastating the country around. With heavy breathing and long dramatic pauses, Tancredi told us that Alexander had returned and had stood rooted as a statue among the boulders, half-hidden in the scrub and crying bitterly. He looked, Tancredi said, sucking in his mouth with awe, most heathen and uncanny, much as a camel had appeared long ago at an outdoor performance of Signor Verdi's *Aida* at Prato. The temporary stage at Prato, it seems, had given way under the camel, during the Grand March, to the animal's furious consternation and it had perforce remained hump-high to the audience for the remaining acts of the opera. The singers had found its presence difficult to negotiate and this, Tancredi wanted us to know, had greatly affected the dramatic action, but exactly how he was not sure, as he had not seen the work since. The camel had sung strangely throughout the performance and so had Alexander, among the rocks. It was a very heathen thing, Tancredi said, to hear and see Alexander thus, for the ram had been in great fear when dragged in and he had bolted, glittering, among the trees perhaps never to be seen again by mortal man, for he had been turned into gold.

I confess this saga of Tancredi's has remained with me more clearly than what Addle had to say about Pier-Francesco's infancy and I irritated Addle by telling him so. He can be touchy at times. He said he wished I would not refer to Freud as his old friend, because he had never met Freud and in any case he had been talking about Jung. Just to be polite I said that his old friend Freud believed that a man's goals were honour, power, wealth, fame and the love of women. I said I had had all those things for forty years and I could tell his friend Freud that there was more to life than those modest goals. What, I asked, had I been doing all this time, if that was all there was?

He became very quizzical and sardonic. "Power, you have?" he asked, smiling lopsided.

"Certainly."

"Over Pier-Francesco?"

But Pancho drew up at the house just then and I was spared the need to counter that sally. Pancho got out and carried Lens in very tenderly and Estelle took the drooping Moustique and they went upstairs, for Estelle to see that Lens was comfortable and Moustique comforted.

"I wonder," Addle murmured, when we were in the good Duke's hall, "why you named him Pier-Francesco."

"After Piero della Francesca, naturally," I replied at once, since I could not remember why.

"I did not think it was after Pier-Francesco Fiorentino."

"That dog's dinner of a madonna-manufacturer?"

"There are times, old friend," said Addle, "when your capacity to be obtuse makes you seem as stupid as painters are supposed to be.

There are only three ways for Piero to regard you. One is as a jealous and remote god, so isolated from the common run of people that you are wholly beyond any cognition of human problems. You are, after all, so far beyond such matters as money or fame and so clearly loved by women that at times none of us can put up with you."

"But you do. What are the other ways?"

"He can regard you as dishonourable, as a fraud."

"All artists are liable to be that. It is very difficult to tell, all the time, that one's integrity is intact and even what it is."

"Or he could regard you as hopelessly spoiled and therefore distressingly like him."

"Go to bed, Addle."

"I do not think he regards you as a fraud. He is not a philistine, despite his pose, but I think he does not know what to do with you and he feels he must revenge himself for your failure to pass on your talent to him."

"Oh, for Christ's sake go to bed, Addle, old friend."

"He wishes you to suffer. He wishes that you were human."

"And don't I? Aren't I?"

"Not so far as he can see. I sometimes wonder myself."

"I am old. Isn't that enough to suffer?"

"No."

"Does he suffer? He dishes it out."

"Yes."

"Yes what?"

"Yes, he suffers and he makes everyone suffer except, it seems, you. It is very frustrating for him."

"I have not the time to suffer for Piero's benefit. I have not the time now to do anything but what I do."

"You suffer from vanity."

"I have much to be vain about and I do not suffer from it, but I do not have time now even to suffer from that if I felt I should."

"*Hubris*. You are not your own god."

"I am an archetype, as you said."

"An archetype is nothing so self-conscious as you are, my dear Capo. It is a much more indeterminate and flexible thing. You are an archetype only in so far as others are disposed to believe you to be. An archetype is a vinomould, a negative jelly in which un-worked waxes are fabricated."

"Others take my word for it, or rather my unresolved image."

"You know, I think perhaps you have become isolated even from yourself, my friend, or been isolated by your fortune. It is the same with Pablo. The circumstances have been too much for both of you. Even your speech is restricted to aphorisms."

"You are one of those circumstances and you are often too much."

"Or perhaps I am a consequence. Meanwhile, you are being very sententious and as pompous as Aesop's bullfrog."

"You are right. Go to bed."

"You have come to believe that no one knows you except as your image."

"I wear, Addle, the ass's ears of Midas. Jeannot even drew them on to me, last night. I am well aware that they can be detected by those who have seen me without my Phrygian cap. I have the golden touch, too, which is doubtless a pity. But, despite all that, I am a man pressed for time and I cannot waste it bathing in some river to wash myself clean of residual gold-dust, or whatever the legend requires."

"Perhaps not, but, as I remember, Dionysus made the suggestion that Midas should do just that."

"Do you think that I did not notice what, by accident, I did to Piero tonight, in his party piece as Dionysus?"

"You touched him. You touched him up, too. He will not forgive it and you should try to give it up."

"I did it to stop him from killing Alexander."

"*Ach,* my old friend, there are always excellent reasons for per-forming acts even when they prove embarrassingly symbolic."

"Go to bed."

And so he went, grinning and marmoreally judicious. I veritably believe that he has survived several million more years than he deserves. He is full of dire wisdom.

For myself, I went into my workshop and looked at Theseus, half built. Much of what that old monster Addle says is true, but I do not need him to tell me.

In the garden, Theseus himself will be asleep, without guilt. He may, for all I know, be a father. He may have generations of baboons, all with two-inch incisors, behind him, but I doubt if he cares what they think of him. I doubt if he loved them. He is a fucking archetype too, after all.

The telephone rings and after a while it stops.

I am in the workshop, which I like best at night with one light bulb only, thrusting harsh shadows everywhere to make all the stuff convincing because then the faults are dramatically disguised. I know the faults from memory, or most of them, but I like to stage-manage this mystery for a few minutes at this time of night, because it is the time before I begin to work and before Estelle interrupts me with her inevitable fried eggs because of my not having eaten enough dinner to suit her. Even during these comforting dark minutes, when I can see the sculpture the way most people see sculpture because they are not looking hard at it, I become impatient. Sitting here on the truckle bed, I like staring at the dim, white, plaster ghost of unfinished Theseus, who looks so subtle and mysterious, even knowing that he will look so lousy when I turn up the working lights and see that he doesn't work properly from various angles and will have to have the axe taken to him and the tin-snips on the chicken wire and a lot of twisting about and plaster cracking off, to be built back. But I get a lift from this old *animus* squatting there and the other bits and pieces hiding in the shadows which are some of them probably manifestations of the *anima* collected in the dark unconscious, but here released beyond wealth and power, being projections of the love of women but honourable, I honestly believe, whilst they remain in this privacy and before they go out of the dark and become public.

I remember a story about Pablo making "automatic drawings" in the dark with some surrealists. When they turned the lights on, he had drawn a woman's head. So they turned the lights off again and had another go and Pablo had no idea, he said, of what he was making. When they turned the light on yet again he had done the same woman's head in reverse. It seems he was surprised. I am not. I would have expected it. A woman's head comes out of Pablo's fingertips more often than anything else since the days of the guitars. If he picks his nose, I would expect the snot to be woman-shaped. Besides, each of us produces a limited vocabulary of forms until, at a certain stage, they look so stereotyped that they have to be given a jerk to reanimate them. It is partly alarm at repeating one's self that makes one reshape things to make them more responsive to their own energy. "A painting of mine," Pablo used to say, "is a sum of destructions." And so it usually is, because he wants to do the same thing again without it appearing to be the same, and so do I. But sculpture to me is a sum of transitions. Besides, if we really were truly able to avoid doing the same thing again, no one would believe in us. No one would be able to say with certainty and satisfaction Ah, I see you have a fine so-and-so, and then where would Addle be?

When in doubt, we communicate urgently with the dead who are so much older and in some ways better off than we are, they being still alive in all the ways that matter to us. Piero takes the line that the dead are dead and therefore no longer interesting. It's not good thinking, although fashionable. I daresay it is rather embarrassing for Piero that Duchamp has died so tactlessly early in my son's life, but it may come to remind him that no human life is complete without a dialogue with the dead. You can't really live without that endless dialogue, however long your creditors have been gone. You can't complete anything without reference to them, however up-to-date your admirers think you look.

That single light bulb on half-built Theseus is very satisfactory. Sculpture exists only in the light it receives and by the light it discards. The Greeks punched out marble in the whitest and clearest light on earth and at their best, before the steel chisel was invented, they splintered it out in particles so that the bruised stone ate the light in minute facets. Then they put it in the sun for sustenance where it still is, or should be. But all that is stone carving. How much sculpture has always been made for the tomb and the mud hut, rejecting the sun? Bronze is for the lamp and the light of torches. It is for the cult statue inside the temple in the half light, as bones show through flesh only where the flesh permits. The gods don't carve the body, they model it. Adam was made from mud, skeleton and all.

"There is not a bone where one cannot find the trace of the thumb, which has not been modelled, except the orbit of the eye," Pablo said. "The edges of that orbit have been broken, the mud has been kneaded around the cavity, pressed between thumb and index finger, then let go at the precise moment when the creator who holds the mud let go, when the element hardened into a fissure, unique in the skeleton; later its indentation permits the eye to be properly fixed." That was Pablo on the skull of a horse and I'm reminded of it by catching sight of a zebra's skull I have on the shelf over there; a remnant of a lion's kill, picked up somewhere in Africa. That remark of Pablo's is the best thing that he ever said about sculpture, so far as I know, because bones are the armature of the body, white when revealed, but hard mud clad in soft mud hidden in the darkness of flesh until death. To me, perhaps, bones are the most mysteriously beautiful of all creations, made as they are from soft into hard.

"Sculpture," Pablo said, "is the art of the intelligence." It is odd, I think, that he isn't better at it. He is intelligent enough. But perhaps sculpture takes too long for him. He is hasty with it.

The shelf where the zebra's skull is, and two pelvises and a group of vertebrae and some large seashells, is where I keep the tins of black and gold and copper spray-paint for "bronzing" plaster to see how it will look when it is cast in metal and to correct the kinks and faults which you don't see in naked plaster. Even in this light I can see that two tins of gold are missing. Piero would have taken the cleaners with him if he'd known what was coming. But then, none of us did know.

I wonder at myself. I have broken my son's hand and sprayed gold in his face and I don't seem to feel as I feel I should about it, or even as Addle feels I should. Perhaps I am heartless, as I sit here brooding about Pablo and bones when I've just cracked Piero's metacarpus, in rage and outrage, with a tin of gold spray-paint.

I should be full of self-disgust and equally full of guilt at having produced so much resentment in Piero and been in a way responsible for poor Moustique getting done by his thugs. I should be filled with shame at being at the centre of such a scene, especially such a public scene, with so much pique and pain in it. Why aren't I feeling it? Perhaps because it was so public—a film, a fiction, a TV playlet—and I don't believe it. But it happened. It has only just happened. And I feel as remote as that chessplayer Duchamp, dead with his dandyism and his disdain. Duchamp, the survivor of the great age of twentieth-century Paris; our contemporary who despised us all and settled in New York to become the hero of the art of trendy youth because, when it came down to it, he designed a special porcelain "ready made" which flushed the baby out with an illusion of bathwater contrived by means of a mechanical tin-can turning for ever, powered by an electric motor, behind the closed door of a peepshow at the Philadelphia Museum, God rest his thin, ironical soul. I maunder, when I should be repenting about Pier-Francesco.

The trouble is that I understand very well about my beloved son who, it seems, keeps asking, in the traditional fashion, why I have forsaken him and seeking the means to get me onto the cross where he hangs to such remarkable effect. I'm not really as shocked as I ought to be because, if I were not fully occupied with all the making of things which he does not want me or anyone else to make, I should behave rather like him, I expect. Or I should have in my day.

There is, of course, a difference. I should have fucked all the time and without any help from my mates, whereas I don't think Piero fucks since his lovely mum fucked him up. I may be wrong, but I get the feeling he has as much contempt for fucking as he has for me and for the idea that I fucked his lovely mother to get him. He goes about like an open razor or maybe it is a safety razor with a loose blade, nicking but not quite cutting throats. His violence is contrived, staged, and I don't believe he has to have it. I don't know. I suppose I shouldn't have clobbered him but it was a reflex anyway, to save Alexander. Or did I mean to hit him for doing that to Moustique, which I did not find acceptable?

I think I would not have done that to a girl when perhaps I could. I think I only feel now that once I might have done because now I cannot manage much in the way of randy conceits. But then Piero didn't screw her himself and at his age I didn't lay on spectacles like an impresario. I should at least have been the actor-manager. Finally I would not like to have taken any woman who did not want me, supposing in fact that there would have been one, and I should certainly not have done it by proxy.

Yet I have the curious sensation that Piero and I are in some sort of unacknowledged conspiracy with one another: that we are sharing some sort of competitive joke and that Piero is going through the motions assuming that I know the form. Aside from accidents like tonight, I think perhaps I do. He rejects sex or disdains it, to score off my reputation for enjoying it, which I never made any bones about; it being the bones' own dance. That's simple. He knocks the Greeks and extols the Romans and I remember perfectly how that started. It was when he got involved with my set of Piranesi's *Carceri* etchings in the days before he took up his anti-art stance, an antic which he is far too educated to be going to sustain. Piranesi invented those dark prisons of his which trap a part of me too in the intricate labyrinths of his tomb-turned mind, and Piero caught them like measles. It wasn't so long ago and, being Piero, he delved into the subject and came up with Rome versus Greece, all or nothing. The Greeks were all vanity and prettiness, he said. He even used Piranesi's own phrase, *vana leggiadria,* about the Greek ornament. Rome was all grandeur and blood and power; very much to Piero's address and a short sword to stick into me, for being born at Paestum.

What is all wrong is Addle's notion that Piero is at me because he feels inferior and is overwhelmed by me. He doesn't. He simply plays me as if I were an old swordfish. Or does he see me caught in a Piranesi prison of my own reputation because I am not free, as he is, to do nothing? Is that why I broke one of his hands? And all this Duchampery. That's a new one. Nice that he's got beyond tinkering with Zen and mystical camp-following or has he, playing at Dionysus, come from the East? Is that a gloss? Fads bore him as quickly as they do me and I know his speed. The not-yet-dead will represent the up-to-date for him until he becomes deadly bored with them. I was like him at his age except that his hands won't work for him and perhaps he dislikes putting his prick anywhere, knowing that I have worn mine out.

Marcel was not the best of the Duchamp brothers, nor was Jacques Villon. It was that horseman Raymond who chose to be called Duchamp-Villon, being twice the other two, who had the real goods. The *Grand Cheval* was the real goods; in 1914. Perhaps the best sculptor France produced in those times, and dead at forty-two, was that young man.

The phone is ringing again. Who has to phone at this time of night? Stopped.

As for my fellow-countrymen, they weren't Duchamp-Villon. Poor Boccioni, another casualty, had a stab at being, but *Futurismo* was too rhetorical to produce anything better than the *Dynamics of a Bottle*. Balla's simultaneity was almost simultaneous with everyone else's. I am wandering again. Piero. Piero has a sixth sense. Not surprising, everyone has and animals have many more. But Piero's sixth is not a sense of balance. He is a victim of trends. I remember the whole team from Lautréamont and Petrus Borel to now, I suppose, Warhol the new master of *ennui,* who can make a moral virtue out of tedium; a good trick. Or am I just old? I think there is some method in Piero's antics which I do not grasp, perhaps it is my hardening arteries and his recognition that my cock is never so hard any more as once it was. I shall stop worrying about Piero and build hands for Theseus. Hands are not to Theseus quite what they are to me. Thumb opposed to fingers, yes, but mine a holder of tools sometimes my own, while he is only a thrower of stones. No very great anthropoidal jump from chimps to *Capo habilis* but maybe a longer one for Theseus and Piero, neither of whom can really use tools. Thumb opposed, son opposed.

Is it his mother he is really getting at? He certainly switched off her *beau monde* for her, which is more than I ever could, and with a gratuitous savagery which even the most sophisticated dinner guests came to avoid after one demonstration. What did I do, when Madeleine wanted me dressed up and paraded? I pleaded work and those tactics only served to turn on the lion-tamers, until I quit Madeleine and her entourage with her. Piero just spat in their plates. Very final. Why? Her set disgusted him as they disgusted me, but he won and silently. I lost. I shall stop thinking about him.

The bloody phone again. Estelle will come in at any moment, to tell me about who is calling. I need not think about that either. She will have dealt with it. The inevitable fried eggs will turn up at any minute and perhaps I may as well let Theseus wait for his hands until I've eaten.

I'm puzzled by Moustique. To be honest I never really thought of her being screwed, ever. And I am sad at the brutality because Piero knows better, or used to. It wouldn't have mattered, even with Kir.

No, that's not true. It would. But at least Kir is made for it and likes it. Talent is what I think that child would have, and talent is more important than anything else in the matter. I had a girl like Kir once, who could move an exhausted eunuch at a touch, or even a glance. It was her appetite and her genius. If she had chosen to be a whore she could have had a career like Cora Pearl or La Paiva, but she wouldn't let herself be made into an object. She could have been had by a bus-tour if it amused her, and it would have, except that she wouldn't let herself be made into an object. She and Estelle used to play together for me and she liked Estelle more than me, in fact, which was curiously delightful in the giving. I think Kir would be like that. Jeannot should grow up into her and perhaps he will. They are leaving, Estelle says, because I have overlaid him. Probably she is right, but I shall miss them. I'll give them the cottage and my joke with it, sooner or later.

But Moustique, with her odd little voice and her parsnip legs non-sexed, which is what I thought she was; she was brave and I hope is not destroyed. Rape comes so seldom to art historians, except in the learned journals, that I fear she may be damaged. Piero's cold frenzy was not a benison. Could I have done that to her when I was of such an age? Perhaps I could. I, too, have been a savage and I, too, have cruelty, but I used it all up because it was easy for me to take it out on objects, which I made out of subjects. It is better to take it out even on machines. To that extent Duchamp was right. I do not need to practise this ritual humiliation on people, who are subjects not to be made into objects. I would not need to do that to a woman, unless I had stopped thinking. Or do I mean feeling? I don't think I could have done it. Yet truly I don't care about Moustique, even if I should. Not to say really care.

If Kir were not wholly concerned with Jeannot, could she put Moustique back? I suppose not. Yet she has the quality to restore and could, if they were not so far apart. These are useless speculations. We must keep Moustique here and restore her, if we can. Estelle perhaps can, and I have the advantage for the child that I am a subject for her, in what I make as objects. I can never, I think, really discover what she is. It is too late for me and I have no time.

Those consequences I made us play: why did I do that? To pass the evening and show off, as I can never resist, or was there some more hidden purpose? To hive off the Swiss couple and keep them from pushing me? To irritate Addle, which he accepts as my recreation? Piero came and won and lost. It was unexpected and a consequence which unfolded itself. Thank God the film thing is over. I do not know why I agreed to do it. Pablo would not have done, but then he really is old and has his gift for ostentatious privacy to protect him. I have disappointed myself. I am an old clown, still.

Estelle is arriving. I can hear her. She is coming with the eggs and the news of the phone calls.

I am thinking, here in my freedom which is so large because I am beyond the goals old Freud set of wealth and power and honour and all that lot; I am thinking of Piranesi's invention of the *Carceri* which are dark gaols endlessly clenched, which are endless passages moving among and through each other, without the means to escape; which are the piled-up ruins of the heart's prison with the veins caught in the blackest dry-point burr and shut, shut, shut. Why, when he was so young, did Piranesi dream of all those vast, damp vaults in the earth, when all Rome's sky-shining ruins awaited his bright needle? Is it the red knitting-needle that was Theseus' point of departure, that has prompted me? Or is it that I am old beyond my needle's pricking? I think I need the eggs.

And here they are, but Estelle has scrambled them, which is unusual. Perhaps it is appropriate to this particular night. They look very good. She too looks very good. She sits on the bed with me and gives me the tray and I begin to eat and the eggs are very good.

"Alexander has turned up."

"Where?"

"He somehow found Pancho who is a friend of his and Pancho is cleaning him. The gold comes off quite easily, Pancho says, and Alexander needed a bath. Did he need one? I thought sheep had dips."

"I'm glad. It was a near go."

"Addle came to see how Moustique was, on his way to bed and he said, '*Vocatus atque non vocatus, deus aderit.*' I think I have remembered it correctly. He would not tell me what it meant."

"Bloody old oracle."

"What does it mean?"

"It means: 'Invoked or not invoked, the god will be present.' It was spoken, in Greek and not in Latin, by the Delphic Oracle."

"He said to quote it to you and made me repeat it, twice."

"I bet he did. His old friend Jung had it carved over his door."

"He said you were feeling badly and that the saying would be a help."

"Well I'm not and it isn't."

"You have egg on your face."

"I daresay I have. This evening I had egg all over my face."

"Better than spray-paint."

"How is Moustique?"

"She is asleep. It took time."

"Is she upset?"

"Fool. Yes."

"And Lens?"

"She, too, is certainly asleep."

"Ah."

"And Addle is now also asleep, I should think. He said we could take out an injunction."

"Against whom? Piero?"

"No, against the film being finished or shown."

"Oh that, I had forgotten."

"He says it must be cut."

"The Moustique bit?"

"Yes, but not only that."

"I seem to remember Pablo tried to take out an injunction against Françoise. It came unstuck."

"This is different. Also Madeleine rang."

"Yes, I imagined she would."

"She wanted to speak to you."

"I don't doubt it."

"She is going to make Piero sue, because of his hand."

"What does Addle say to that?"

"He said to take no notice. He can't sue with the film as witness."

"Then how can we take out an injunction against the film people?"

"Yes, there is that."

"What is the use anyway? I am public. I have been public for forty years. What the hell."

"Finish the eggs and wipe your face."

"Yes, yes."

"Moustique could get an injunction."

"Then let her."

"I think she should."

"Good. How is she?"

"You have already asked. She is sore and she is humiliated. Oddly, she does not seem as frantic as I would expect."

"How do you know?"

"I know. Also she gave me this book, which was in her bag."

"What book?"

"It is by Euripides and it is called *The Bacchae*."

"Have you read it?"

"How could I have done? She has only just given it to me. But it is about Dionysus, who is a god. Addle spoke about him to me last night."

"What did he say?"

"He said you weren't him. He said he was more like Pablo."

"Ho."

"Tell me about him."

"He was the son of Zeus and his mother was called Semele and she was burned to death at Thebes by a stroke of lightning sent by Hera, who was jealous of her."

"Hera was the wife of Zeus."

"Yes."

"Wives can be very difficult."

"Dionysus was born of a lightning flash, too. That may have been what gave Piero today's idea, although he was not brought up in my leg!"

"How do you mean?"

"Well, he thought he was playing Dionysus tonight, and Dionysus spent his infancy inside Zeus' thigh. Perhaps it was the storm that set him on, and the lightning."

"Why did he want to do that? I don't mean about growing up in your thigh."

"Well, you know Piero. He improvises. And it was a full-blown storm, with lightning, and he had Alexander and the props and his revelling rout, which was what Dionysus went about with."

"Yes, I know about that. But Piero is not as beastly as Dionysus."

"Only now and then, perhaps. He is anxious to be a god or a legend. The usual alternative to Dionysus is Apollo who behaved with almost equal brutality often, but has a reputation for order and sobriety. The whole thing is rather capricious."

"It seems rather silly."

"Piero and I are both that, in different ways."

"I know. But what is the point?"

"It is sometimes called the divine spark."

"Bushwah, as Lens says."

"But bushwah is not to be underrated. Art is divine bushwah made for bushwah-loving gods."

Estelle smiles and pats me as if I were a poodle. She is supremely unsilly, Estelle. Very down-to-earth-mother.

"Go on about Dionysus and why should Piero want to go through all that nonsense; cruel nonsense too?"

"Legend is all he has."

"And you?"

"I have hands."

She touches my hands, as if to tidy them.

"Dionysus is a part of men and he balances Apollo. He is the god of release, of irresponsibility, of fierce reaction to order. And order is all very well, but tiresome."

"You have bits of Dionysus, then."

"He used to manifest as a bull. Tonight he became a ram, which is me in a sense, since I am not a bull any longer. Alexander who became a god in his own right, being unusually talented, won the bout."

"I know you know all about this, because of your father and everything, but is any of it to do with us?"

"Yes."

"Why?"

"Because we live by myth and inhabit it and it inhabits us. What is strange is how we remake it."

The phone goes and Estelle takes it. It is Sandy, the director.

"He says they have finished and that they will come to take the video things out of the house tomorrow."

"Dear God, you mean they are still here, running in this room?"

"It seems so."

"I thought they were gone. They must have everything on them that I have thought and said, tonight as well."

"Have you thought or said anything special?"

"Of course I have."

"Well, then it is in the little boxes."

"Christ all bloody mighty . . ."

"He doesn't seem to be quite relevant, does he?"

"But . . ."

"You might as well go on about Dionysus and Piero. What's the difference?"

"You are being very *fausse-naïve*. You know much more about the whole thing than you are letting on."

"Maybe, but this is what they call 'for the record.' "

"Do we want a record?"

"You do. You want everything known, really. Hence Addle and Moustique and even the Schlegels."

"Vanity, vanity."

"Yes, darling. It is irresistible, isn't it? So go on about the legends."

"Dionysus came out of the East. He came from Lydia rich in gold, Euripides said, and he was given a place next to Apollo at Delphi. His particular role was to be a liberator and to have his following surrender to the supernatural, being drunk and disorderly. Women would follow him into the mountains and there tear animals and even men to pieces with their bare teeth and hands. Rather like Madeleine."

"So that was what it was about with Moustique and Alexander?"

"Yes, but reversed. That was a remake of the myth."

"How?"

"Dionysus gave Midas the gift to turn everything he touched to gold. But it was I, and always has been I, who turned Piero into gold. That is what has been so wrong."

"And Moustique?"

"That too was reversed. It was the Bacchae, the women, who

killed; the women who tore men apart. Not the men who raped virgins, even if she wasn't."

"And what else?"

"Why, Madeleine. In your book you will find that Agave tears her son to pieces and brings his severed head to show for it. But I think perhaps it is Madeleine whom Piero most wanted to injure."

"Not you?"

"Less me than what people call 'them.'"

"That was the consequence."

"It was."

"All that was aimed at you, wasn't it?"

"No, it was not so much me. It is Madeleine who hates me and Piero does not really like her to. It unmans him and makes him demonstrate."

"Was that a consequence?"

"It has been one of them."

I have eaten all the eggs and toast and wiped my face. Theseus waits.

"But all that was not the full consequence," Estelle says.

"What is, then?"

"You are, my dear. You are the victim, not of Piero or Dionysus nor of any mythical deities. You are your own victim."

"Who is not?"

"I'm not. Nor is Kir, nor perhaps will Jeannot be."

"No, perhaps you aren't. Perhaps they're not. I would not want victims, not being a god but, rather, a kind old person with abundant talent."

"You are a sacred monster and a gay monster, which is better than being a sentimental bore."

"And you are a monstrous cheat, my love, aren't you? With your pretended simplicity and 'Who is Dionysus, please explain?' and quoting Voltaire to me?"

"Did I?"

"Hah."

Silence and the archaic smile are all I get in response to this derisive snort.

"Maybe we had better get that injunction. If we don't, all the cultured viewers will learn that I am learned and you are cultured and that we are not the semi-sacred idiots that artists and their women are supposed to be. It could be a disaster for us all."

"Well, I'm glad you ate your eggs."

"What else could I do?"

"As I remember, Midas, whose name comes from *mita*, meaning a seed, was the son of a satyr whose name is forgotten."

"Was he? How did you know?"

"Well, the metaphor of you and your Midas touch is not exactly new and seed is something I have always enjoyed."

"So?"

"So if the legend was reversed this evening, it will be Piero whose name will be forgotten."

"Reversals like mirrors are not so straightforward. If they were, we should see ourselves in the looking-glass not only reversed, but also upside down. And we don't."

"Why not?"

"Nobody knows."

"Then again it was Midas who promoted the cult of Dionysus in Phrygia, wasn't it? And, if I remember right, it was Apollo who gave Midas ass's ears for objecting to his getting the music prize and voting for Marsyas. So Dionysus would be more popular with Midas than Apollo."

"You are a blue-stocking and I am only learning it after all these years. I have been swindled or you have got all this from Addle."

"I doubt if Pancho will whisper your secret into a hole in the riverbank, which would make the parallel complete, or that Moustique will pass it on if she is the reed who grows by the river."

"Why Pancho?"

"He shaves you. It was Midas' barber who whispered."

"Pancho would not whisper into holes in the ground and Moustique is no broken reed. Besides they will hardly need to if the movie gets shown."

"Publicity is so much more widespread, these days. And in any case you are not, like Midas, going to drink bull's blood and die in disgrace. There is no way to disgrace you that would not get you even more admiration than you get already."

"Bitch."

"It's true though, darling."

"Go to bed."

"Poor old Capo."

"I am the victim of a woman who understands me. I am turned to parcel gilt by the Estelle touch."

"What can you do?"

"There is nothing I can do now."

"No, love, there isn't but I'm glad you ate your eggs and of course you are loved."

"This whole conversation is repulsively sweet."

"Perhaps you deserve it for being so potent."

"Me? Now?"

"Yes, darling. You, still."

And she touches my cock which is limp and unresponsive down there, as it has been in general—except a little for Kir—since whenever.

"It is elsewhere, though," says Estelle.

"Every man of genius should have two, his own and a real one."

"Well, at least you haven't turned it into gold."

"It might be more of a utility if I had."

"It would be like a bathroom fitting."

And on this note, Estelle picks up the tray and goes out to make sure, I suppose, that everyone is tucked up in bed and Alexander is given hay and oats, or whatever he likes, from a gold manger.

It is sad to think that Kir is going away with What's-his-name, just to protect him from me, just because no one is certain of how good he really is and that he might be ruined by being here with us. I imagine Estelle and Kir both think he might, not knowing, as how could they, what the chances are and how little anyone else could spoil or succour what there is for him to do if he can do it.

I am not tired. I shall begin on Theseus' hands as I have been trying to do for hours and I shall shortly be interrupted by Madeleine, who will telephone to tell me what I have done and that Pier-Francesco has gone and cannot be found and that it is all my fault. It will not be the first time. The irritating thing is that because of the sentiments expressed in the rather nauseating dialogue that Estelle and I have been having, all of which have been recorded in sound and on vision, in the bloody little black boxes, I shall not have the heart to wait for Estelle to wake up and take the call, and I cannot let the phone ring or she will, and then she will come down again and tell me not to get overtired.

I have worked through the night and am not overtired, just dead beat. I have peered out and seen that the men have come to take out the film equipment, of which there seems to be a ludicrous amount, considering all that they were packing up last night down at the restaurant, but now they are going to and fro across the hall, trundling things on wheels and clanking with lights and carrying huge bits of meccano and boxes of bits and pieces. So far as I can tell, they have not done any damage much. I have not heard the sort of notes that the Chola bronzes or the Shang pieces would strike if they hit the floor, nor the crack that the African carvings would make if shattered. They may have hit the etching press, I suppose; I heard one metallic crunch and there have been bumps. Is the Marino horse crippled, or the Henry Moore holed, I wonder? Or did they catch a lamp-standard thing against the frame of the Balthus?

I do not, for a fact, know what there is standing about in there. A sperm whale's skull, of course, which I wouldn't like harmed, and Pablo's stuffed bull, which would certainly stand up to a bang or two. What else? Packing-cases full of things which may be important or useful. There might even be a Duchamp in a packing case, perhaps a "ready-made" such as the *Fountain* signed "Mutt" or, better still, an unsigned one.

On the floor everywhere, when I peered out, there were bits of white tape stuck down or curled up, for marking where the cameras should have moved to, I suppose. Also wires, endless coils of flex coming out of boxes and coiling about on the floor, in a dangerous way, which must also be part of filming. I don't think any of it belongs to me. But I can't ask, because they think I am still asleep in here, behind the door of the good Duke's hall of audience, and they are taking great care not to wake me. The technicians, all tact and care, are creeping round and my relatives and their relatives are on tiptoe and whispering, as they pad about among all the treasures that have washed up on my beach, like flotsam on the building-site down by bloody Poitevin's. Only the monkeys, whom I named for critics, and the parakeets, called after museum directors, or vice versa, keep up their interminable chatter and I am known to be used to that. Alternating shrieks of abuse or approbation affect me in much the same way and have for years; that is to say, not much.

None of the *gratin* is up yet. Perhaps they had an exhausting evening. Pancho I can see through the shutters, on the terrace, massively calm, and with Alexander, clean as a whistle but unwilling to stir from his heels. This is because, although Pancho is a tower of strength, Alexander is a nervous wreck.

Because the film shooting is more or less all done now and I suppose the film is in cans on its way to the plane and thence to the cutting-rooms and whatever they do that they call processing, the director called Sandy sounds as if he is congratulating himself on the telephone, long-distance, to someone called Janos.

It remains, then, for the men to come in here and dismantle the videotape box things and to reveal the hiding-places of the little boxes which contain, in their spools or sprockets or whatever, the deep secrets of my private life and the meaningless rubrics I recite, the songs I sing and the grunts and anguished cries which I make while I work. All these are, presumably, cobbled on to my creative thoughts and deep insights and manual skills, recorded simultaneously in sight and sound. I cannot think what this will look and sound like as an end-product, but so long as it is enigmatic and peculiar enough, it will do no harm.

So behind these great doors Capo, that is I, am wide awake and I wait to see where these black-boxed mechanical spies and informers are hidden, except the one that I broke in the bog. I am sitting now on my narrow bed, very austerely contemplating Theseus in plaster, and when the film is finished and shown, you will become aware of how much progress I think I have made during the night, because the boxes are still running for a little while longer. I am not absolutely dissatisfied with Theseus emerging and I am looking enigmatic with my eyes slitted like a mysterious oriental, to take the glare out of the plaster, which is banded with the sunlight blazing through the closed shutters. Although it is probably after midday, it is cool in here and the heaps of plaster, lumps and chippings round Theseus, nearer finished, are piled in clumps and cradled in white dust, like broken sugar icing, rock-hard and inches deep.

Theseus now has arms and hands roughed in and the axe is no

longer his antagonist. He is for the riffles now and the cheese-graters and the sureforms, which clog less than rasps and all these lie round on the bed beside Capo, who is me and who has not been to bed except for cat-naps and will not go there until all the men have gone, in case I talk in my sleep.

"The trouble with plaster," I say to myself, "is not only that it dries faster, but that it looks like plaster. You cannot relax . . ." And I cannot relax until it is stages on and can be shellacked with three thin coats, diluted with meths. Thereafter, I can spray it to resemble bronze, which I enoy to do. Usually, at least, I greatly enjoy this process, if perhaps not so much today as usual. The time has not come yet for it, anyway, and won't for a week or two.

And these are the last shots before what Sandy calls the wrap-up and it is all that is left to do with this documentary, apart, of course, from the dubbing and the music-track and the weeks of editing that they have told me about and which is not my problem.

Sandy, a pro to the last, has come off the phone and has his little hand-held camera whirring, the way good directors do, like they tell me Kubrick does, nowadays, in case something atmospheric or poetic has somehow been overlooked. On the terrace is Ariadne, my marmoset, fast as a mosquito, performing a little dance before Theseus, who has come out from the bushes and is sitting in the archaic pose of great baboons of ancient lineage, as they have all sat, straight-backed and hands on knees, since long before that Egyptian god wore the mask of Thoth.

It would be peaceful now, or I would have expected it soon to be, with all the little men nearly gone and the black boxes with them, but up the drive from the gates two lorries are coming and they are trying to approach the castello, and to avoid running down the boy from the post office who has just learned how to ride a bicycle dangerously and seems to be carrying some urgent communication to convey, I hope, not to me. He is weaving his way here at breakneck speed. This is not easy, with all the filming machinery littering the driveway, and the shouts and horn-honking are such that even I cannot be believed to be asleep any more, especially since I know perfectly well what these *poids lourds* contain. One is from Castiglioni in Paris and the other is from the Berlin foundry. Both contain newly cast bronzes which will have things wrong with them.

It is odd, but however hard I try to get the different foundry people to come on different days, they always turn up at the same time, to hate each other. One lorry will be driven by a vanman who knows nothing whatever except a bovine loyalty to his firm. The other will also be driven by vanmen who know nothing, but that will be followed by a limousine with Castiglioni himself in it, and there he is, bouncing out of his shining Rolls-Royce, like a balloon filled with hydrogen. As he bobs towards the house I shall think last thoughts into the black boxes for you, about the perils, splendours and miseries of being a sculptor in bronze and you will surely hear what Estelle has to say, too, because the moment the spherical Castiglioni touches down on the terrace she will be there to greet him and tell him where he has gone wrong in patinating and where there are faults in the moulds, if there are any, and where the joins are rough or visible. And Casti will cower and cover up and excuse himself and explain. It always happens. Estelle has the eyes of a hawk for flaws and Castiglioni has the eyes of a pigeon, natural prey of hawks.

The next stage will be the unpacking of the work from Helgen's, and Castiglioni will criticise it to point up the excellencies of his own castings and the crass deficiencies of all Germans. If, as sometimes happens, the other French foundry delivers within ten minutes, there will be more covert sneering and eloquent silences than anyone whose money it is being spent, which is me, can take. So I wait for that. I do not know how three cottage industries, all of whom are two months or more late on deliveries, can all manage to coincide their arrival here, each stuffed with the sense of rivalry of which they are so proud. But they do and they do and once again they have, or at least two of them have.

But here is the hard life of the sculptor in bronze and what he endures, as I promised silently to tell you. First, there is the time factor. You make a model in plaster, or wax, or even in clay, which involves one further process. You lavish love and care and talent on the model until it is ready to be moulded. Then it goes to the foundry and there, when I was younger, I went too. The foundry used to piece-mould, and now rubber-moulds the model, and they prepare the wax from their mould. You correct and refine the butter-pat of an object they then produce from simulating your model, and you complain continually that the moulder cannot tell his arse from your elbow, nor understand the forms enough to see how they articulate even at their simplest. The founder, once you have re-worked his wax, then invests the thing in a fireproof mantle, which he puts on wet, in layers of different texture and density, but, before this, he has run in tubes of wax, reasonably called runners, to join the freestanding elements of the sculpture and ensure a fast and even flow of hot metal through the mantle in due course. And he has put "risers" in, to allow the hot gasses to escape when the metal pour occurs. That is fine if he puts the runners in the right places and doesn't lose projections like fingertips because the hot bronze has cooled and clogged and hasn't pushed through to them prop-erly. Anyway, the work is now out of your hands and lost to you and you begin to worry. I believe that that is really why the process is called "lost wax." Weeks then pass and you go on and do other things and wait. In the course of this time, the foundry burns out your wax model and pours molten bronze into the negative left in the mantle by that wax, now "lost." And the foundry waits for the metal to cool and they break off the husk of the mantle with hammers and there is your bronze, pretty rough and waiting to have the runners and the risers cut off, because they too are now bronze, where the metal flowed through them. Simple, you might say. But slow. Then comes the cleaning off of the surplus mantle, unless you are Marini and want your bronzes as dusty looking as stale bread. This cleaning then done with dilute hydrochloric acid, the acid is cleaned off and then comes the chasing, the disguising of faults, the masking of joins, the smoothing away of scars where runners were, together with the grinding away of stumps, the chasing of surfaces and the patination of those surfaces with chemicals, of which "liver of sulphur" is the one which produces those deep browns that look like molasses, until you yourself have burnished the treacle away to give light back to the metal. You will have told them exactly what depth and kind of patination you want and they will have done something that they wanted, which is not the same. And then will come the day, the three-months-late day, when you see your new work in metal. When you first see it, it will look wonderful, almost every time. It will be an hour later that it will not, because by then you will cease to be dazzled. And your disgust will form because your diligent foundrymen forgot, or have lost, your notes which explained the surface and how it should be finished. Then you will sweat with frustration, as bronze sweats tin, like leprosy, if the core wasn't properly dried in the kiln, and the first thirty years will have been no worse than the present decade, or rather better, in retrospect, of course, because of the decay of craftsmanship everywhere these days and the fact that you alone are served by morons with no sense of their medium.

In the old days I used to go to the foundry most weeks, but now I use three and all in different places so that they deliver to me instead, in order to save me time, which it doesn't because the real time is between the making of the model and the completion of the cast and then there is the time I must spend on every wax and every complete cast in every edition, which no one can spare me. Even though there are people here who do the first work on the bronze with the wire-wool and the wire brushes in rotary drills, it is still all for me to finish.

They are unpacking both lorries now and there are a dozen small bronzes, including duplicates of the Theseus maquettes which Piero pinched, and they are in sixes, half editions, all looking fine at the moment. There is the four-foot head, cast sand because very simple: a "one off" of this and, by the look of it, that's all in that container. This means Helgen haven't finished the *Interlocked Figures,* as I might have known. Castiglioni is sniffing at the work. No foundry has a good word for anyone else's castings, except when talking to each other. It's a tradition.

The other lorry is unpacked now, so that there is quite a batch of oven-fresh Capiscos on the terrace. The Castiglioni casts are polished bronze and there are four of them, gleaming away. From this distance they look flawless, because Castiglioni is the best foundry for polished bronze, which requires a perfect surface and seldom gets it. If there are flaws, Estelle will see them before anyone else.

A voice on the other side of the doors says, "All bloody nudes." To which another replies, "Randy old bugger."

These commentators are film technicians, I imagine. Of course, they are right, in a sense. Most of what I do is founded on, or derived from, the nude, the stripped human body, as is most of the good bronze sculpture in this world. Where the boys are wrong is to believe that my impulses are primarily sexual. If they were only that, I would indeed be an old bugger, because many of my sculptures are male, including the four-foot head, although that would be very difficult to bugger. But if the nude human body in sculpture is about sex, it is also about Time, or rather it is especially not about Time. It is the only way to deal with the human image, male and female, without precisely dating it; clothes and even drapery being the badges of specific times. A bronze figure in drapery is either classical, or neo-classical, or baroque or what-have-you and clamped to its period. A nude, because the human body has not evolved more than to square its shoulders at times and stick out its belly at others, is the human species through and in the midst of time, *sub specie aeternitatis* as you might call it, which is perhaps where I have always wanted to be: more now than ever, I think, my being old and little inclined to bugger around. The nude is also about structure, the human form being so perfectly worked out and complex and precisely articulated to perform all that is required of it, until it gets worn out.

Estelle is on the terrace now, with Castiglioni bowing over her right hand, while the boy from the post office is delivering a cable or something into her left, and I shall wait a little for her to suggest, tactfully, what is wrong that I cannot see properly from here. By the look of her, she cool, and of him, he bobbing and flapping, there are pits in the polished surface of *Stressed Man*. She has not opened the cable, but is using it as a baton to conduct Casti's eloquence and to control it.

The film people, who are still going to and fro with their bits and pieces, are gathering round Estelle now and hemming in poor Castiglioni, who wears a Poitevin expression as of one innocent of everything and only trying to make an honest living and to pay for his other Rolls-Royces. He does not believe that Estelle knows more about bronze than he does and probably more even than his one really great chaser, a craftsman he seduced away from Helgen's.

I must now put a stop to it all, because there is the Sandy person filming away with his little camera and if the casts are not good, I do not want them on film. So I go out and stop him.

Estelle has now told Castiglioni where the pits must be plugged and, as a result, the whole surface of each bronze must be repolished and he is shaking his head sadly.

"My dear Casti," I say, all benevolence, "I know that you will do this little thing for me. Send the men down tomorrow and especially Bertolucci, who is the chaser beyond all chasers."

"We are so busy," says Castiglioni.

"What a superb car, Casti. No wonder you must keep so busy to buy so many such cars."

"I have only two."

"Nonsense, Casti. I have seen four here at different times, and besides I sympathise. How else would we consume our large profits and show how important we are? You will do this little thing for me?"

"We are choked with work just now, Capo," he says, having earned the privilege of calling me that on some rare occasion when I was pleased with him.

"Of course you are and I am most grateful that, in the circumstances, you will send Bertolucci tomorrow. We have the equipment to repolish here."

"I cannot promise him so soon. He has so little time. We are all so pressed."

"Casti, you have all the time in the world, apart from all the money. You are a young man."

"But, Capo . . ."

"It is I who have no time, Casti. I am very old. Estelle, I am very old, aren't I?"

"Yes, darling."

"Consider, Casti, two things. I may not live to see the work of mine you have in cast for me now at this minute and which has been overdue since March. I may not have time. Also it is possible that if the bronzes arrive after I am gone you will not be paid until all the lawyers have cut me up."

"Oh, Capo, you are joking. You have many years of work ahead of you."

"Do not be too sure. It is an agony to have to wait so long for every bronze, knowing, as I do, how easy it would be for me never to see your magnificent work on my last things."

At this moment in the conversation, when I am wilting sadly and not looking round to see if any of my relatives or Estelle's friends are weeping quietly, or hearing if any of the film people have broken into sobs, Estelle puts her arm round my shoulders and leads me away.

"I will give you exact notes of what must be done, Casti, as soon as I have made Capo comfortable," she says over her shoulder.

No one is weeping as I pass weakly back into my workshop. It is heartless of them. The vanman from Helgen's is standing open-mouthed as we pass. We pause. "I shall have notes for you to take back to Helgen's when I have finished with Monsieur Castiglioni," Estelle says firmly. "Do not leave. Furthermore, you may tell Herr Kleist that he should telephone us on Wednesday and that Monsieur Capisco will require him to come in person with the next delivery."

And as I totter inside, I catch sight of the hands on the little *Mirrored Figure* and see that they are all made up with silver solder. "Tell Kleist to telephone tonight," I say fiercely, as I falter towards my sanctum, leaning heavily on Estelle.

"Yes, darling," she replies. "I will phone as soon as the film people leave the telephone alone."

"He's getting on, you know," I hear the girl who does the continuity say to the assistant director. And I suppose I am.

"It is all very, very sad," Estelle says.

"Screw you," I retort courteously in a whisper. "And screw Helgen's and my compliments to that distinguished craftsman Balthasar Castiglioni, that pattern of courtesy and ineptitude, and screw him."

"Hush, darling," says Estelle. "You mustn't tire yourself."

"I have been working all night and I am as fresh as a daisy."

"Then I shall put you to bed."

"I have had no coffee this morning and nothing to eat, and until I have had both and inspected with minute care the grotesque objects which the foundries have delivered as representing my work, and dictated exactly what is to be said to them about it, I shall not go to bed."

"No, darling. I will get breakfast."

"Tell Pancho, or one of those women, or tell Pancho to get one of those women who are everywhere, to get breakfast. And tell all those film people to leave, and why haven't Kir and Jeannot come? Aren't they even going to say goodbye? And where is that old crook, Addle?"

"Darling, wait until the film people have gone."

How, I wonder, did they get all this stuff on the terrace on to a tape in a black box? Or didn't they? And then I can see that two men are holding video boxes, still trailing wires, so still hooked up. I get no privacy, even in public. They must have dismantled everything in my workshop while I was on the terrace and now I'll never know where they hid the things apart from the one I broke, or indeed if they left once secretly, to churn out the remainder of my life.

I am not certain whether my thoughts and actions are going to be my own again ever. It makes me very frail and vulnerable to look at, or I hope it does. After all, I'm getting on and this should inspire veneration in everyone, except those who know better.

On the way in I pick up a Theseus maquette, which I don't really need any more for the big one, and give it a rub with my palm and look closely at it with my failing old eyes and it is not bad, except for his tail, which is not curving properly, but which I can bend out on this scale with pliers if I do it gently. I put him in the pocket of my dressing-gown. And then on I go into the shadows with my helpmeet propping me up and we leave Castiglioni to sweat on the terrace while the film people go on packing up. Doubtless Pancho will fetch a chair and a drink for our distinguished visitor to sweat in and on.

In the doorway of my workshop is who but Sandy, not quite going in, to squirt his little penis-substitute camera at plaster Theseus. I bow Sandy in with dignity and patronage. I open the shutters for him, so that old Theseus shines white enough to prevent Sandy from getting anything but flare on his lens. The image he gets will be enigmatic, dramatic, mysterious and without contrast, so that he won't be able to use it, which is as it should be with unfinished work. I shake him warmly by the hand. Estelle shakes him warmly by the hand and then we push him gently out and shut the door.

On the bed, of all places, is one little black box trailing wires: the last one? I view it with distaste. I shall take it and put it outside until someone finds it, or the rain gets into it or something. And then, or, rather, pretty well now, Estelle will take me out of here, before I go on riffling Theseus and working out where Kleist from Helgen's will make his saw cuts to dismantle this great ape for casting. Kleist is peculiarly expert at sawing up. He is better than anyone I know. Castiglioni would not even know where to begin.

"Come along, darling. You really must go to bed in the big bed upstairs. You haven't had a full night's sleep in real comfort for days."

"I am as fresh as paint and I need coffee, woman, and I need breakfast."

But, truth to tell, I am perhaps a little tired. I need silence and not to be public again after all this business and after Piero having done this thing. Silence is to hide in and must be manufactured and guarded against the endless dialogue which is to be heard and in some sort, paradoxically, to be seen in the presence of people, of whom I have too many. I am interested in man, who is the single mainspring of what I do and the model I use for everything, except of course, women, whom I also use. But in some ways it happens against my will, since all that disgusts me, man produces. I am myself disgusting, as I am disgusted with the junk I pick up on the rubbish heap to make my metamorphoses, but that is logical. I remake human detritus and purge it by putting it back into use as sculpture. The rubbish is made by man, discarded and flung away by man, cast up on the beach by natural forces and I, being a natural force in some degree, remake it and recast it in materials, man-manufactured, but mined from the core of the world which, like man, is also a sort of hot rubbish.

"Capo, darling, what are you mumbling about?"

"I am being sententious to myself."

"Yes, darling."

"I am saying that I am both contemptuous and fearful of man, including myself, and I am saying that all I understand, or anyone understands, is human beings and their works, since all else in nature is comprehended through the human filter. And I am saying, my love, that for my alarm and revulsion I am rewarded with adulation, which is odd. Also I am saying that Addle's old pal believed that the human psyche is beyond time and space while all I do is fill space to take up my time, and that I must remember to tell Addle that what counts for him is that I should produce what will remain beyond immediate time for long enough to augment his investment."

"I think it is time you were in bed. You are rambling. But it is nice for me to have my bottom pinched like that. It is like old times."

"Why don't you read the cable?"

"What cable?"

"The one you have been holding in your hand, since it arrived, that envelope you have been prodding Casti with."

"Oh, this?"

"Yes, that."

"I don't suppose it is important."

Suddenly I am cold. After all it is only April. It is not summer.

"Open it, anyway."

It is odd how cold it is, suddenly.

"Capo."

"Yes."

"It is from Mougins."

She has crumpled the telegram up. I cannot think why.

"From Pablo? No, that old bastard wouldn't cable."

"No, not from Pablo. It is about Pablo. He has died."

"It is not possible. He can't. It is a joke."

"No. He is dead."

"When? I don't believe it. It is too late for him to die. When?"

"The day before yesterday. I think the storm held up the wire."

"Was that the edge of the storm we had yesterday?"

Estelle is looking at me, knowing what storm I mean.

"There was a terrible storm further up the coast yesterday; the post-boy said that all the lines were down."

"It seems right."

"Yes, it seems right. He is dead? It's not some joke?"

"No, Capo. I do not think it is a joke."

"Telephone to Jacqueline."

"No, Capo."

"We had only the tail-end of the storm then."

"It is a long way from Mougins."

208

"Estelle, my love, take that black box off the bed and put it out, would you? Put it on the window-sill, or somewhere."

"Yes, darling."

The little black box on the window-sill is recording still. It is taping the film men carrying out the last of their stuff and they go carefully round the bronzes and round the vanmen and round Castiglioni from the foundry. And they go especially carefully round the living Theseus, who simply sits on the lawn, on his long chain, and watches them. Because of Theseus, the crew make a wide detour out of respect and awe. But Ariadne, who is out of his reach and who taught him the way in at Knossos before he abandoned her to the embraces of Dionysus on the island of Andros, spits at Theseus and leaps and chatters at him with unending anger and contempt.